# timeline retreats

A Collection of Romantic Comedies

## daisy landish

Editing by Veronica Jauregui
Cover by Daisy Landish

BEACHES AND TRAILS
PUBLISHING

# contents

## borrowing a better mara

## becoming a bolder lana

## claiming a braver jules

# sketching a softer nora

# writing a wilder sage

# one meltdown away

. . .

MARA JENSEN HAD EXACTLY six minutes to get out the door, and her seven-year-old had just declared he couldn't find his left shoe because "the cat stole it for vengeance."

"Leo," she said, balancing a travel mug of coffee between her teeth while digging through the shoe bin with one hand and smoothing down her yoga leggings with the other, "we don't have a cat."

Leo shrugged, unbothered. "Then it was a ghost cat."

She closed her eyes. Counted to three. On four, she stepped on a LEGO and muttered something unrepeatable in front of minors and clergy.

It was 7:48 a.m. Her class started at 8. She'd already missed the window for the good parking spots, the good mats, and the good mood. The "Blessed Belly" cortisol detox juice sat untouched on the counter, glowing an unholy shade of green, daring her to believe in wellness again. She took one defiant sip.

It tasted like celery's angrier cousin had been blended with garden hose water and emotional betrayal.

She gagged, wiped her mouth on a dishtowel that said *Live,*

*Laugh, Lunge*, and tripped over something sticking out from under kitchen counter. "Found the shoe!"

Leo grinned, grabbing it like it had been blessed by the gods. "Thanks, Mom! I knew the ghost cat would give it back."

She did not have time to unpack that sentence.

By 8:06, she was sprinting barefoot through the hot yoga studio, clutching her mat like it was a lifeline and not a foam rectangle with a suspicious stain in the corner. The door squeaked dramatically as she slipped inside, and twelve ponytailed heads turned in perfect unison to judge her tardiness.

She offered a breathless nod and took the only open spot—right next to the woman who always wore glittery sports bras and smelled like eucalyptus and superiority.

The instructor, a man named Kylen (with a *y*), greeted her with a serene "Namaste" that sounded suspiciously smug.

Mara attempted to center herself.

She inhaled. She exhaled. She inhaled again and immediately choked on her own spit.

Off to a great start.

The room was set to "gentle sauna" but felt more like "cursed swamp." Within two minutes, Mara's sports bra had fused to her skin, and her bangs were plastered to her forehead in a way that suggested she was doing jazzercise in a monsoon.

"Find your breath," Kylen intoned, "and flow with intention."

Her intention was not to die here, soaked in cucumber-scented defeat.

Then came crow pose.

Mara knew—*knew*—she shouldn't try it. Her wrists weren't ready. Her dignity certainly wasn't. But something about the room, or the pressure, or just the fact that Eucalyptus Supermodel next to her had effortlessly floated into it made her think: *What if today's the day I don't fall?*

Reader, she fell.

She didn't just fall. She toppled forward into her mat, knocked over her water bottle, and narrowly avoided headbutting a woman in downward dog.

A collective hiss of sympathy swept the room.

Kylen, from his pedestal of enlightenment, offered a gentle, "Let's remember: ego has no place on the mat."

Mara gave a thumbs up from the floor. "Noted."

By the time she left the studio, she was raw—emotionally, physically, possibly spiritually. Her leggings were riding in unholy places. Her water bottle had a new dent. And her aura, if it had ever existed, was now dented, too.

She sat in her car, blasting the AC at her face, and stared at her reflection in the rearview mirror.

"You are okay," she told herself.

Then she burst out laughing. Not a cute giggle. A loud, barky, *this-is-fine*-while-everything-is-on-fire kind of laugh.

"Sure," she said to no one, "okay."

Her phone buzzed with a calendar alert: **10:30 a.m. – Q2 Team Check-In (Don't forget to smile!!)**

She sighed, cranked the AC higher, and wondered what it would be like to disappear for a week.

Not forever.

Just…long enough to remember who the hell she used to be.

Willow Ridge Park smelled like sunscreen, mulch, and whatever emotional residue clung to the baby swing set. It was, objectively, a nice day—blue skies, light breeze, birds singing a little too cheerfully for Mara's current mood.

She sat on a weathered park bench that leaned at a slight but ominous angle, like it had survived one too many winter storms or existential breakdowns. Her yoga mat was still rolled under one arm like a tragic accessory. Her hair was damp. Her mood was feral.

Across from her, Lana looked fresh as a daisy. Her black cat-eye sunglasses screamed competence, and her oat milk latte glistened like a weapon of calm.

"I fell in hot yoga," Mara announced.

Lana didn't blink. "Like, metaphorically? Or into another emotional pit?"

"Physically. Crow pose. There was a noise. I think I startled a woman into rethinking her life choices."

"That's very on-brand for you."

"I know." Mara groaned and flopped back on the bench, staring up at the blue sky like it might swallow her whole. "Also, I'm ninety percent sure I still have detox sludge in my bra. I smell like spinach regret."

Lana crossed one leg over the other and sipped. "You're the only person I know who tries to biohack her way to inner peace while rage-texting her ex about pick-up times."

"I am multi-dimensional," Mara said, then added under her breath, "and under-medicated."

A shriek rang out from the monkey bars—Leo's voice, triumphant and slightly dangerous. Mara glanced over just in time to see him attempt a move that could only be described as "parkour-adjacent." Her heart skipped, thudded, then resigned itself to the reality that Leo, like his mother, had never once heard of subtlety.

"He told me yesterday that he's going to be a YouTuber slash paleontologist slash ninja," she muttered. "Then asked if that came with dental. He's seven, Lana."

"Well, he's got range."

Mara exhaled through her nose and leaned forward, resting her elbows on her knees. "Do you ever just... feel like you're one bad Target trip away from fully snapping? Like, you'll be fine, fine, fine, and then suddenly someone's in your way in the seasonal candle aisle and you're ready to hurl a pumpkin-scented votive at their head?"

"Sweetie, I once cried in a Michael's because I couldn't find the right shade of glitter. You're among the broken and the blessed."

Mara smiled, weakly. "My therapist would love you."

"I *am* therapy, just without the copay."

There was a beat.

Mara sniffled.

Then—disaster struck.

The juice box. The *freaking juice box*—Leo's backup apple, lovingly squished into her purse at 7 a.m.—had ruptured. Warm, sticky liquid seeped out like an offering to the gods of defeat.

She yelped and pulled her hand out of the bag, dripping in fruit-scented syrup. "Oh, for the love of—"

In her flail to extract it, her knee clipped the side of the already unstable bench. A loud *thunk* echoed. The whole thing shifted under her with the comedic grace of a cartoon chair collapsing.

It didn't break. But it made a sound of *threat*.

She froze. Looked at Lana. Then down at her soaked hand. Then back at Lana.

And finally—finally—it happened.

The meltdown.

Not a sweet, demure tear gently rolling down one cheek.

No. This was The Cry™.

The messy, hiccupy, can't-tell-if-it's-laughing-or-sobbing release of a woman hanging by the thread of her Google calendar. Her shoulders shook. Her chest heaved. And in the middle of it, she muttered, "I'm going to start a new life as a moss-covered hermit named Fern. I'll learn to knit, grow potatoes, maybe marry a gentle bear."

Lana reached into her tote, calmly handed her a tissue, and said, "You'd last fifteen minutes without Wi-Fi."

"*Twelve,*" Mara corrected, dabbing at her eyes. "Tops."

They sat like that for a while. Leo howled in the distance, victorious over the playground. A dog barked. Somewhere, a child wailed in protest over a granola bar that dared to have texture.

A gust of wind stirred the mulch at her feet, carrying a scrap of paper across the park path. Mara barely registered it at first—just another coupon or lost PTA flyer. But when it stuck to her yoga mat like it had been magnetised, she peeled it off and squinted at the oddly thick cardstock.

Cream background. Gold lettering. A tagline in elegant serif font:

TIRED OF YOUR TIMELINE? TRY ANOTHER.

She frowned. No logo. No phone number. Just a shimmering infinity symbol, small and strange in the bottom corner.

"What the heck…" she murmured.

Lana glanced over. "You say something?"

Mara crumpled the card instinctively and shoved it in her tote bag. "Nah. Just tired."

And then, like the wind had delivered a cosmic punchline, the card was forgotten—at least for now.

Mara sucked in a breath. "I'm so tired, Lan. Not like sleepy tired. Just…world tired. Like every morning I wake up and I'm already at zero."

Lana's voice softened. "I know."

"I keep trying to fix it. The juice thing. The yoga. The VR vacation where a dolphin in a bowtie told me to 'embrace my shadow self.'" She shook her head. "But none of it sticks. Nothing feels better."

"You need a real break," Lana said. "Not a thirty-minute savasana or a bath bomb. Like... a pause on being Mara for a minute."

Mara tilted her head, amused. "What, like, loan my life to someone else?"

"I'm just saying," Lana said with a shrug, "if there's a Time-Share for souls, I'd happily guest-star as you for a week. You'd come back to find Leo speaking fluent Spanish and your inbox at zero."

Mara laughed, watery and a little unhinged. "That actually sounds amazing."

Which, of course, is *exactly* when the woman showed up.

The park had that strange mid-morning lull where the toddlers were all melting down, the coffee had stopped working, and the sun had turned from *warm* to *personally aggressive*. Mara was just starting to remember she had a work meeting in forty minutes and no emotional bandwidth to fake being "passionately aligned with Q2 strategy," when a shadow crossed her lap.

Not a cloud.

Not Leo swinging back into her orbit.

A person.

She looked up—and immediately clocked three things:

1. The woman's eyebrows were **perfect**. Not Instagram-perfect. Not *microbladed within an inch of their life* perfect. These were celestial. Ethereal. Possibly *enchanted*.

2. She wore an all-linen ensemble that looked equal parts spa uniform and high-fashion cult.

3. She was smiling like she knew things. *Big things*. Like which timeline you should've chosen in 2012 and what your soulmate smells like.

"You look like someone who needs a break from this timeline," the woman said, like she was offering Mara a Tic Tac.

Mara blinked. "I'm sorry... do I know you?"

"No. But I know you." The woman's smile deepened. Not creepy. Just... like she was in on something Mara hadn't been invited to yet.

Lana muttered, "Okay, what in the *Goop*-sponsored—"

The woman ignored her, holding out a business card between two elegant fingers.

Cream-colored cardstock. Gold lettering that shimmered ever so slightly, like it was made from stardust or expensive toner.

### Timeline Retreats
*For When Your Life Just Isn't It*

No phone number. No address. Just the logo—an infinity symbol that looked suspiciously like it had been doodled by someone bored in a quantum physics lecture. Just like the flyer Mara had just tucked into her bag.

Mara took it, mostly because her mother had taught her not to be rude to people holding cryptic invitations to alternate dimensions.

"This is a... therapy group?" she asked.

The woman tilted her head. "It's a temporary relocation program. A reset. A limited-time trial of a better you."

Lana raised her sunglasses. "Okay, but like... in a *gently dystopian tech startup* kind of way, or more of a *divine intervention meets Etsy witchcraft* situation?"

The woman actually chuckled. "I suppose that depends on your interpretation."

Mara tried to hand the card back. "Sorry, I don't really have time for—"

"You don't need to *do* anything," the woman said, her voice soft but unnervingly direct. "Just sleep. We'll handle the logistics."

"Wait, what?"

"If you're selected, the switch will occur automatically. One week. No strings. Full immersion. If you don't like it, you return. If you do…" She shrugged, like the rest was obvious. "We talk options."

"Okay, but what *is* it? Like—what am I even agreeing to?"

"A glimpse into the life you almost lived," the woman said, eyes twinkling. "The one where you chose differently. Stayed. Left. Said yes. Said no. You know the one."

Mara opened her mouth to argue, to laugh it off, to say something very practical about time travel and scams and *The Matrix*. But all she could manage was:

"…I think you have the wrong person."

The woman smiled again—warm and patient, like a preschool teacher who also controlled the fabric of the multiverse.

"No, Mara. You're exactly who we're looking for."

And then—*because of course she did*—she turned and walked away.

Just like that. No dramatic exit. No puff of smoke or shimmer of light. Just linen pants swishing peacefully in the breeze as she strolled down the park path and out of sight.

Mara stared after her.

Then down at the card in her hand.

Then at Lana.

"You saw that, right?" Mara asked, voice pitched somewhere between confused and mildly haunted.

Lana reached over and plucked the card out of her fingers. Examined it.

"...Okay, yeah, this feels either magical or like a very niche MLM."

Mara snorted, still dazed. "Do you think she slipped me a microdose or something?"

"No, babe. You're just tired. Your brain's trying to manifest a better version of your life."

She paused. Handed the card back.

"But honestly? If there *is* a timeline where you're rested, rich, and still have all your ligaments intact after crow pose—I say go for it."

Mara laughed. But it was shaky.

She slipped the card into her purse.

She wouldn't call, obviously. Wouldn't fall for some weird linen-clad woman's reality escape fantasy.

Still...

That night, when she set her alarm and lay in bed, she pulled the card out again.

Held it between her fingers like a secret.

Then turned out the light.

# it's not kidnapping if it's a vacation

. . .

MARA KNEW something was wrong the moment her eyes opened and her sinuses weren't angry. No distant hum of traffic. No ceiling fan rattling like it was held together by hope and expired warranty tape. No seven-year-old launching himself into her bed like a caffeinated spider monkey. Just quiet. Soft light. A linen canopy she absolutely did not own. And sheets—real sheets, high-thread-count sheets, smelling faintly of eucalyptus and what she could only assume was upper-middle-class peace.

She sat up slowly, expecting back pain. None. She was in a robe. A plush, cloud-soft, offensively luxurious robe tied around her with suspicious elegance. Her feet found cool hardwood floors instead of discarded laundry. Her panic finally clicked into gear.

"Okay," she muttered. "Either I'm dead or someone broke in and did...home improvement. Like a kidnapping but with feng shui."

The room was all soft curves and neutral tones, like someone had asked an algorithm to design "serenity with tasteful Wi-Fi." A bonsai tree sat peacefully beside a pitcher of spa water. Her phone was nowhere to be found. No laptop, no to-do list scribbled on the back of a grocery receipt. Just her. And her confusion. And her weirdly smooth skin.

Then the far wall shimmered.

Not *opened*. Not *slid*.

Shimmered, like someone had installed a portal disguised as a minimalist art piece.

From it stepped the woman—still serene, still linen-clad, still wielding those suspiciously symmetrical eyebrows like a quiet weapon. She looked exactly as she had in the park, except now she also looked like she belonged here. Like maybe she was the CEO of Calm.

"Good morning, Mara," she said, her voice as silky as the robe. "My name is Celeste. I trust you slept well?"

"Okay, see, I was really hoping this was a metaphor or a stress dream," Mara said, backing slightly toward the spa water in case it doubled as a weapon. "You can't just wake up in a robe. That's not normal. That's cult behavior."

"You've been selected for a timeline immersion," Celeste said, like she was reading from a very elegant brochure. "A one-week trial in an adjacent life. Yours—if one key decision had been made differently."

Mara stared. "I didn't *agree* to anything."

"You didn't *decline*, either."

"That's not consent. That's...a passive yes at best."

Celeste gave a diplomatic smile. "We prefer to call it 'energetic readiness.'"

"And what, exactly, happens now?"

"For the next seven days, you'll experience life as this timeline's Mara. The original is currently off-grid at a wellness retreat. Everything is stable. You won't be interrupted."

Mara ran a hand through her hair. It was suspiciously clean.

"Let me get this straight," she said. "I've been body-snatched into my own alternate life while other-me is away at a juice-themed spa?"

Celeste inclined her head. "That's...one interpretation."

The kitchen was offensively beautiful. Warm wood accents, matte black fixtures, a backsplash that whispered *I was installed by someone who doesn't cry during tax season.* Everything gleamed in a way Mara couldn't process. There were potted herbs that weren't wilted. A glass bowl of lemons that looked staged. And—she swore on her Wi-Fi bill—fresh-cut flowers. Just...casually. Sitting there. Like joy grew here.

She opened the fridge and nearly wept. Mason jars lined up like they were auditioning for a lifestyle blog. Containers labeled in someone's actual handwriting—*quinoa salad, almond butter energy bites, zucchini fritters.* She hadn't made zucchini fritters in this life or any parallel one.

Behind her, footsteps padded in. She turned, half expecting Celeste again. But it was Leo—same mop of curls, same sleepy eyes, same velociraptor clutched under one arm. He yawned and blinked at her like it was a regular Tuesday.

"Morning, Mom," he said, already climbing onto a stool at the island.

"Hi, baby." Mara's voice cracked. She tried to sound normal. "Sleep okay?"

He nodded and rubbed his eyes. "Is today the book fair?"

"...Yes," she said, guessing correctly by the sheer luck of context clues. "Do you want pancakes?"

He lit up. "The smiley ones?"

"Obviously." She had no idea what that entailed, but she found a non-stick pan and went for it. The batter was prepped in the fridge. Of course it was. She ladled it carefully, drawing a face with a squeeze bottle of...chocolate sauce? *Alt-Mara, you magical kitchen witch.*

As Leo dug in, she leaned against the counter and spotted a sleek tablet charging nearby. It buzzed, screen lighting up with a name.

> Eli: Morning, sunshine 🌞 Don't forget fig bars for Mrs. K—her sugar crash tantrums are real.

> Also, if you wear that striped top again, I reserve the right to be hopelessly distracted.

Mara blinked.

That was—was that flirting? It had been so long since someone texted her without asking for lunch money, tax documents, or photos of a rash that wasn't going away.

She typed nothing. Her thumbs hovered. She locked the screen.

Leo was humming, swinging his legs, chewing through a smiley face like a tiny god of chaos.

"You're acting weird," he said without looking up.

"I'm...not," she lied. "I'm just well-rested."

"You never say that."

And he was right. She *never* did.

She looked around again. At the life that should've felt like cosplay. But somehow—it didn't.

It felt like someone had cleaned her house, prepped her meals, and handed her back her child *without the mental hangover*.

It felt like cheating.

But also?

It felt like breathing for the first time in years.

The hallway was lined with photos she didn't remember taking.

Mara moved slowly, a mug of something cinnamon-scented in

hand—tea or bone broth or some alternate-Mara elixir of calm. She wasn't sure. She hadn't made it. It had just been waiting on the counter like everything else in this timeline. Ready. Warm.

Her fingertips brushed a frame. Leo, a little younger, barefoot on a beach at sunset, his smile so unguarded it hurt. Another one showed her—well, *this* her—at a ribbon-cutting ceremony in front of a shop window that read: **Bookish & Bold**. Her hair was styled. Her shirt didn't have a single visible stain. She was laughing. With people. Publicly.

And then one that stopped her cold.

It was her again—but not laughing. Just…standing. Next to Eli. His arm draped loosely around her shoulder, her hand tucked into the front pocket of his jeans. They looked like a couple on a holiday card. Relaxed. Intimate. Like two people who knew each other's coffee orders and Netflix passwords and had survived some serious *life* together.

She swallowed.

This version of her had taken a chance. Or said yes. Or not run. Whichever choice it was, it led here. To this hallway. This robe. This tea. This man who texted her sunshine emojis like they were private jokes.

She wasn't envious. Not exactly.

She was *aching*.

How close had she come to this version? Was it one decision? One afternoon? Did Alt-Mara just not flinch when things got hard? Or did she flinch and stay anyway?

Mara turned, catching sight of herself in a mirror hanging between the frames.

She looked the same. Mostly. Maybe a little more rested. Maybe a little less like she was perpetually bracing for bad news. But the dark circles were still faint echoes. The worry lines hadn't vanished. This wasn't a makeover. It was just…a pause.

"I don't know how to be you," she whispered to the woman in the mirror.

The woman stared back, quiet and calm. A maybe-better version. A maybe-braver one.

Behind her, a wind chime sounded—soft, ethereal. Not magical. Just...*intentional.*

Mara didn't believe in fate.

But she was starting to believe in second chances.

# meet-cute... take two

. . .

THE LIBRARY WAS BUZZING with energy and the soft, anxious hum of children hyped up on free bookmarks and limited supervision. Mara stood behind a booth labeled **"Bookish & Bold"** and tried not to have a full-on identity crisis in public.

The table was already set up when she arrived—because of course it was. Brown-paper-wrapped mystery books tied with twine, a sign inviting readers to "fall back in love with fiction," and a ceramic dish filled with—were those fig bars?

She leaned forward to read one of the flirty handwritten notes on the back of a wrapped book:

*If you liked your last breakup spicy and your protagonists with healing trauma + tattoos, this is the one.*

"Oh my God," Mara whispered. "Other Me is cool."

Kids darted past her booth, dragging reluctant parents toward the origami station. A woman in a flowy cardigan shouted something about story time in five minutes. Mara fumbled through the tablet on the booth, trying to find an inventory list or at least a cheat sheet.

Nothing.

She was on her own.

"Cool Mara," she muttered under her breath, smoothing down her sweater. "You just have to pretend you're Cool Mara."

Cool Mara, presumably, had a spreadsheet for this. Cool Mara wore boots that didn't give her blisters. Cool Mara definitely didn't wipe her hands on her jeans and knock over an entire stack of poetry anthologies in the process.

Mara reached to steady the pile, caught one book mid-fall, and —wham—bumped the edge of the neighboring display. A tower of romance novels teetered like it was personally offended by her clumsiness.

She lunged.

Too late.

Three paperbacks slid off the edge and landed—splat—straight into a kid's lemonade.

The child wailed like she'd just drowned his puppy. "MY DRINK!"

"I—hang on—okay, it's fine!" Mara grabbed the dripping books, fumbling for a napkin that didn't exist, mopping with a promotional tote bag. "They're... hydrated! Literary self-care!"

A nearby mom gave her a look that could sour milk.

She tried to laugh it off, cheeks blazing.

"Excellent save," said a voice behind her.

She turned—and froze.

Eli.

Same warm brown eyes. Same smirk. Same cardigan that looked like it had opinions about indie coffee shops.

Of course he looked good. Of course he was holding a clipboard like he'd just redesigned the Dewey Decimal System for emotional accessibility.

And now he was watching her with an expression that could only be described as: intrigued and lightly amused.

"Hi," she said, clutching a soggy tote full of regret. "Welcome to my TED Talk on how not to run a booth."

He grinned. "You're crushing it."

Eli crouched beside her to help gather the damp books, his arm brushing hers as he reached for a dripping copy of *Beach Read*. Mara inhaled sharply—because either his laundry detergent was called "Kind Man With Intentions" or her brain was short-circuiting under the pressure of his casual closeness.

He looked up at her, holding a soggy paperback in one hand. "I'm assuming this one isn't part of the hydration-themed promotion?"

"Technically no," she said, trying to sound breezy and not like a woman currently experiencing cardiac confusion. "But if it helps, this version comes pre-cry-ready."

He chuckled—warm and low—and dear god, it did something to her spine.

Once the crisis was semi-contained and the lemonade child pacified with a free sticker, Mara stood behind the table and tried to collect herself while Eli leaned one elbow on the edge, clipboard forgotten.

"Didn't expect to see you running a booth this year," he said. "Last time, you swore the emotional labor of organizing was 'above your pay grade as a chaotic neutral.'"

Mara blinked. "Did I?"

"You did." His grin was crooked. "I still have the text. And a voice memo where you yell about font choices like it's a war crime."

"Oh," she said, with a weak laugh. "Wow. I sound...fun."

He tilted his head, studying her. "You okay today?"

The question was simple. But not casual.

He wasn't asking like someone who needed a quick "fine." He

was asking like someone who knew her tells. Someone who'd seen the frayed ends and figured out how to tuck them in.

Mara tried to smile. "Just a little distracted."

"You seem... different," Eli said, voice soft now. "Not bad. Just...more in your head than usual."

She panicked.

"I got a new bra," she blurted. "It has memory foam. For my boobs."

There was a beat.

A long one.

Eli laughed. Like, actually laughed—tilting his head back, letting it roll out in waves.

"Oh my god," she muttered, covering her face. "I swear I used to be mysterious and cool."

"You've never been mysterious," he said, still smiling. "But you've always been you."

Mara's heart made a strange, fluttery noise she didn't approve of.

He was looking at her again. Really looking. Like maybe something had clicked for him too, or almost. His brow furrowed slightly, like he couldn't quite pin her down.

"I should—uh—check in with the poetry tent," he said finally. "Apparently the haiku kids have unionized."

"Power to the poets," Mara said, voice higher than she intended.

He paused at the edge of her booth. "You're doing great, by the way."

"Lying is kind," she muttered.

"I'm not lying." He winked. "Just...delightedly confused."

And then he was gone again, weaving through the crowd like this wasn't a moment Mara was going to replay in her brain like a highlight reel for the next decade.

She exhaled.

And realized she wanted to see him again.

*Soon.*

Which was a problem.

Because this wasn't her life. Not really. And whatever was blooming here...wasn't hers to keep.

Mara found a quiet spot behind the nonfiction stacks and leaned against a bookshelf like her knees weren't fully reliable anymore. Her heart was still doing jazz hands in her chest. Her face felt flushed. And her tote bag was still damp from the Great Lemonade Incident of 9:42 a.m.

She had survived. Barely.

But it wasn't the booth or the toddlers or the minor literary flooding that had her reeling. It was *him*.

Eli.

He was warm and steady and familiar in a way that made her chest ache. He'd looked at her like she was *his person*. Not just someone he liked. Someone he *knew*. Someone who'd earned his jokes and his trust and his soft, fond glances across crowded book fairs.

And the worst part?

She liked it. She liked *him*. And not just timeline-Eli, not just hot-alt-boyfriend energy. *This Eli*. With his clipboard and cardigan and subtle flirtation and dumb perfect face.

She slid down the wall into a squat, hugging her knees.

"This is fine," she muttered. "Just a casual emotional emergency in the large print biography aisle."

Her mind flashed to the text from earlier. The "striped shirt" comment. The emoji. The easy shorthand that came from *years* of inside jokes and slow mornings and probably shared dessert.

She didn't have that.

Not with him.

She had forty-eight hours of borrowed history, a slightly melted fig bar, and a growing knot of guilt coiling tighter every time he smiled at her like she was the real deal.

And she smiled back—because she didn't know how not to.

But she also couldn't hold his gaze for long.

Not when it meant pretending this was real.

Somewhere else in town, Eli stirred the last of his latte, untouched.

Lana sat across from him, sunglasses pushed into her hair, a brow arched in that particular way she saved for men who were clearly Not Okay.

"She's back," he said. "But it's like... not really."

Lana sipped her drink, slow. "She seemed pretty Mara to me. Smelled like that same essential oil panic and coffee breath combo."

Eli smiled faintly, but it didn't stick. "No, I mean... she's *here*, but she's not *her*. Or not the version I know. She's lighter. Calmer. Like someone peeled a layer of stress off her skin. But also... kind of like she doesn't know me."

Lana was quiet for a moment. "Maybe she's just trying again. Starting over."

He shook his head. "It doesn't feel like a restart. It feels like a rewrite."

He didn't say what scared him more:

That he liked this version of her.

Or that she might not stay.

Celeste's words echoed in her head— "The original is off-grid. Everything is stable."

But *was* it?

Because Mara didn't feel stable. She felt like a knockoff handbag trying to pass inspection. Like any second now, someone would tap her on the shoulder and say, *"Excuse me, ma'am, you're not supposed to be here."*

Maybe not today.

But eventually.

And when that moment came—what would she do?

What would Eli do?

She covered her face with her hands and let out a low groan.

This wasn't just a vacation anymore. This was dangerous.

Because she wasn't just pretending to live someone else's life.

She was starting to want it.

# hot mom summer (for one week only)

. . .

FOR THE FIRST time in what felt like years, Mara Jensen didn't wake up to an alarm, a screaming child, or an inbox full of existential dread.

She woke up to sunlight filtering through gauzy curtains, the smell of something lemony and divine from the kitchen, and her name gently spoken by a home assistant that didn't glitch or call her "Margo."

*"Good morning, Mara. Today is Wednesday. Your priorities include brunch with Lana, shipping confirmation for the fig bar order, and an evening event marked 'Karaoke: DO NOT CANCEL AGAIN.'"*

She blinked at the ceiling. "Did I finally sell my soul?"

The assistant chirped: *"Would you like to play your Feel-Good Morning playlist?"*

"Obviously."

Cue music. Cue montage.

She was thriving. At least for now.

There were yoga classes where no one judged her form. Smoothies that didn't taste like pond water. A team of cheerful bookstore employees who somehow didn't mind when she blanked on Alt-Mara's filing system and whispered, "What do I do with returns?" like it was a secret shame.

Leo was happy—like *truly* happy. He hummed to himself at breakfast, hugged her without prompting, and asked questions like, "Can we read more of that Greek myths book tonight?" instead of "Can I live on chicken nuggets forever?"

And then there were the texts from Eli.

Every day, something small.

> Eli: Reminder: story time at the shop tomorrow. Wear your glasses so I can pretend not to swoon.

> Eli: I made a Spotify playlist that starts with 'Lovefool' and ends with that obscure jazz track you pretend not to like. You're welcome.

> Eli: Are you free tonight or emotionally unavailable with flair?

She kept saying yes. Even when she knew she shouldn't.

They went for walks. They sat on the back patio drinking wine while Leo built a pillow fort that somehow didn't collapse in under ten minutes. He kissed her once at sunset and once in the stockroom while she accidentally knocked over a cardboard cutout of Jane Austen.

She laughed more this week than she had in the last two years combined.

And somewhere between the trivia night where she aced an entire category on 2000s rom-coms and the quiet moment on the couch where Leo fell asleep with his head in her lap, Mara stopped trying to act like Cool Alternate Timeline Mara.

She just…was.

And that was the most dangerous part of all.

The night began with trivia and wine.

Mara didn't remember agreeing to go out, but apparently Alt-Mara's calendar was smarter than she was, and "Eli & M – Midweek Mischief 🍷🎤 " had popped up with a reminder that included directions to a cozy bistro she'd never heard of and a note that read: *"YES, YOU LIKE THIS PLACE. YES, WE ALWAYS GET THE FRENCH FRIES."*

It was already her favorite night out.

Eli was waiting by the hostess stand when she arrived, leaning against a chalkboard sign advertising $8 sangria and "Musicals & Mixed Nuts: Themed Trivia Night." He was in his usual flannel, sleeves rolled to the elbows, one curl falling onto his forehead like he knew what it did to people.

"You wore the boots," he said, eyes dipping to her ankle. "Bold move."

"I've accepted the possibility of rolling an ankle in the name of fashion," she replied. "I'm brave like that."

They were seated in a corner booth with a view of the tiny stage and a very earnest duo setting up a mic stand and tambourine. Their team name—**Wuthering Bites**—was apparently a recurring bit. Eli pulled out a pen and scribbled hearts around it like it was the most natural thing in the world.

"Are we...flirting via Jane Eyre puns now?" she asked, sipping her sangria.

"Please," he said. "We graduated to full literary foreplay two summers ago."

Her face burned, but in the nicest way.

The trivia was chaotic. Their team lost spectacularly, thanks in part to Mara confidently insisting *Legally Blonde* came out in 2004 (it didn't) and Eli misidentifying a *Wicked* lyric as "something from Rent." They heckled each other gently. Shared fries. Stole glances.

After the trivia, the mic was left open for karaoke.

"I will Venmo you $100 not to sign us up," Mara said.

Eli already had the sign-up sheet in hand. "You say that every time, and every time, you sing 'You Oughta Know' like it's your battle cry."

"I'm wearing a sweater. I'm emotionally stable. Don't make me unhinged on a Wednesday."

He smiled and handed her the pen.

They sang a duet.

It was bad. *Gloriously* bad. She forgot half the lyrics. He added extra harmonies that sounded vaguely threatening. Someone gave them pity applause that turned genuine by the end.

And when they stepped off the stage, adrenaline still buzzing between them, he leaned in.

Not a dramatic kiss. Not dipped-back, Hollywood-style.

Just close.

Confident.

Like it had happened a hundred times before, and this was simply the next.

His lips brushed hers, soft and warm and slow, with the careful certainty of someone who knew just how she liked to be kissed— and had earned the right to know.

She kissed him back.

Not because she should.

Because she wanted to.

Which, of course, made it worse.

Mara couldn't stop smiling on the drive home.

Her lips still tingled from the kiss, her cheeks ached from laughter, and her phone buzzed every few minutes with Eli texting more inside jokes about their karaoke performance (*"I'm just saying, if this bookstore thing doesn't work out, we'd make a killer Alanis cover band"*).

The windows were down. The night was warm. And for the first time in a long time, she didn't feel like she was being chased by her own life.

But the second she stepped into the house—quiet, tidy, perfectly hers and not-hers—the smile began to fade.

Leo was asleep, already tucked in. A small lamp glowed in his room. A book rested on his nightstand. One she'd never read to him. But *Alt-Mara* had.

She walked through the kitchen, fingers trailing along the smooth countertop. Everything was where it should be. Nothing out of place. Like someone had pressed pause and left the scene open for her to step into. A role. A routine.

She should've felt grateful.

Instead, she felt like a trespasser.

She sat down at the table and pulled out her old phone from the bottom of her purse. She hadn't touched it in days. Not since that first morning.

It flickered to life slowly, battery nearly dead. One missed call from Lana. A few texts from work—her real job, the one that paid in deadlines and stress dreams. A picture Leo had drawn at school: a stick figure labeled "MOM" with wild hair and what appeared to be a coffee IV.

Her throat tightened.

She loved this life. This calm, curated, fig-bar-scented dream of a life.

But it wasn't hers.

Not really.

She hadn't built it. She hadn't earned it. She hadn't stayed up crying over spreadsheets or patched things up with Eli after a fight or figured out how to calm Leo down when he panicked about monsters under the bed.

That was *her*. The other her. Alt-Mara.

And tonight, she'd kissed someone else's boyfriend.

The guilt landed like a weight in her chest. Heavy. Sharp.

She opened her tablet and found another message from Eli.

> Eli: I know you get weird after good things. I'm just gonna say it—tonight was one of my favorite nights ever.
>
> And no, it's not because of your singing.
>
> (Okay, a little because of your singing.)
>
> But mostly because you seemed happy. I've missed that. I've missed you.

She stared at the message.

And for the first time since she arrived in this alternate life, she didn't feel lucky.

She felt like a fraud.

# this timeline has a warranty, right?

. . .

MARA WOKE UP TO BIRDSONG, the smell of cinnamon toast, and the unsettling feeling that her life had become suspiciously easy.

Which was, of course, when Celeste reappeared.

Not through a wall this time—just casually perched on the back patio like she'd wandered in off the cover of a high-end meditation retreat brochure. Linen pants, herbal tea, the faint scent of sage. Her entire presence said: *I definitely know where your chakra alignment is stored and I will not hesitate to reformat it.*

"Morning," Celeste said, smiling like a TED Talk about destiny was about to begin. "You look...adjusted."

Mara stepped outside, mug in hand. "Is that a compliment or a warning?"

"Just an observation," Celeste replied. "You've acclimated beautifully. Some participants struggle to let go of their original context. You? You've stepped in with full energetic presence."

Mara took a sip of coffee, unsure whether to say *thank you* or *help.*

"I kissed him," she blurted instead.

Celeste didn't blink. "Yes. I saw."

"You *what*?"

She waved a hand, vague and mystical. "We monitor emotional milestones. It's part of the transition evaluation."

"Right, of course," Mara said, gripping her mug like a lifeline. "Milestones. Like...kissing a man who thinks I'm someone else and maybe falling in love with his Goodreads account."

Celeste's expression softened. "Love isn't bound by origin points. It's bound by resonance."

Mara blinked. "Okay, what does that *mean*, but in human?"

"It means," Celeste said gently, "that you're ready."

Mara's stomach flipped. "For what?"

Celeste reached into her linen tote (of course she had a linen tote) and pulled out a sleek, gold-edged envelope. The front was embossed with a familiar swirling infinity symbol.

### Timeline Transfer Eligibility: CONFIRMED
*One-Time Offer. One Permanent Choice.*

"You've reached your immersion midpoint," Celeste said, sliding the envelope across the table. "You may remain in this life—permanently. If you accept, the current timeline's Mara will be...reassigned."

Mara squinted. "Reassigned to *what*, exactly? The Mail Room of the Multiverse?"

"She'll be relocated to another timeline with appropriate energetic compatibility. Fully supported. Smooth transition."

"That sounds...vague. And vaguely ominous."

Celeste smiled, pulled a tuning fork from her tote, and tapped it against the mug.

A faint chime sang through the air like a decision being made.

"It's not ominous," she said. "It's...delicate."

Mara stared at the envelope. It shimmered faintly in the sunlight.

A real choice.

Stay in this beautiful, functional life with its clean kitchen and warm texts and karaoke kisses...or go back to the chaos and cortisol of reality. Back to the version of herself who never figured it out.

Back to a life that was still *hers*.

Celeste stood.

"You don't have to decide yet," she said. "But the moment will come."

And then, like all mildly terrifying magical life coaches, she vanished into the early morning mist with the quiet grace of someone who definitely owned wind chimes.

Mara sat alone with her coffee, the envelope, and the uncomfortable truth:

She could stay.

It started with juice.

Specifically, the fact that Mara poured it into the blue cup instead of the red one.

Leo blinked at it like it had personally offended him. "That's not the right cup."

"It's the same juice," she said, cheerfully sliding it across the counter.

He squinted. "But it tastes better in the red cup."

Mara opened her mouth, closed it, then leaned forward, serious. "Is this, like, a color-based flavor conspiracy? Are you telling me you've been lying about apple juice tasting the same this whole time?"

Leo shrugged, clearly torn between maintaining the illusion of logic and the truth of his tiny gremlin brain. "It just feels wrong."

"Fair," she said, swapping cups. He sipped. Nodded. Peace was restored.

Or it should have been.

But then he looked up at her and said, "Are you still my real mom?"

The question was casual. Offhand. Like he'd asked if they were out of string cheese.

Mara froze. "Uh. What?"

"You just seem different this week," he said around a mouthful of cereal. "Not bad. Just...different."

Her stomach did a slow, nervous somersault. "How do you mean?"

Leo tilted his head, spoon in hand. "You've been singing a lot. And you made pancakes two days in a row. And you didn't forget library day or yell about toothpaste being on the ceiling. And you —" he dropped his spoon, face lighting up— "danced in the kitchen yesterday. You never dance."

Mara swallowed hard.

This was supposed to be a good thing. The calm. The pancakes. The dance she barely remembered—just a spin, a song on the radio, a little joy that bubbled up before she could shove it down.

"I guess I'm just...trying something new," she said gently.

Leo narrowed his eyes. "Did you get a brain swap?"

"What?"

"Like in that movie. With the robot girl who secretly controls the weather."

"I'm not a robot," she said, laughing a little.

"But you *could* be," he said, serious. "You know where the first-aid kit is and you used the real vacuum. That's suspicious."

She crouched down to meet him at eye level, one hand on the counter, one on her heart. "Cross my circuits, I'm still your mom."

He considered this, then nodded. "Okay. But if you start floating or controlling squirrels with your mind, I'm telling Grandma."

"Fair warning."

He went back to his cereal.

Mara stood, heart thudding.

He took another long sip from the red cup, then looked up at her with that wide-eyed sincerity only kids and saints possessed.

"Thanks for fixing it, Mom," he said. "You always fix the broken things."

Mara froze.

Because original Leo had said that exact phrase two weeks ago —curled up next to her on the couch, a scraped knee under one hand and a juice box in the other. Same inflection. Same warm trust in his voice.

You always fix the broken things.

She blinked fast.

It was a compliment, sure. A kindness. But here, from this version of him, in this glossy, borrowed life—it hit different.

Like someone had copied and pasted her son into a world she didn't earn.

And suddenly, the juice wasn't the only thing making her stomach turn.

It was a joke.

Just a silly moment.

But still—he knew.

Not in words. Not in facts.

But in that deep, intuitive kid way.

Something about her had shifted.

And even if she was doing everything *right*, it didn't quite *fit*.

Because Leo didn't just know who she was when she had it together.

He knew who she was *when she didn't*.

It started with a sticky note.

Bright pink. Tucked under the bookstore register. Written in

looping, confident handwriting that was definitely hers—but also...
not.

> *Mara—Don't forget to reshelve the Banned Books display. Eli says if one more copy of The Handmaid's Tale ends up in Sci-Fi, he's going to riot.*
> *(Also: order more fig bars.)*

Mara stared at it for a long moment.

She hadn't written it. Not in this life, anyway.

Which meant Alt-Mara had.

She slipped the note into her pocket, unsure why it made her feel like she'd just found a receipt for someone else's happiness.

The bookstore was warm and bustling. People smiled at her. A woman with cropped pink hair waved and said, "Thanks again for the self-pub panel—you were right about the vampire barista subplot. It *totally* worked."

Mara smiled, nodded, and added "vampire barista" to her list of things to Google later.

She tried to shake the unease.

But it followed her.

Little things.

Her employee, June, asked, "Did you still want to write that grant proposal this weekend?"

Mara blinked. "Grant?"

"You were all fired up about it last week," June said. "Said you were ready to stop playing small."

"Oh. Yeah. Definitely," Mara said, voice too bright. "So ready to...not play small."

Then there was the customer who brought over a stack of novels for the "Fierce Female Leads" table. "I saw your blog post about this theme—so good," she said. "I shared it with my book club. I love how you write about women getting messy and still winning."

Mara nodded numbly.

She hadn't written a blog post in two years. Not since Leo's birthday party ended with a trip to urgent care and a flaming dinosaur cake.

That night, after Leo was asleep and the dishes were done and the house was once again suspiciously spotless, she opened the laptop in the office and stared at the browser tabs already open.

There was a half-written article titled **"Burnout Isn't a Personality Trait: Reclaiming Rest Without Permission."**

It read like something she *wanted* to say. Something she'd almost said a dozen times. But never had the time. Or the energy. Or the nerve.

She closed the laptop.

Sat very still in the quiet.

The envelope from Celeste was still on her dresser.

It hadn't moved.

But somehow, it felt...closer.

Like the choice inside it was pulsing now. Louder.

Because this life?

It was incredible.

It was fulfilling.

It was full.

But every compliment, every memory, every perfectly organized thing—

It wasn't hers.

She let the sticky note slip from her fingers, untouched.

Even her handwriting didn't feel like her own anymore.

# a timeline built on lies (and lattes)

. . .

ELI BROUGHT HER COFFEE.

He did that sometimes—just showed up at the shop with a to-go cup labeled *"For: M. From: The guy with excellent taste in women and espresso."*

Today's cup said:

**"WARNING: Contents may cause emotional vulnerability. Sip responsibly."**

Mara stared at it for a full thirty seconds before taking a tiny, traitorous sip.

It was perfect. Of course it was.

Eli leaned against the counter, watching her with that quiet, careful smile. The one that said *he saw her.* Not just her jokes. Her rhythms. Her heart.

It made everything harder.

"I need to tell you something," she said, setting the cup down like it might explode.

Eli's brows lifted. "Should I sit down?"

"Maybe," she said. "Or run. Either is valid."

He took the stool next to the register, hands clasped, face open. "You're scaring me a little."

"Good. You should be," she said. "Because this is...not normal. Like, this week—me. I'm not acting like myself."

He laughed. "No offense, babe, but you're always a little off."

"No," she said, too quickly. "I mean—I'm really not myself."

He tilted his head. "You okay?"

"I'm not *this* Mara," she said, voice trembling now. "I mean, I *am*, but I'm not. I'm just...visiting."

Silence.

"Like...emotionally?" he asked.

"No. Like dimensionally."

Eli blinked. "Is this a metaphor?"

Mara ran a hand through her hair. "No. I mean...I came from another timeline. I switched places with a different version of myself who made better choices and has a more consistent skincare routine."

He smiled slowly, waiting for the punchline.

None came.

"Wait," he said. "You're serious?"

"Dead serious."

"Okay." He stood. "So, you're telling me...the woman I've been dating—the woman I kissed two nights ago—isn't you."

"It's complicated," she said.

He nodded once. Too calm. Too quiet.

"Right," he said. "So, what is this? You freaking out again? Deciding you're not ready, and instead of saying it, you make up some multiverse thing to soften the blow?"

"What? No—Eli, I'm not trying to ghost you via sci-fi allegory!"

"Well, you *are* trying to disappear," he said, eyes flashing now. "And honestly? I expected it. You always run when things get real."

She stared at him, stunned.

"I'm not running," she whispered.

"Yes, you are," he said. "Even if this whole story is true, even if there's some alternate version of you with a better life...you're still the one who's scared to stay in it."

He walked out before she could say anything else.

The doorbell jingled behind him, soft and final.

Mara stood alone with her coffee, her half-confession, and the slow, dawning horror that she might've just broken something she'd never get back.

Mara didn't cry at first.

She wandered the bookstore in a daze, wiping down counters that were already clean, straightening bookmarks that didn't need straightening, muttering apologies into the quiet like they might retroactively time-travel and fix everything.

"You always run when things get real."

The words didn't just echo. They sank. Heavy. Familiar. Like someone had read out loud a thought she was trying to smother.

But the worst part wasn't that he'd said it.

The worst part was that he wasn't wrong.

Her first instinct had been to bail. To avoid. To deliver the truth wrapped in sarcasm and hope no one noticed she'd packed a parachute.

She sank into the armchair in the reading nook—the one labeled "Reserved for Fictional Crying." Fitting.

The fantasy was fraying at the seams.

It had started out magical: better hair, calmer kid, dream job, perfect boyfriend who knew how to make espresso and respect boundaries.

But now?

The house was too quiet. The texts were too perfect. The smiles she'd faked all week were starting to echo.

And beneath all of it—beneath the fancy pants and fancy

pancakes—was the gnawing realization that this life wasn't flawless.

It was curated. Carefully. Painstakingly.

Alt-Mara hadn't stumbled into success.

She'd worked for it. Sacrificed. Struggled. Maybe even broke down in this exact chair once or twice.

And somehow, Mara had glossed over that. She'd stepped into someone else's highlight reel and assumed it was real time.

She stood and walked to the stockroom, needing something to do with her hands, her heart. She opened a drawer and found another note—this one in a different handwriting. Eli's.

*"Get some sleep. You're not as invincible as you pretend to be. x - E"*

She stared at it, something in her throat catching.

Alt-Mara had been tired too.

Alt-Mara had gotten overwhelmed.

Alt-Mara hadn't floated through this life. She'd *fought* for it.

And Mara? She'd walked in and treated it like a vacation with benefits.

She blinked back the sudden sting behind her eyes.

Maybe the most important part of this life wasn't the polished surface. Maybe it was the cracks. The effort. The people who stayed even when things got messy.

And maybe—just maybe—it wasn't too late to stop running.

But first, she had to do something she should've done days ago.

She had to find the person whose life she'd borrowed.

She had to find *herself.*

The decision wasn't dramatic.

There was no thunderclap. No wind ripping through the room. No ghostly voice whispering *"Choose wisely."*

There was just Mara. Sitting on the edge of the bed in her borrowed linen pajama set, staring at the gold-edged envelope on the dresser like it was judging her in calligraphy.

She'd spent six days trying to blend in.

Trying to believe she could slip into someone else's life and be *enough*.

And maybe, for a minute, she had been.

But this wasn't her story. Not yet. Not really.

If she was ever going to have a version of this life that was *real* —earned, not borrowed—she had to go back to the beginning.

And the beginning?

Was a woman with her face and her name who'd carved this whole thing out of chaos and therapy and probably a lot of fig bars.

She had to find *that* Mara.

She had to find *herself.*

She tapped the interface on her sleek alternate-timeline tablet— because of course it had a spa concierge *and* interdimensional tracking—and searched:

**Timeline Retreat: Wellness Facility – Current Location of Alt-Mara Jensen.**

A blinking pin dropped on a digital map.

A wellness retreat.

Of course.

She should've known.

No one who organized a color-coded pantry and emotionally available relationships got there without a few days of herbal steam and reflective journaling under a waterfall.

She grabbed her bag.

No dramatic speech. No goodbye note. She didn't even look at the gold envelope again.

Instead, she threw on a hoodie from the other Mara's closet that read **"It's Not Avoidance, It's Strategic Rest,"** stuffed her old phone in her pocket, and headed for the door.

As she stepped outside, the sun was rising—pink and gold, the kind of sky that looked fake, like a set designer had gone a little too hard on the ambiance.

"Okay," she whispered. "Let's meet the woman who made me possible."

She didn't know what she was walking into.

But for the first time since this whole strange, sparkly trip began—

Mara wasn't afraid of what she might find.

# the other woman is... me

. . .

THE WELLNESS RETREAT looked exactly like Mara imagined a place called **"The Stillness Center"** would.

Muted pastel buildings nestled among wildflowers. A koi pond that probably had its own Instagram account. A tiny gift shop selling bath salts with names like *Trauma Release Blend* and *Chakra Soothe: For When You've Been Through It*™.

The woman at the check-in desk wore a tunic and a look of deep, judgment-free serenity. Mara handed her the tablet with the coordinates from Celeste and tried not to sweat through her hoodie.

"I'm here to see someone," she said. "Mara Jensen."

The woman didn't blink. "Which one?"

Mara blinked back. "I... what?"

"Original or Alternate?" she asked, as if this were a coffee order.

"Original. The Mara from here. The one who—uh—built the life I've been crashing in like a confused houseguest with boundary issues."

The receptionist nodded and tapped a few things into a shimmering interface. "She's in Reflection Cabin Three."

Mara took the keycard and a deep breath.

She walked the gravel path toward the cabins, heart hammering in her chest like it was trying to knock its way into another timeline altogether. Trees swayed gently above her. Birds chirped like they'd achieved inner peace. Somewhere, someone was definitely meditating aggressively.

Cabin Three was small and beautiful. Clean lines. Big windows. A rocking chair on the porch.

And in it sat a woman.

Same hair. Same posture. Same nose that went all scrunchy when she was concentrating.

She looked...older, somehow. Not in years. But in *miles.* Like she'd done the work. Like she *carried* things and didn't try to hide it. She wore no makeup. Her sweatshirt read **"Feelings First, Logistics Later."**

She looked up as Mara approached.

No surprise. No tension.

Just the kind of half-smile Mara had only ever seen in the mirror —when she was exhausted but trying anyway.

"Hey," Mara said, awkwardly, as she reached the porch steps. "So... this is weird, right?"

Alt-Mara smiled faintly. "Only if you think it is."

And just like that—Mara met herself.

Not the dream version. Not the fantasy.

Just a tired woman in yoga pants with a lot of mileage and the strength to still be here.

They sat on the porch in silence for a moment, two versions of the same woman sipping herbal tea like this was a normal Tuesday.

It wasn't.

Mara cleared her throat. "So... how do we do this? Hug first? Cry? Fight? Rock-paper-scissors for who gets to keep Eli?"

Alt-Mara smiled softly. "You're not the first version of me I've met."

Mara blinked. "Oh. Wow. Okay. Are we just...out here crossing timelines like it's a book club?"

"Apparently I'm very popular with the burnt-out crowd," Alt-Mara said, then took a sip of tea. "You're number four."

"Seriously?" Mara sat back. "There are three other 'me's running around this spa?"

"Mostly crying into smoothies, yeah."

That pulled a laugh from Mara—small but real. Then quiet settled again, heavier this time. Not uncomfortable. Just...full.

"I thought you had it all figured out," Mara finally said.

"I don't," Alt-Mara replied. "I've just had more time to stop pretending I have to."

Mara looked out at the trees, voice softer now. "I've been living your life. And I thought it was perfect. Like...you'd cracked the code."

"I haven't cracked anything," Alt-Mara said. "I've just stopped making myself small for everyone else's comfort."

She paused.

"Which was hell, by the way. It wasn't one magical decision. It was years of therapy and grief and letting people think I was difficult. And dropping a lot of balls. And asking for help. Loudly."

Mara swallowed hard.

"I kissed Eli," she confessed.

Alt-Mara smiled, wistful. "Good. He deserves another chance to fall in love with you."

Mara blinked. "You're not mad?"

"Why would I be?" she said. "You're me. You're exhausted. You needed a break. And if kissing a good man in a timeline with better lighting helped you remember who you are underneath all the panic? Then I say—thank you."

Mara exhaled, something breaking open in her chest.

"I've felt like a fraud this whole time," she whispered.

Alt-Mara looked at her, really looked. "You're not a fraud. You're tired. And the world keeps acting like just surviving isn't enough. But it is. Sometimes, that's the bravest thing."

Mara's eyes burned.

"I don't know how to go back," she said.

"You don't have to go back and fix everything," Alt-Mara said. "Just...go back. Take one thing off your plate. Let someone help. Say no. Sleep."

Mara laughed, watery. "Sounds fake."

Alt-Mara leaned over, touched her hand. "It's not. It's just hard. But you've already done harder."

And just like that, something shifted.

Not in the air.

In Mara.

She didn't feel fixed.

She didn't feel whole.

But she felt...seen.

By the one person she'd spent years ignoring.

They didn't hug.

Not because they didn't want to, but because some things are too heavy for a gesture that simple.

They stood at the edge of the porch while the trees rustled and a pair of doves—because of course there were doves—flew past like the universe was staging an emotionally nuanced Hallmark moment.

"I don't know how to thank you," Mara said.

Alt-Mara smiled. "You don't have to. Just don't waste the version of us who gets to go back."

Mara nodded. "So... what happens now? Are you...reabsorbed into the timeline matrix or whatever?"

Alt-Mara raised an eyebrow. "I'm going to take a nap and then eat three kinds of gluten and not feel bad about it."

Mara laughed. "That's honestly aspirational."

She started to turn, then paused. "Hey… if you ever want to visit *my* timeline…it's messy. And underfunded. But I know a great place to get late-night fries, and my best friend makes a mean 'emergency mimosa.'"

Alt-Mara grinned. "Careful. I might take you up on that."

They stood there a second longer.

Mara didn't want to leave—but she also didn't need to stay.

Not anymore.

She'd come looking for permission.

But what she found was something way more powerful:

A reminder that she already had it.

She gave one last wave, turned, and headed down the path— dust clinging to her shoes, sun on her shoulders, the envelope from Celeste still tucked inside her bag.

But this time?

It didn't feel like a ticking clock.

It felt like a second chance.

And this time, she was going to use it.

# the real thing (even if it's messy)

. . .

MARA WOKE up to the sound of Leo yelling about waffles and the cat they didn't own scratching at the back door again.

So... not a dream.

Her ceiling was cracked, her smoke detector was still blinking low battery, and the air smelled faintly of syrup and mildew.

And yet—

She smiled.

Because this time, she wasn't waking up *dreading* the day.

She was waking up *in it*.

She rolled out of bed—still in her old pajamas, the ones with the hole in the thigh and the faint smell of microwave popcorn—and padded into the kitchen, where Leo had managed to both pour cereal and get it on the ceiling.

"Hey, kiddo," she said, scooping up a rogue Cheerio.

Leo looked up, surprised. "You slept in."

"I did," she said. "And it was glorious."

He narrowed his eyes, suspicious. "Are you back to being Weird Mom or still Fancy Pajama Mom?"

She laughed. "Somewhere in the middle."

She grabbed two bowls, filled one with cereal, and—just because she could—tossed a handful of blueberries on top. Leo's eyebrows shot up.

"You're putting *fruit* on things now?" he asked. "Did you hit your head?"

"Only my heart," she said, ruffling his hair.

Her phone buzzed on the counter. Five work emails. Two unread Slack messages. One calendar alert titled: **"9 AM – Internal Strategy Huddle (bring positivity + metrics!)"**

She stared at it.

Then hit snooze.

Then opened a new tab.

**Search:** part-time positions with flexible hours + health benefits.

She had no plan.

But for the first time in years, she had a starting line.

And a spine.

She turned to Leo, who was now arranging his cereal pieces into a smiley face. "Hey, want to help me pick a new chore chart?"

He blinked. "Is that a trap?"

"Nope. It comes with stickers. And maybe bribery."

"I'm listening."

They grinned at each other.

Her phone buzzed again.

She left it.

Just sat there with Leo, letting him build a cereal fort on the table.

And for once, she didn't reach for control.

She just stayed.

Mara quit her second job during a lunch break, with half a

sandwich in one hand and a Google Doc of talking points in the other.

She didn't even cry.

"Wellness over worship," she typed in the farewell email, followed by a smiley face that was only mildly passive-aggressive. She reread it, added a semicolon for emotional balance, and hit send before she could talk herself out of it.

Her chest felt tight.

But also—lighter.

She made three more bold moves before 3 p.m.:

1. She finally called the respite care coordinator she'd been avoiding for six months and signed Leo up for Saturday sessions.

2. She texted Lana *"Can you come over tonight? I need help and possibly wine and definitely emotional supervision."*

3. She unfollowed the mommy blogger who made parenting look like a minimalist Pinterest board with curated tantrums.

Then she sat on the couch with a mug of tea that was still warm and just...*breathed.*

The apartment was messy. The laundry pile had evolved into a hostile sentient being. Leo had spilled glitter glue down the side of the fridge. And the living room still smelled faintly of hot dogs for reasons no one could explain.

But she didn't feel buried by it.

Not today.

Today, she felt *present.*

Lana arrived an hour later in leggings, a messy bun, and a tote bag labeled **"Emotional Support Snacks."**

"Did we survive the timeline hijinks?" she asked, kicking off her shoes.

"Barely," Mara said. "I came back changed."

"Emotionally or interdimensionally?"

"Both."

Lana handed her a mini bottle of champagne and a bag of popcorn. "Then let's toast to that."

They flopped onto the couch.

Mara didn't launch into a monologue. She didn't even try to explain.

She just sat there.

Real.

Tired.

But not hiding.

And that, Lana understood completely.

"By the way," Lana said later, through a mouthful of popcorn, "You've got major main character energy right now."

"Is that code for 'you look like you just cried in your closet'?"

"Yes," Lana said, smiling. "But like... in a powerful way."

Mara laughed. Actually laughed.

And when she caught her reflection in the TV screen—a little messy, a little puffy-eyed, hair doing its usual rebellion—she didn't hate what she saw.

She looked like someone who'd stopped waiting for things to get easier.

And decided to start anyway.

The bookstore was tucked between a vintage record shop and a café that claimed to have invented the dirty chai. Mara had passed it a hundred times and never gone in.

Today, she did.

The bell above the door gave a hopeful little jingle, like even it was rooting for her.

Inside, it smelled like paper and cinnamon and possibility. Shelves stretched high, fairy lights wound around displays, and in the corner—a small table with a handwritten sign that read:

*"Blind Date With a Book: Take a Chance, Break Your Heart, Heal Anyway."*

Her breath caught.

It wasn't *the same* bookstore. But it had *the same spirit*.

A man was restocking the romance shelf. Tall. Brown curls. A well-loved flannel. He turned, holding a paperback in one hand and a coffee in the other.

"Hey there," he said, smiling politely. "Looking for anything specific?"

She stared at him, stunned.

Same eyes.

Same voice.

Same vibe that said *I alphabetize my trauma and would gladly talk about it over a croissant.*

"Actually," she said, finding her voice, "I think I'm just...trying again."

He tilted his head, intrigued. "At reading?"

"At life."

He grinned. "Cool. No pressure, but we do have a special on existential fiction and accidental self-discovery."

She laughed, and it felt different this time. Not forced. Not stolen. Just *hers.*

She glanced at the display table.

Picked up a book.

Held it out to him.

"I don't know if we've met before," she said, "but I think we were supposed to."

Eli blinked, caught somewhere between confused and charmed. "That's a hell of a line."

"Yeah, I'm working on the delivery."

He took the book from her. Their fingers brushed. And in that simple, quiet contact, something opened.

Not a memory.

Not a spark.

A *possibility*.

"You want a recommendation?" he asked.

"I want a lot of things," she said. "But let's start there."

They stood in the middle of the shop. Books stacked all around them. Lives waiting in pages. And for the first time in a long time, Mara didn't feel behind.

She felt ready.

Ready to start over.

Ready to choose.

Ready to stay.

Eli handed her a book.

She took it.

And smiled.

"Just let go," she whispered—

—and this time, she meant it.

# epilogue

. . .

ONE YEAR *Later*

There's a sticky note taped to the front door of *Bookish & Bold*, now co-owned by Mara Jensen and Eli Navarro.

It reads:

**Closed Today** – *Owner needed a day off. Miraculously, took it.*

Inside, the lights are off, the couch in the reading nook is taken over by pillows and takeout containers, and Leo is halfway through a Percy Jackson reread with his head in Mara's lap.

Eli walks in balancing iced lattes and a bag of fig bars.

"We could've opened late," he says, nudging Mara's foot.

She shrugs. "I'm practicing imperfection. And naps."

He grins, drops the bag on the table. "Therapy today?"

"Already went. Talked about boundaries. Cried into a stress ball shaped like a croissant."

"Proud of you."

They clink lattes.

Leo sighs. "You two are so *weirdly healthy* now. It's gross."

Mara smirks. "You say that, but you still requested 'smiley face pancakes' for dinner."

"That's called tradition," Leo says, very seriously.

Outside, the bookstore sign creaks gently in the breeze.

Inside, Mara glances at Eli. At Leo. At the life she chose—still messy. Still loud. Still *hers*.

No magic this time.

Just a little time.

And the decision, every day, to stay.

The End

# support role fatigue

. . .

LANA MORENO ADJUSTED the mimosa tower for the third time, because apparently even champagne pyramids had imposter syndrome now.

"Just tilt the top flute a hair to the left—no, *my* left, babe," Grace called across the courtyard, her voice lilting with the effortless authority of someone whose eyebrows were microbladed into perfect confidence.

Lana smiled. Not because she felt particularly smiley, but because she'd been Grace Patel's best friend since middle school, and smiling was muscle memory by now. Plus, they were five minutes from guests arriving and someone had to look like they weren't one lemon macaron away from a breakdown.

"Got it," Lana called back, steadying the glass as Grace flounced past in a seafoam wrap dress that probably cost more than Lana's car battery. She left behind a waft of peony and mild panic.

The backyard sparkled—literally. Fairy lights strung through citrus trees, delicate signage in calligraphy fonts, individual seating cards shaped like seashells. *Confetti & Grace* had done it again. Or rather, Grace had. Lana was just the human tape dispenser.

"Can you grab the bride's lavender spritz from the cooler?" Grace asked, not breaking stride as she adjusted a throw pillow and kissed the air beside the event photographer's cheek. "It should be marked 'main character hydration.'"

Of course it was.

Lana wiped her hands on her linen shorts and ducked behind the bar cart. Her phone buzzed. A text from her mom asking if she could "pop by and fix the Wi-Fi again, sweetie." Another from her boss, wondering if she was "still planning on updating the fundraiser deck?" Today was supposed to be Personal Time Off.

She grabbed the bottle, straightened, and—oh. There was Charlie.

He was setting up folding chairs near the archway, sleeves rolled, sunglasses on, and looking like someone who carved his own furniture and *meant* it. He bent slightly to test one of the chairs for wobbles, and Lana's brain misfired just long enough for her to forget how hands worked.

The spritz slipped.

It hit the grass with a soft thunk, not quite a tragedy—but enough for her to flinch.

Charlie looked over. "You okay?"

"Totally," she chirped, crouching to retrieve the bottle and her pride. "Just testing gravity. It works."

He smiled, that quiet kind he reserved for shared jokes and sweet dogs, and turned back to the chairs. She watched him for one extra beat.

Then—

"Oh my *god*, it's happening!" Grace squealed from the patio. "She's here! Lana, cue the playlist!"

Of course it was Lana's job to hit play. Just like it had been her job to assemble party favors, wrangle RSVPs, and unstick Grace's Spanx in the church bathroom once.

She hit the button on the Bluetooth speaker, and bright, bubbly acoustic pop filled the air.

Everyone clapped. The bride glowed. Grace floated.

Lana stood behind the bar cart, alone with the lemon rinds and her suddenly unshakeable thought:

What if this was it?

What if she stayed like this forever—silent, helpful, just off-camera in someone else's beautifully filtered life?

And what if... she didn't want to anymore?

Her phone buzzed again. Another work ping. Another some-one-needs-you text.

"Lana, can you top off the mimosa bar?" Grace called brightly. "It's looking a little... less-than."

Lana rose to do it, just in time to hear a guest murmur, "Is she the help?"

No one corrected them. Grace gave a tight smile but didn't step in.

Lana found a moment to herself in the powder-pink guest bathroom, the one Grace had styled "for aesthetic emergencies." It smelled like lemon verbena and mild stress.

She stared at her reflection. Her eyeliner had migrated. Her curls were frizzing in strategic rebellion. There was a lipstick smudge on her chin from sipping someone else's drink in a panic two minutes ago.

She was background at best. Wallpaper. The sort of person who showed up early, stayed late, and was tagged in Instagram stories only when she happened to be holding someone else's bag.

The playlist outside shifted into some dreamy acoustic cover of a Beyoncé song. Lana sighed. *Of course* Grace had licensed the ethereal Spotify version. Nothing could be loud here unless Grace made it look effortless.

Her phone buzzed again—Mom, again, with a gif of a blinking

router and the words "HELP ME TECH WIZARD 🌐🧙 ." She turned it facedown.

She thought about the scene earlier. Charlie, crouched in the sun, laugh lines softening his usually serious face. He'd smiled at her like he *knew* her—like maybe he still thought of her as more than Grace's dependable sidekick.

That used to be her secret favorite part of events: catching Charlie in the quiet moments between his sister's whirlwinds. Setting up folding chairs. Bringing the bride's grandma a chair with arms. Handing Lana a can of ginger ale without asking, because somehow, he always knew she preferred it to soda water.

They never *talked* much. But she noticed. And sometimes, she let herself believe he noticed back.

She'd never told Grace. That was its own can of guilt-sparkled worms. Best friend's older brother was a trope for a reason, and Lana had no interest in playing the cliché.

But in the privacy of her own thoughts, she'd imagined it. What it might be like if someone like Charlie looked at someone like her and saw *more*.

She bit her lip.

Then—voices outside. Applause. Grace must have launched into her "love is a curated experience" toast.

Lana splashed cold water on her cheeks and forced a smile back onto her face. Not the bright, boss-babe kind Grace could do in her sleep. Just… passably okay.

She adjusted her top, smoothed her hair, and opened the door.

Time to be The Reliable One again.

Lana ducked behind the hydrangea hedge for five blessed minutes of shade and silence. Her sandals *peeled* from her feet with every step, like even her shoes wanted out. One of Grace's interns had just asked if she could "run out and grab more biodegradable confetti." From where, exactly? The artisanal glitter fields?

She crouched on a low garden wall, tucked in next to a stone cherub that looked just as exhausted as she felt, and closed her eyes.

She said, softly, to no one in particular, "I'm so tired of making other people's dreams photogenic."

A lemon rind floated down from a tree that hadn't rustled. The breeze shifted, oddly warm for spring.

She looked up—and there was a shimmer in the air, like heat off pavement.

And then, suddenly, she wasn't alone.

The woman wasn't *there* before. Lana was sure of it. But there she was now—linen-draped, sunlit, and unbothered by the heat like it personally respected her.

She looked like someone who only drank tea from glass cups and spoke in allegories. Her eyebrows were celestial. Her energy? Mildly unsettling but weirdly reassuring. Like a therapist who also hosted dinner parties in the astral plane.

"Rough day?" she asked, voice smooth as the pressed linen she wore.

Lana blinked. "I'm sorry—do I know you?"

"No. But I know you."

Of course.

The woman extended a card. Cream. Heavy stock. Gold lettering.

### Timeline Retreats
*For When Your Life Just Isn't It*

Lana didn't take it.

"Is this… a wedding vendor?" she tried.

The woman smiled, just slightly. "It's not an invitation to a wedding, no. It's an invitation to you. A different version of you."

Lana huffed a laugh. "I don't have time for soul-searching, sorry. I've got a mimosa tower to maintain and a unicorn piñata emergency waiting in the wings."

"And what if, for once, someone else handled the tower?" the woman said, gently. "What if you stepped out of the background and into the center of your own story?"

Lana didn't mean to. But her fingers reached for the card.

It was cool to the touch, unnervingly blank on the back. Just the infinity symbol in the corner, looped like a secret.

"One week," the woman said, watching her. "In a version of your life where you said yes. Where you took up space."

"And what," Lana asked, voice cracking slightly, "if that's not who I am?"

The woman tilted her head. "Maybe it's not. But maybe it could be."

Lana glanced back toward the courtyard. Grace was leading a photo op. Charlie was in the background, holding a tray of cupcakes. No one had noticed she'd disappeared.

She looked down at the card again.

Maybe this wasn't a scam.

Maybe it was a sign.

"Do I have to decide right now?" she asked.

The woman's smile deepened. "You already did."

And with that, she turned and walked away—vanishing into the sun like she *belonged* there.

Lana stared after her.

And in her hand, the card glowed faintly.

That night, she Googled "Timeline Retreats."

Nothing official. Just a cryptic site with a one-page scroll: *"Step into the version of you who said yes."*

There were no testimonials. Just a looping symbol. And a button labeled: *Begin.*

# new life, new look

. . .

LANA'S first thought upon waking was that someone had replaced her bedding with clouds and her ceiling with… Instagram.

Soft morning light spilled in through gauzy curtains that were definitely not hers. Neither was the linen duvet or the geometric pendant lamp above her or—she sat up slowly, heart pounding—the neon-pink wall sign glowing faintly across the room.

## LOUDER, LANA.

"Oh no," she whispered.

She glanced down. The pajamas were leopard print satin with a tag that screamed luxury brand and a neckline that said, *you own confidence now, sweetie.* Her nails were almond-shaped and painted a glossy mauve. Her skin was suspiciously luminous.

This wasn't her apartment. This wasn't her life. And judging by the oversized ring light, the mic setup near the window, and the sleek desk calendar labeled "PITCH DEADLINES // BRAND COLLABS," this version of her wasn't hiding in the background.

Her reflection stared back at her—cheekbones sharp, lips

painted, eyes wide with someone else's certainty. She didn't just look seen.

She looked staged.

A knock startled her.

Then a voice—chirpy and professional—called through the door: "Ten-minute heads-up, Lana! Live in fifteen. Makeup team's in the kitchen. There's beet lattes and the morning energy shot!"

*Makeup team?!*

She stood too fast and had to clutch the headboard to steady herself. "Live *what*?!"

Her phone buzzed from a wireless charger shaped like a disco ball. The lock screen was a close-up selfie: her, but with winged liner and the kind of cheekbone situation that said she took herself seriously now.

A calendar alert popped up.

**LIVE TAPING: "Say It Like You Mean It" – Ep. 212**

**Guest: Dr. Shanae Young, PhD, Confidence Coach & Human Confetti**

"What," Lana muttered, scrolling madly, "is happening—"

Another alert.

**PRE-READ: Top listener Qs**

**– How do I find my voice?**

**– What if I'm scared to be seen?**

**– Is confidence real or a scam?**

Outside her door, footsteps. Laughter. Someone said, "TikTok numbers are wild this week." A coffee grinder whirred. The scent of beetroot and ambition wafted in.

Lana dropped the phone and reached for the nearest robe, which turned out to be black silk and embroidered with tiny gold lightning bolts.

She caught sight of herself in the floor-length mirror by the closet.

And for a moment… she paused.

The woman staring back at her had her face—but less hesitation. Better brows. And a little sparkle in her eye like she knew something Lana didn't.

Or maybe she'd just stopped apologizing for existing.

"Okay," Lana whispered. "I don't know what's going on, but… she's hot?"

A knock again. "Two minutes!"

Lana inhaled.

Exhaled.

And stepped into the hallway.

Because apparently, today… she was going live.

The set was brighter than any room had a right to be before 9 a.m.

Fairy lights framed a pink velvet armchair. A branded tumbler labeled *LOUDER, LANA* sat on a side table next to a tiny succulent wearing rhinestone sunglasses. And Lana—still mentally clutching her old Target coffee mug—was perched in a glam robe and fuzzy slippers, surrounded by a very professional-looking production crew.

"Ready for mic check?" a woman with a clipboard asked, gesturing at Lana's collarbone like it had betrayed her.

"Sure," Lana said, because what else could she say? "Let's mic it up."

Someone adjusted her hair. Another dabbed concealer under her eyes with terrifying efficiency. A third handed her a cue card she couldn't read fast enough.

### EPISODE 212: SAY IT LIKE YOU MEAN IT

Guest: Dr. Shanae Young

Focus: Authenticity, Visibility, Volume

Hot Quote: "Quiet women aren't weak—they're just recharging."

A producer made a twirling gesture. "We're rolling in three—two—"

Lana smiled blindly at the camera.

"Hey, hey, hello," she said, her voice coming out oddly smooth, like her throat had been coached by a thousand affirmations. "Welcome back to *Louder, Lana!* where we say the things we've been too scared to say… until now."

Oh god. Where was that coming from? Was this muscle memory? Timeline possession?

The screen behind her sparkled to life as applause audio piped in. Across from her, a woman in bold glasses and a jewel-toned blazer gave her a warm smile. This must be Dr. Shanae.

"So," Lana continued, somehow still speaking, "let's talk about taking up space. And what happens when you finally stop shrinking yourself to fit other people's comfort zones."

Dr. Shanae beamed. "Absolutely. Lana, your story last week about the conference panel—where you refused to be cut off—resonated so deeply."

Lana blinked.

*I did… what?*

"Oh, right, yes," she said, nodding like a bobblehead on a rollercoaster. "I… stood up for my speaking time. Like a boundary ninja."

The audience—real or piped-in—chuckled.

Dr. Shanae leaned in. "You said something beautiful in that moment. About how silence used to be your default—but now, it's your *choice*."

"I did say that," Lana said slowly, trying not to look directly into the teleprompter where a very helpful line read:

**(REMIND AUDIENCE: YOU USED TO BE INVISIBLE)**

She faked a laugh. "Yeah, the old me couldn't even order lunch without apologizing for existing."

The chat screen beside her exploded with heart emojis.

Lana clung to the chair's velvet arms and kept going.

She didn't know what she was saying. She didn't know how she got here.

But the audience believed in her.

Worse?

A small part of her was starting to believe it, too.

After the taping, Lana fled to the balcony like a woman avoiding both enlightenment and beet lattes.

The air was soft, tinged with jasmine and traffic. Far below, a delivery bike zipped by, blasting a remix of something she was probably supposed to know the lyrics to. She clutched the *Louder, Lana* tumbler like a lifeline and tried to remember how breathing worked.

A phone—*her* phone—buzzed on the side table next to an open planner covered in color-coded stickers:

　　brand call

　　voiceover studio

　　pilates (cancel?)

She swiped without thinking.

A notification blinked up from Instagram.

**gracepatel.events**: *Sometimes the people we cheer the loudest for leave us clapping alone.*

#growthisgrieving #confettiandboundaries #gracefultruths

Lana stared.

It was a photo of a champagne flute, half-full, abandoned on a lawn chair. In the background: fairy lights. A familiar garden.

*The bridal shower.*

She tapped to read the comments.

**@bridesandblooms**: Girl. Been there.

**@cakedbycass**: Let 'em go if they ghost you in glitter.

**@yourvibrantvenus**: Rooting for you, always 💔 ✦

Lana's heart gave a lurch.

In this life, she hadn't just drifted from Grace. She'd dropped her. Walked away. No explanation. No apology. Just... vanished into volume.

She flipped to her DMs and scrolled up.

Nothing recent. Just a thread from months ago.

> GRACE: Just call me when you're ready to talk.

> GRACE: I miss you.

> GRACE: I didn't think I was temporary.

> GRACE: ...are you okay?

Lana closed the app.

In the studio, the next guest was getting mic'd up. A producer offered her a smoothie with her name on it—well, this version of her name. Curly script. Gold straw.

Lana smiled, accepted it, and stepped back inside.

But her stomach churned.

The lights were flattering. The compliments were flowing.

But somewhere, just outside the sparkle...

She'd left someone behind.

# oh no, he's hot

· · ·

THE MAKERSPACE SMELLED LIKE SAWDUST, espresso, and something faintly herbal—probably from the indoor plant wall that looked like it had a therapist.

Lana stepped inside, heels clicking against polished concrete, sunglasses still on. She hoped she looked casually important. She was here to "film a collaboration," according to the calendar in her phone. What kind of collaboration? Unknown. The email was... vague. Or possibly deleted.

"Hey, you made it!" called a bright-eyed staffer in paint-splattered overalls. "Lana, right? We've got the woodturning demo setup out back, and the interview spot's pre-lit. Charlie's out there now."

*Charlie.*

The name hit her like an unexpected drop in a workout playlist —jarring, a little thrilling, and completely disorienting.

"Sorry—Charlie?" she echoed, trying to sound breezy and not like her organs were suddenly doing parkour.

"Yeah, he's running the shop today. You two have *great* chemistry, by the way. That reel from the Valentine's campaign? Iconic."

Lana's mouth went dry. She didn't remember a campaign. Or a reel. Or ever being "iconic."

She followed the staffer down the hall, past shelves of hand-made cutting boards and curated chaos. The sliding door to the back patio opened and—

There he was.

Charlie Patel.

Rolled-up sleeves, work boots, one knee braced on a stool as he adjusted a camera tripod. His forearms were exactly as unfair as she remembered. His hair had that artful mess that only came from real effort or sheer magnetic personality.

He looked up.

Paused.

And in that pause, Lana felt the ground tilt just slightly.

"Hi," she said, like she hadn't ghosted him in this reality.

His jaw tightened. "Hey."

One syllable. Heavy as a hammer.

She swallowed. "You, uh… run this place?"

"For five years now," he said, straightening. "Since the Kick-starter. You—" A beat. "You used to come by more."

Ouch.

"I've been busy," she offered, hating how small it sounded.

"Yeah," he said, turning back to the tripod. "I noticed."

Lana stepped closer, watching him adjust the lens. His hands were steady. Skilled. Familiar.

"You okay with filming?" she asked, trying to find her footing. "It's just a short segment."

"Sure," he said, without looking at her. "Not my first time being your content."

Her breath caught.

Oh.

They weren't just friends in this life.

They were *something more.*

And she'd ended it.

They stood side by side behind the woodworking table, just close enough that Lana could smell sawdust, cedar, and whatever magic shampoo Charlie used to smell like calm mornings and bad decisions.

The cameras were rolling. A producer signaled silently for "energy." Lana plastered on a smile and turned toward the lens.

"I'm here with Charlie Patel," she said brightly, "co-owner of Ridge & Grain, carpenter extraordinaire, and today's guest star in my attempt to not lose a finger on camera."

Charlie gave a tight smile. "We're making a tray today. Straight lines, no bloodshed."

The audience—somewhere online—would probably find their dynamic charming. Banter-y. Maybe even flirty.

But Lana could feel the static.

Every glance Charlie threw her way came with a second, hidden sentence. Every silence felt like it used to hold laughter, or kisses, or the kind of inside jokes that only happened on long, quiet mornings.

"Tell me what you love most about working with your hands," she prompted, just following the script on her tablet.

Charlie hesitated.

Then set down his sanding block.

"What I love," he said slowly, "is watching something take shape. Knowing every piece matters. Nothing wasted. No shortcuts."

She nodded, unsure.

"But it only works," he added, eyes locking with hers, "if you stick with it. If you don't walk away when it gets messy."

The silence that followed wasn't on the script.

Neither was the way her cheeks burned.

"Okay," she said softly, turning back to the camera. "So, uh... tools. Let's talk tools."

Charlie exhaled like he'd been holding something back for too long. "You used to know them all by name. You loved the lathe."

Lana blinked. "I did?"

He looked at her then—really looked. "Yeah. You did."

She scrambled for a recovery. "Well, a lot's changed."

"Clearly," he said, not unkindly. Just... honest.

A beat passed.

Then: "Is this part of the show?" he asked. "Pretending you don't remember?"

"I—no. I just..." She floundered. "Things have been a blur lately."

He studied her for a second longer. Something softened in his expression. Not forgiveness. But something close to wondering.

"Well," he said quietly, "you're still good on camera."

The producer called "Cut!" and Lana stepped back, heart pounding, pulse in her ears like a warning bell.

Charlie didn't say anything else.

He just turned back to the table.

And began sanding again.

Lana lingered after the cameras stopped.

The crew packed up quickly—cords coiled, tripods collapsed, someone asked for a boomerang and got a polite, practiced smile in return. And then it was just her and Charlie again, the silence between them no longer buffered by content strategy or curated charm.

She leaned against the worktable, running her fingers along the edge of the half-finished tray. "You really do make beautiful things."

Charlie didn't look up. "It's not complicated. Just measure twice, cut once, and finish what you start."

She flinched, just slightly. "Is that a metaphor?"

He shrugged, still sanding. "You tell me."

Oof.

She took a step closer, toeing the line between safe and sorry.

"I don't remember what happened," she admitted, voice low. "Between us. But... I feel like I hurt you."

That made him pause.

For a long second, he didn't speak.

Then—softly— "You didn't just hurt me, Lana. You disappeared. No explanation. One day we were... *something*, and the next, you were on a stage talking about how you had to 'shed distractions to grow.'"

She winced. "That doesn't sound like me."

"It didn't sound like you then either."

The workshop was warm. Dust motes floated in the sunbeams slicing through the back windows. Lana could feel the press of memory—not hers, but hers somehow anyway.

She reached out instinctively, her hand brushing his wrist.

He froze.

And in that breathless half-second, something flickered between them.

Familiarity.

Regret.

Possibility.

His eyes found hers. And for a moment, she felt it—all the versions of her that might have said yes, might have stayed, might have built something real instead of branding it.

Then he stepped back.

Carefully. Kindly.

But still—a step.

"Whatever this is," he said, voice quiet and even, "it's not where we left off."

She nodded, throat tight. "I know."

He offered the faintest smile, tired at the edges. "But… it's good to see you."

And then he turned back to his tools.

Just like that.

Like they hadn't almost been something.

Like maybe they still could be.

But not yet.

# influencer chaos & inner conflict

. . .

LANA'S FACE stared back at her from the homepage of *The Current*, a trendy digital mag known for listicles, late-night horoscope drops, and declaring people "voices of the moment."

Her headline?

**"LOUDER, LANA: The Podcast Princess Turning Self-Doubt into a Movement."**

*"She's bold, branded, and possibly powered by beet lattes."*

She blinked. Sipped her beet latte. Blinked again.

There she was: bold lipstick, fierce pose, laughter mid-freeze. The kind of photo that said *I woke up emotionally hydrated and unbothered*. Except... she hadn't.

The article raved about her confidence. Her clarity. Her catchphrases.

"She makes truth feel stylish," the profile read. "In a sea of curated calm, Lana Moreno reminds us that being loud is a form of love."

"Lana?" her assistant—no, her *brand coordinator*—poked her head into the studio. "We just hit half a million downloads. Also, the *Rising Voices* panel confirmed. You're officially on stage with Sadie Bloom and Dr. Lex Hart."

Lana blinked. "Sadie Bloom—the TEDx poet with the sleeve tattoos?"

"And Lex Hart. The woman who rebranded rage as empowerment."

"Oh."

The coordinator smiled. "You okay? You don't *look* nervous."

That's because she wasn't sure how to look like a woman halfway through an identity crisis in a cashmere jumpsuit.

"I'm great," Lana lied smoothly. "Thrilled. Empowered. Radiant."

The door clicked shut.

She stared back at the homepage again.

And suddenly, the words felt… foreign.

*Podcast Princess. Movement. Voice of a generation.*

But who was writing the script?

Not her—not really. Her show had producers. Her captions had "tone guides." Even her outfits came from mood boards now. She wasn't *sharing*—she was *performing vulnerability* with five talking points and an affiliate code.

Her phone buzzed with new followers, glowing praise, and curated hearts. But no one asked if she was okay. And the hollowness crept in like fog under a door.

She closed the article.

Walked over to her mic.

And whispered, "I don't think I belong here."

The moderator smiled brightly. "We've got time for one more audience question."

A woman in the second row stood, adjusting thick glasses and clutching a tiny notepad. "Hi, Lana," she said nervously. "Um… your confidence is really inspiring. But I guess I want to ask…"

She hesitated.

Lana smiled, professional and polished. "Go ahead."

The woman's voice wavered. "What happens when you lose the people who mattered to get here? Is confidence still worth it then?"

The question landed like a stone in a still pond.

Lana's throat tightened.

Every script in her head evaporated.

She could say something packaged—about growth and sacrifice and finding your tribe. Something safe.

Instead, she blinked and said, "Honestly? Sometimes I wonder the same thing."

The room stilled.

She added, more quietly, "I lost someone I thought would always be there. And I'm still figuring out whether I chose the spotlight… or just ran from the shadows."

A beat.

Then a soft murmur of acknowledgment from the crowd.

The woman nodded, eyes glassy. "Thank you."

Lana exhaled, smiled with less polish this time. "Thanks for asking the question no one puts on a mug."

The recording light stayed dark.

She didn't hit record.

Lana was halfway through a mood board caption about "radical presence" when she realized she hadn't spoken to Grace in this timeline at all.

Not a text. Not a tag. Not even a sarcastic "don't forget to hydrate, queen" voice memo.

She'd been too busy. Too branded. Too curated.

She opened her photos app, searching by keyword: *Grace*.

Nothing recent.

No brunch selfies. No backyard chaos. No blurry late-night shots of glitter and gummy bears and ambition.

Just one old video, low-res, buried in a folder called "Stuff to Keep."

She hit play.

The scene: a picnic table. Grace in oversized sunglasses, blowing bubbles through a straw into her iced coffee. Lana laughing so hard the camera shook. Grace yelling, "I *am* Confetti & Grace!" like a battle cry.

It was a nothing moment.

But it felt like *everything*.

She scrolled further. DMs. Emails. She found an archived thread she'd missed—probably on purpose. Or maybe Timeline Lana had just ignored it.

> GRACE: You said this version of you would make room for the people who mattered. But it feels like she only made room for applause.
>
> GRACE: I hope you're happy. I'm still here, by the way. In case you ever remember who we were.

Lana's chest ached like the wind had been knocked out of her.

She hadn't just ghosted Grace.

She'd replaced her—with followers, fans, and flattering lighting. But none of them had seen her cry over almond butter at midnight. None of them knew her coffee order *and* her coping mechanisms.

And worst of all?

She hadn't missed her until now.

Lana closed the thread.

For the first time since arriving in this timeline, she didn't feel bolder.

She just felt... alone.

The makerspace wasn't technically open, but the door was unlocked.

Earlier that day, she'd skimmed an email from her team:

*Re: Ridge & Grain Collaboration – ready to greenlight for social push?*

Lana tapped back a quick yes.

Even as something in her chest tugged.

Charlie hadn't responded to the original concept. Maybe he didn't even know.

But it was clean. Strategic. Glossy.

And Lana was tired of second-guessing herself.

Lana slipped in quietly, like someone sneaking into a memory.

The lights were low. Tools hung neatly on pegboards. A half-sanded bench sat mid-project, patient and unfinished.

She found Charlie in the back corner, brushing sawdust off a newly built frame. He looked up when he heard her, then went right back to work.

She didn't blame him.

"I just…" she started, then faltered. "I wanted to say thank you. For the shoot."

He didn't respond right away. Just kept wiping down the frame, methodical and calm.

"You're different," he said finally, not looking at her.

Lana's stomach twisted. "Different how?"

He paused. "You used to show up and ask a million questions. About finish options. Grain patterns. What kind of glue was secretly the best." A soft smile, barely there. "You called my toolbox the 'emotionally unavailable boyfriend of the shop.'"

A laugh caught in her throat. "I did?"

He nodded. "You were curious. Focused. Kind. And I was proud of the way you saw things—little details no one else noticed. I thought maybe we were building something together."

He shifted, finally looking at her. "Then you sent over that brand collab offer. It was big. Corporate. All about making the shop look glossy instead of real."

Lana blinked.

"I turned it down," he said. "Didn't hear from you again after that."

His voice wasn't accusing. Just matter-of-fact. Like sand smoothing into wood grain.

She flinched. "And now?"

He finally turned to face her. "Now you're... polished. Strategic. Everything you say feels like it's meant to be clipped and shared."

She swallowed. "I didn't mean to become a soundbite."

He shrugged. "Maybe you didn't mean to. But you did."

Silence stretched between them like wood that hadn't quite been sanded smooth.

"I'm trying," she said, barely above a whisper. "I want to be... better. Braver."

Charlie's eyes softened. "I think you already were. You just didn't know it yet."

That landed deep. Like a chord in her heart someone had finally strummed.

She blinked back something sharp. "What did I do, Charlie? Why did I leave?"

He hesitated.

Then: "You said you needed more. That you couldn't grow while being someone else's 'sweet chapter.' That if you were ever going to be *louder*, you had to leave the quiet things behind."

He said it gently.

Like he didn't want it to hurt.

But it did.

Because maybe the "quiet things" weren't holding her back. Maybe they were the only parts that had actually been real.

He set down the frame. "You didn't owe me forever. I just wish you hadn't made me feel like a footnote."

Lana opened her mouth.

Closed it.

There was nothing to say that would make it okay. Not yet.

So, she just whispered, "I'm sorry."

Charlie nodded. Not a forgiveness. Just an acknowledgment.

And then he did what he always did—he picked up the work. Not for her. Not to impress. Just… because it needed doing.

She glanced toward the corner, where a small wooden tray sat half-sanded.

The edges were uneven. The handles mismatched. But she recognized it—it was the one she'd tried to design with him once.

Her fingers traced the outline.

"You kept this?"

"Never got around to finishing it," he said.

"Maybe you were waiting for the right help," she offered.

He hesitated. "When Grace and I were kids, I learned real quick that letting her shine meant staying out of the way. I didn't mind, but… it stuck. I got used to being in the background."

He glanced at her. "With you, I thought maybe I didn't have to be."

Lana stood there, watching the man she'd once walked away from.

She remembered the first time he showed her how to sand an edge—like it was a meditation, not a chore. The air in the workshop had smelled like cedar and sweat, and she'd worn old paint-streaked joggers she would later pretend she didn't still sleep in sometimes.

"Hold it like this," Charlie had murmured, sliding behind her, hands guiding hers on the block.

Her breath had hitched. Not because it was romantic—though it was, undeniably—but because it was safe. Solid. The kind of closeness that made her forget to be self-conscious.

"What if I mess it up?" she'd asked.

"You will," he'd said. "That's how it gets good."

She'd snorted. "Wow. Very Mr. Miyagi of you."

He'd smirked. "Call me Sensei and I'm walking out."

She'd laughed so hard she'd dropped the sandpaper. And he'd

just crouched to pick it up, still smiling like she was the best part of his day.

She didn't remember kissing him, exactly. Just that at some point, their mouths had found each other—and it hadn't felt like a first kiss. It had felt like a callback.

She'd wanted to build more than trays with him.

And then she'd convinced herself she wasn't ready.

Now, across from him, Lana felt that ghost of a memory settle behind her ribs like a question she still didn't know how to answer.

She cleared her throat. "I ever tell you how much I hated sanding at first?"

Charlie didn't look up. "Yeah. You called it 'therapeutic trauma.'"

That pulled a smile from her. "You remember?"

His sanding slowed. "I remember a lot of things, Lana."

# backstage breakdown

· · ·

LANA'S NAME shimmered in gold on the event banner:

**"Louder, Lana LIVE: Confidence Is a Choice"**

Presented by *GlowHaus* and *The Current*.

The stage was intimate, lit by pink uplighting and optimism. A hundred folding chairs faced the branded backdrop. Rows of ring-lighted fans waited, phones out, hearts full. Lana stood just offstage, mic in hand, heart pounding like it was trying to warn her.

"You good?" her assistant asked, clipboard in one hand, crisis smile in the other.

"Totally," Lana said, adjusting the silk wrap dress she still didn't quite believe belonged to her. "Just... running the script in my head."

Except she hadn't looked at the script.

She couldn't.

Not when her brain was full of Grace's old texts and Charlie's quiet disappointment and the echo of a life she didn't remember choosing.

The emcee's voice rang out: "Put your hands together for the one, the only, Lana Moreno!"

Applause.

She stepped out. The lights were warm. Blinding. The audience blurred into a sea of curated faces and flickering camera lenses.

She inhaled.

She smiled.

And then she blanked.

Totally.

Utterly.

Nothing.

The teleprompter flashed her opener:

**"Confidence isn't volume—it's ownership."**

She stared at it.

Then at the crowd.

Then at her own hands, which suddenly didn't feel like hers at all.

"I..." she began, voice catching. "I was going to talk about confidence today. About how I built mine. How you can too. But..."

A murmur swept the crowd—curiosity, not concern.

Lana gripped the mic tighter. "But the truth is, I don't remember how I got here. Not really. I just woke up one day and everyone said I was brave, so I tried to act like it."

Silence.

A few phones lowered.

She swallowed hard. "What if the louder I got, the less I listened? What if I made noise to cover up the fact that I don't feel like I deserve any of this?"

A chair creaked.

Someone coughed.

And then—one sharp, awkward clap from the back. Lana winced.

The soundboard glitched. Her name stuttered in the background track: *Louder, Lana. Louder—*

Her throat tightened. She gripped the mic like a lifeline.

"I miss her," she said. "The version of me who didn't need an audience to matter. Even if she was quiet. Especially because she was."

No one spoke.

And then, mercifully, the lights dimmed.

The venue had a garden.

Of course it did.

A curated, Instagram-friendly corner full of potted lavender and string lights and those little ceramic signs with affirmations like *You are the moment* and *Don't let your crown slip, babe.*

Lana sat on a bench beneath a lemon tree, dress bunched awkwardly around her knees, mic still in her lap like it might start whispering the answers.

She hadn't cried.

Yet.

But she felt hollow. Like her confidence had been peeled off and left backstage with the branded swag bags.

Then—soft footsteps.

She didn't look up. She already knew.

"Rough set?" came a woman's voice, like a silk scarf brushing pavement.

"I bombed," Lana said flatly.

Celeste eased onto the bench beside her, linen immaculate, gaze fixed on the koi pond like it was telling secrets.

"I've seen worse," she said mildly. "Once, a woman stood on a TEDx stage and forgot her own name. She improvised a ten-minute talk on ducks."

Lana huffed something like a laugh. "And did it change her life?"

"Not really," Celeste said. "But she's very good at improv now."

A beat passed.

"I thought this was the life I wanted," Lana said quietly. "The glow-up. The voice. The spotlight."

"And now?"

"I feel like a fraud. Like I borrowed someone else's confidence and stretched it until it tore."

Celeste tilted her head. "Confidence isn't a costume, Lana. It's a *muscle*."

"Well," Lana muttered, "mine's pulled."

Celeste smiled, small and knowing. "You think being loud made you strong. But strength doesn't always shout."

"I thought I had to change everything about me to matter."

"No." Celeste looked at her then. Really looked. "You just had to stop hiding."

Lana blinked. Her eyes burned.

Celeste reached into her pocket and handed her a card. The same one from the park. Cream. Gold. Infinity.

Lana turned it over.

It now read: *You're almost ready.*

"What happens now?" she asked.

"Now," Celeste said gently, "you decide if the version of you who stayed small was any less worthy of love."

Lana didn't answer.

But she held the card tight.

And for the first time since arriving, she felt something settle inside her—not certainty. Not clarity.

But maybe... choice.

Lana curled into the corner of her couch like she was trying to make herself smaller.

The lights were off. Her silk wrap dress had been swapped for an oversized hoodie she found in the back of the closet—faded, comforting, and smelling faintly of sandalwood and regret.

Her inbox glowed on the tablet in her lap. She wasn't sure why she'd opened it. Muscle memory, maybe. Or maybe some part of her knew the reckoning was overdue.

She scrolled.

Fan messages. Brand requests. A collaboration offer from an oat milk company she was 99% sure she'd mocked on air.

And then—**one flagged message**, unopened.

**From:** Grace Patel

**Subject:** Still here

She stared at it.

Her thumb hovered.

Then tapped.

*Lana,*

*I wasn't going to write again. I told myself you were too busy, or too important now, or too sparkly to look back.*

*But today I saw a clip of your live event.*

*You looked beautiful.*

*You sounded... hollow.*

*And I realized something I wish I'd said sooner:*

*I miss the version of you who didn't have it all figured out. Who made color-coded snack trays and sang off-key to Lizzo in my kitchen. Who listened like it was her job and held space like it was her superpower.*

*You didn't need to be louder, Lana.*

*You just needed to believe you were worth hearing.*

*I don't know what happened. Why you left. Why you stopped calling. Maybe you outgrew me. Maybe you thought that kind of closeness would hold you back.*

*But I never wanted to keep you small.*

*I just wanted to grow with you.*

*So here it is. One last note from the quiet friend who never stopped clapping for you—even after you walked offstage.*

*Come back, if you want.*
*Or don't.*
*Either way, I hope you find your voice again.*
*The one that doesn't need a mic to matter.*
*—Grace*

Lana didn't cry.

Not at first.

She just sat there, blinking at the screen, breathing like it hurt a little.

Then she whispered, "I'm so sorry."

To no one.

To everyone.

And maybe, finally… to herself.

Charlie was already there when Grace walked in—leaning against her kitchen counter, sipping one of her lavender tonics like it wasn't aggressively floral.

"I saw the clip," he said.

Grace kicked off her heels with a sigh. "The part where she froze? Or the part where she basically throat-punched her own brand?"

"Both."

She dropped her bag on the table. "She looked… not okay."

Charlie nodded. "Yeah. But also? More herself than I've seen in months."

Grace shot him a look. "Don't get soft on me now. She disappeared, Charlie. Ditched me. Ditched you. All because she found a camera angle that finally liked her."

"She didn't just disappear," he said quietly. "She unraveled. Loudly."

Grace grabbed a spoon and stirred her tea with too much force. "So what? We just forget everything? Clap and forgive?"

"No," he said. "But we remember who she was before all this."

Grace's voice caught. "She was my person."

Charlie stepped closer. "She still is."

Grace leaned on the counter, eyes tired. "She hurt you, too. Don't pretend she didn't."

He didn't deny it. But he said, softly, "People hurt each other all the time. What matters is whether they come back."

Grace blinked fast. "She doesn't even know how."

"Then maybe we show her," Charlie said. "Together."

# best friend showdown

· · ·

CONFETTI *& Grace* was hosting a soft launch event for their new "Intentional Glam" line—a curated blend of color palettes, party kits, and personality quizzes with taglines like *"find your shine without dimming your circle."*

Lana didn't RSVP.

She showed up anyway.

She wasn't in a power outfit. No bold lip, no influencer hat. Just jeans, a sweater she'd forgotten she loved, and a heart full of complicated hope.

The venue was peak Grace: pink velvet couches, floral installations shaped like quotation marks, and pastel cocktails with names like "Radical Bloom" and "The Unbothered Spritz." It smelled like jasmine, ambition, and just a hint of rose gold resentment.

Grace stood near the step-and-repeat, surrounded by clapping guests and a pop-up ring light. She wore lavender silk and her most practiced smile—the one that came out during press photos and personal betrayals.

Lana waited until the crowd thinned.

Then approached.

Grace's eyes widened for a split second. Then the smile snapped back into place like armor.

"Wow," she said coolly. "The icon returns."

Lana winced. "Hi, Grace."

A pause. Long enough to be awkward. Sharp enough to draw blood.

"Are you lost?" Grace asked. "This event's for soft launches, not hard exits."

"I know I have no right to be here," Lana said. "But I had to see you."

Grace folded her arms. "So now you show up? After what—six months? A brand deal later? One emotional breakdown livestreamed to your entire following?"

Lana flinched.

"I wasn't okay," she said. "And I didn't know how to admit that without unraveling everything I'd built."

"So you unraveled *us* instead?"

That hit.

Hard.

"I thought I had to change," Lana whispered. "I thought small meant invisible. I thought I had to be loud to matter."

"And you didn't think I'd understand?" Grace's voice broke, just slightly. "Lana, I've *always* been loud. But I never needed you to shrink. I just needed you to stay."

Lana's eyes stung. "I missed you. I miss us."

Grace shook her head. "You can't miss someone while pretending they're just a footnote in your origin story."

Lana stepped forward. "I'm not pretending anymore."

Grace's expression softened—but didn't melt.

"You hurt me," she said. "And it wasn't with a fight. It was with silence. You left a Grace-shaped hole in your life and called it growth."

Lana didn't defend herself.

She just nodded.

"I know."

They stood there, not as brand personas or polished narratives —but two women who'd built something real, then lost it under the weight of who they were trying to become.

And maybe—maybe—this was where healing began.

Not with forgiveness.

But with *truth*.

The music inside shifted to something slower—lo-fi beats over strings, soft enough to make space for hard truths. Grace led Lana out to the side patio, where a half-deflated balloon arch and a row of mood-matching mocktails waited, neglected.

No one followed. No audience. Just them.

"I read your email," Lana said gently.

Grace looked away. "It wasn't for your feed."

"I know. That's why I didn't respond with a reel."

A pause.

Then, tentatively, a laugh from Grace—small, grudging, but there.

"I meant every word," she said. "Even the dramatic ones. I was hurt. Still am."

"You're allowed to be," Lana said. "I was so focused on becoming someone bigger that I didn't realize I was shrinking the people who helped me get there."

Grace sat on a white wire chair, plucking petals off a flower arrangement like it owed her money. "You made me feel disposable. Like I was part of your 'before.'"

Grace looked down at her drink. "You think I always feel loud and shiny? I curate for a living, Lana. Half the time I'm praying no one notices when I stumble."

She gave a soft laugh. "I'm confident because I rehearse it. Just like you."

"I never wanted to leave you behind."

"You didn't leave me behind, Lana. You erased me. Quietly. Like it would hurt less."

That hit like truth always does: low, direct, impossible to deflect.

"I was scared," Lana admitted. "Terrified that if I stopped performing confidence, I'd disappear again. That being seen meant being perfect."

Grace looked up. "And now?"

"Now I think... being seen means being known. And maybe even loved anyway."

For the first time, Grace's expression softened completely.

"You broke my heart, you know." She set the flower down.

"Remember the rooftop party?" she said suddenly. "The one where we made a vision board out of pizza boxes because the printer broke?"

Lana blinked. "You drew a tiara on mine with ketchup."

"And you made mine say 'CEO of Glitter & Grit.'"

Grace smiled, just barely. "I haven't laughed like that in a long time."

Lana nodded. "You were the first person who ever made me feel like I mattered. And I treated you like a marketing casualty."

Tears welled in Grace's eyes, but she didn't let them fall. "I don't need a grand apology. I don't need a public reconciliation. I just need you to remember who we were. And who we could still be."

Lana sat beside her, hands folded in her lap.

"I remember everything now," she said. "And I want to try. I don't expect you to just... let me back in. But I'd love the chance to earn your trust again."

Grace looked at her for a long moment.

Then nodded—slowly, not quite a smile.

"Okay," she said. "You can start here. One real moment at a time."

The event was winding down.

Guests trickled out, high on mocktails and affirmations, clutching tote bags stamped with *shine like you mean it*. Staff were packing up ring lights. The balloon arch had finally given up and drooped like it understood emotional exhaustion.

Lana stepped outside, the air cool against her skin. Her chest felt lighter, raw in a good way—like she'd finally exhaled after months of holding it in.

And there he was.

Charlie.

Leaning against his truck parked across the street, arms folded, expression unreadable.

Lana hesitated, heart skipping in that way it always did around him—even in this life she barely remembered.

"You heard everything," she said as she approached.

He gave her a soft half-smile. "Not on purpose. But yeah."

She looked down. "You came anyway?"

"I wasn't sure if I should. You've been busy being... a phenomenon."

She laughed quietly. "Feels more like I've been busy being a cautionary tale."

He shrugged. "Even those have value."

She looked at him then, really looked. The way his hair curled at the nape of his neck. The paint smudge on his shirt. The way he was *here*—when he didn't have to be.

"I'm sorry," she said. "For walking away. For leaving without a map back."

Charlie's eyes didn't waver. "I wasn't mad that you left, Lana. I was mad that you didn't think I could walk with you."

Her throat caught.

"I thought I had to do it alone," she whispered. "To prove I was someone worth staying for."

"You always were," he said. "Even when you whispered. Even when you didn't see yourself."

Tears burned behind her eyes. "I don't know who I am yet. I'm still figuring it out."

"That's fine," he said simply. "I'm not here for the finished version."

She stared at him.

And then—because it felt right, because it *was* right—she stepped closer.

He didn't kiss her.

Not yet.

He just reached out, tucked a curl behind her ear, and let his hand linger there.

"I'm not going anywhere," he said softly.

"Even if I mess up again?" she asked.

He smiled. "Especially then."

For the first time, she believed someone could love her before the ending.

Even in the middle.

Especially in the middle.

# stage dive

. . .

THE STUDIO WASN'T PACKED.

There were no flower walls, no celebrity guests, no pre-show hype team in matching hoodies. Just a handful of folding chairs, a few curious fans, and a livestream link that might still be buffering.

Perfect.

Lana stood behind the mic, one hand wrapped around a mug instead of a branded tumbler. Her notes were blank. Her phone was off. The neon *LOUDER, LANA* sign behind her flickered once, like it knew its days were numbered.

She looked out at the small crowd.

Someone smiled. Someone waved.

And for once, she didn't worry about how she looked.

She cleared her throat. "Hey. It's... me."

A ripple of polite laughter.

She smiled. "Not 'Podcast Me.' Just... me-me. The version of myself I've been avoiding behind soundbites and smart blazers."

She took a breath.

"I started this show because I was tired of feeling invisible. I thought if I got loud enough, people would finally see me."

A pause.

"And they did. But I didn't."

The room quieted. No one looked away.

"I became a brand. A message. A movement." Her voice wavered, just slightly. "But somewhere in there, I ghosted the parts of myself that weren't shiny. The parts that stammered and stayed small and said the wrong thing at the wrong time."

She looked down at her mug. Her hand. Her *real* self.

"I want her back."

A beat.

Then: "So if you've ever felt like you had to be louder to matter —if you've ever shrunk yourself to fit into someone else's spotlight —this is for you."

She smiled, soft and certain.

"You don't have to shout to be brave. Sometimes showing up at all is the loudest thing you can do."

The light above the mic flicked from red to green. Live.

She hit *stop recording*.

And the room erupted into the kind of applause that wasn't loud, but felt like *everything*.

Lana stepped back from the mic.

This wasn't her biggest show.

But it was the one she meant.

The studio was quiet now.

The neon sign had flickered off completely—burned out, or maybe just done with its job. Lana stood in the stillness, hands wrapped around her lukewarm tea like it might anchor her to this version of herself for just a moment longer.

No makeup crew.

No assistant.

No curated applause.

Just... her.

And then—

"I liked that one," said a familiar voice from the back row. "It was quiet. But honest."

Lana turned.

Celeste sat alone in the third chair of the second row, hands folded in her lap, linen perfectly pressed as ever.

Lana didn't ask how she got in. Or how long she'd been there. At this point, questioning Celeste felt like arguing with gravity.

"I wasn't sure anyone would stay till the end," Lana said.

"Anyone worth staying did."

A beat passed.

Celeste stood and walked toward her. "How do you feel?"

Lana considered. "Small," she admitted. "But... like I finally belong to myself."

Celeste nodded, pleased. "Then you're ready."

The air shimmered again. The studio blurred, just slightly, like someone had wiped their thumb across the scene.

Somewhere behind her, the sign blinked—once, twice—then disappeared.

Lana looked around the studio—at the quiet stage, the unplugged lights, the still air that no longer buzzed with expectation.

She didn't want to stay here.

She didn't want to escape, either.

She just wanted to *live*.

Her fingers hovered over her phone like it might burn her.

Charlie's name sat at the top of the message screen—untouched, unanswered, a digital doorway to something she wasn't sure she deserved to knock on.

She'd typed and deleted three different versions of the same message:

*Are you still at the shop?*

*I miss talking to you.*

*I don't know what I'm doing, but I keep thinking about that tray.*

She stared at the blinking cursor. Her thumb trembled over the send button.

Then—

She hit backspace. Slowly. Deliberately.

The message dissolved.

She locked the screen and turned the phone face down.

Some doors you wanted to open. But only if you were brave enough to walk through them.

"What happens now?" she asked.

"You go home," Celeste said, as if it were the simplest thing in the world. "You carry what you've learned. And you decide what you want to build next."

"Do I get to keep anything?"

Celeste raised a brow. "Do you think confidence can be boxed and packed?"

Lana smiled. "Maybe not. But I'm leaving with better posture."

They stood in silence for a beat longer. Then Lana stepped forward.

"I'm ready," she said.

Celeste didn't blink. "You always were."

And just like that—

The studio dimmed.

The room shifted.

And the world tilted back toward the life Lana left behind.

# quiet is still bold

. . .

LANA WOKE to the sound of her old ceiling fan rattling like it was being held together by good intentions and a single paperclip.

She opened her eyes.

No velvet bedding. No curated lighting. No branded water bottles promising clarity in cucumber.

Just her duvet. Slightly lumpy.

Her phone, face-down on the nightstand.

And the faint smell of whatever body wash was currently winning the shower caddy war.

She sat up slowly.

No silk robe. Just her favorite oversized T-shirt—soft from years of laundry cycles and self-soothing.

The room was quiet.

The world was normal.

And Lana?

She didn't panic.

She didn't immediately check her feed.

She just… breathed.

A glance at her phone confirmed it: one missed call from her mom, one spam text about her car warranty, and a calendar reminder for "brainstorm solo project???"

She smiled.

It was the kind of smile that didn't need witnesses.

Padding into the kitchen, she made her usual coffee—no adaptogens, no cinnamon oat foam. Just caffeine and comfort. She pulled her notebook from the stack of mail she kept meaning to sort and flipped to a blank page.

At the top, she wrote:

**Soft Volume.**

She didn't know what it would be yet.

A blog? A podcast? A newsletter? Just a place to think out loud without having to shout?

But it would be hers.

Her voice. No filters.

And for the first time, that felt like enough.

Lana sat at her kitchen table, laptop open, fingers hovering above the keys like they were waiting for permission.

The cursor blinked.

Blank screen. Blank mind. But not blank heart.

She exhaled, cracked her knuckles (because confidence sometimes sounded like knuckle pops), and clicked "New Project."

Title:

**Soft Volume: A podcast about being heard—without having to shout.**

She stared at it for a moment.

Then typed:

**Episode 1: The Sidekick Steps Up**

*I used to think being in the background made me safe. But it also made me small. This is for the people learning to speak up—not with volume, but with truth.*

She didn't delete it.

She didn't overthink it.

She just hit *Save Draft* and opened her inbox.

New Message →

To: herself

CC: no one

Subject: Idea

Body:

*You're not ready yet.*

*But you're ready enough.*

She smiled.

Then—because sometimes boldness looked like accountability—she added Grace to the email.

And hit send.

The coffee shop wasn't fancy.

No reclaimed wood tables, no oat-foam art, no curated playlist named something like *"Productivity Vibes, But Make It Melancholy."*

Just chipped mugs, a slightly squeaky fan, and the comforting hiss of the espresso machine steaming away in the background.

Lana sat near the window, hands wrapped around a plain latte in a very unbranded ceramic cup.

She was early.

Not out of anxious habit.

Out of something else. Something quieter. She liked the way it felt—being present without needing to perform it.

The bell above the door jingled.

She looked up.

Charlie stepped inside, wind-flushed and smiling. Casual jacket, jeans, a book under one arm. The sight of him made her stomach flutter, not with nerves—but with something warmer. *Permission.*

He saw her.

Smiled wider.

And made his way over.

"No VIP setup today?" he teased, nodding toward the absence of microphones or mood lighting.

She grinned. "Turns out I don't need a spotlight to be heard."

He sat and placed his book on the table: *The Art of Simple Things.*

Of course.

They sipped in silence for a moment, the kind that didn't ask to be filled.

Then he glanced at her notebook. "Still working on Soft Volume?"

She nodded. "It's small. Quiet. Might only reach ten people."

"That's not nothing," he said. "Ten people hearing you is louder than ten thousand hearing a version of you that isn't real."

She blinked. That landed hard in the best way.

He hesitated, then added, "You know, I liked you then. I like you now. But this version..." He smiled, soft and sincere. "Feels like you like you, too."

Lana looked down, touched her notebook gently, then looked up at him.

"I do," she said. "Finally."

He leaned in, elbows on the table. "So... want to tell me what happens next?"

She smiled.

Not the show smile.

The real one.

"I don't know," she said. "But I think it starts with coffee."

Charlie raised his mug in a small toast. "Then let's begin."

Behind them, the café window caught a glint of morning light—just for a second, a shimmer.

Lana turned, half-expecting to see linen and infinity.

But there was only sunlight.

Still, her smile deepened.

Some magic doesn't vanish.

It just lingers.

# epilogue: after the applause

. . .

LANA'S APARTMENT was suspiciously humid.

She sniffed the air.

"You watered the fern again, didn't you?" she said into the phone wedged between her shoulder and ear.

On the other end, Grace gasped. "It was droopy! I gave it a confidence shower."

"You drowned it, Grace. Fernanda's not emotionally overwatered—she's just a plant!"

Lana surveyed the drooping mass of foliage like it had personally betrayed her.

From the open laptop, her audio editing software pinged an error.

Grace was still talking. "Okay, but while I have you—are we still recording Sunday's episode? Because I might have ordered us matching mugs that say Soft Voice, Sharp Mind. Yours is lavender. Mine is sparkle gradient."

Lana sighed, smiling despite herself. "I'm going to regret giving you co-host mic access, aren't I?"

"Oh, absolutely. But I'll sound so good while you do."

Charlie held up a metal pole. "Where does this go?"

Lana, seated cross-legged on his living room floor with a pile of vaguely Swedish instruction pages, squinted at the diagram. "That's either the support beam for the podcast table… or a coat rack for elves."

Charlie gave her a look. "You're very helpful."

She grinned. "I'm growing. I used to be quietly helpful. Now I'm unhinged and hilarious."

They worked in companionable chaos, surrounded by screws, wood planks, and an uneaten almond croissant that kept getting dusted with sawdust.

Finally, Lana wiped her hands on her leggings and said, "You know, we don't have to build the studio in your living room. I can still record from home."

Charlie looked up. His expression was quiet, steady.

"I want you here," he said. "Sawdust and all."

Lana blinked. Then stood. Walked over. And kissed him.

It wasn't a dramatic sweep-you-off-your-feet kiss.

It was soft. Certain. Centered.

Like two people who chose this, and would keep choosing it.

Even through furniture assembly.

Lana's first Soft Volume community meetup was going… mostly well.

The library room was full. Her new mic worked. Grace only cried twice (quietly, on brand). A girl in the back whispered, "You're like the Mister Rogers of adult friendship podcasts," which made Lana tear up and choke on a blueberry scone.

Afterward, while Lana packed up cables, Charlie reappeared with two lattes.

One was labeled "Soft Queen."

The other: "Property of Lana's Sound Engineer Boyfriend."

Lana burst out laughing. "You are ridiculous."

Charlie shrugged. "I just like clear labels."

She took her drink, leaned against him, and looked around at the quiet chaos they'd built.

Messy. Weird. Earned.

"I think," she whispered, "this is what bold looks like for me."

Charlie kissed the top of her head.

"Then bold looks really good on you."

The End

# the overlooked one

. . .

JULES REED ADJUSTED the collar of her blazer for the fourth time in three minutes. The navy fabric was pristine, the shoulders crisp, and the overall effect was exactly what the career development blogs called "polished but not trying too hard."

She'd been trying very hard for six years, three months, and—she glanced at her watch—approximately forty-seven minutes.

"Jules!" The receptionist's voice chirped through the sleek corporate atmosphere of Archer & Bloom Strategic Solutions. "They're ready for you. Conference Room B."

Jules smiled. A real one, not the practiced curve she'd mastered for client presentations. "Thanks, Mei."

"Good luck in there," Mei whispered, offering a discreet thumbs-up. "Though you don't need it. Everyone knows you've earned this."

Jules nodded, grateful but unwilling to jinx herself by agreeing out loud. *Everyone* might know, but *everyone* wasn't making the final decision.

She smoothed her already-smooth slacks and took a centering breath.

Conference Room B waited at the end of the hallway like a glass-walled judgment chamber. Inside, three executives sat around the mahogany table—Diana Archer herself, CFO Trevor Goldman, and... Adam Pierce, who'd started eight months after Jules but somehow had an office with a window.

"Jules." Diana smiled with perfect veneers and perfectly measured warmth. "Come in. Sit."

Jules took the empty chair, placed her portfolio precisely in front of her, and folded her hands. Calm. Collected. Capable. The three C's her therapist had suggested when imposter syndrome threatened to swallow her career aspirations whole.

"We want to thank you for your patience during this process," Diana continued. "The Senior Strategy Director position is critical to our five-year growth plan, and we've been extremely thorough in our evaluation."

Jules nodded, mentally reciting the bullet points from her last performance review: *exceeds expectations in client satisfaction... innovative approach to the Westmore campaign... demonstrates exceptional analytical skills...*

"Your work has been exemplary," Trevor added. "Particularly the Mills Corporation rebrand. That was inspired."

"Thank you," Jules replied, her voice steady. She didn't mention that she'd worked through three weekends and missed her sister's birthday to deliver that project. Or that she'd come up with the entire visual concept while Adam was on a golf retreat with the VP of Operations.

Diana's perfectly manicured fingers tapped once on the table. "However, after careful consideration, we've decided to offer the position to Adam."

Something cold and sharp lodged itself behind Jules' ribcage.

Adam had the decency to look slightly uncomfortable, his expression hovering between feigned humility and barely restrained triumph.

"I see," Jules said, because what else could she say? *Again? Are you kidding me? Do you know I've been doing half his work for a year?*

"It was an extremely close decision," Diana continued, already shifting into the corporate consolation script. "We value your contributions enormously, Jules. In fact, we'd like to create a new position for you—Associate Director of Strategic Implementation."

Jules blinked. "That sounds like an execution role, not a leadership position."

Diana's smile tightened at the edges. "You'd still be part of the leadership team. Just focused on your strengths."

*My strengths*, Jules thought bitterly. *Like doing the work while someone else takes the credit.*

"We'll increase your compensation package, of course," Trevor added quickly. "And you'd have oversight of the junior strategists."

Jules nodded mechanically, already feeling herself folding inward, making herself smaller to accommodate the disappointment swelling in her chest.

"I appreciate the consideration," she said, her voice betraying nothing. "May I have a day to think about it?"

Diana looked mildly surprised, as if she'd expected immediate gratitude. "Of course. We'll need your decision by Friday."

"Perfect," Jules said, standing and gathering her portfolio. "Thank you for the opportunity."

She didn't look at Adam as she left. If she did, she might say something career-limiting.

Instead, she walked steadily back to her office—her windowless, middle-of-the-hallway office—closed the door, and stared at the wall.

Her gaze fell on the corner of her desk, the old brass paperweight shaped like a lion—her dad's. He'd given it to her after her first major pitch.

She had roared in that presentation. Called out a faulty projection from the CFO in real time and offered a bolder, more ambitious strategy.

It had worked. The client loved it.

Diana hadn't.

"It's good to be sharp, Jules," she'd said afterward, eyes cool behind her designer frames. "But next time, let leadership take the lead. Don't outshine the room."

That was the moment. She remembered standing in that glass-walled office, swallowing the urge to argue, to ask why being right wasn't enough. Instead, she'd nodded, thanked her, and left the lion in the drawer for almost a year.

That was the first time she'd learned: being excellent wasn't the same as being seen.

It wasn't that she'd been passed over once. Or twice.

This was the third time.

The third time she'd been told she was *almost* there, *almost* ready, *almost* enough. The third time a man with less experience but more... something... had stepped into the role she'd been meticulously preparing for.

Jules bit the inside of her cheek until she tasted metal.

This wasn't about gender. It couldn't be, not with Diana at the helm.

It was about... what? What invisible quality was she lacking? What magical committee-pleasing skill did Adam possess that she didn't?

Her phone buzzed. A text from her sister.

> Sasha: How'd it go??!! Celebratory dinner tonight???

Jules stared at the screen. She should respond. Should say something. But the truth felt too raw, and lies had never come easily to her.

Instead, she turned the phone face-down and opened her laptop.

The company logo glowed on her screen: *Archer & Bloom — Strategies That Shine.*

For everyone but her, apparently.

She worked mechanically through the rest of the afternoon, updating client decks, answering emails, trying to ignore the pit growing in her stomach. By five thirty, the office had mostly emptied, and Jules was halfway through her third revision of a presentation she didn't even care about.

"Burning the midnight oil?"

Mei stood in her doorway, coat already on, purse slung over one shoulder.

Jules managed a smile. "Just cleaning up some loose ends."

Mei hesitated. "I heard about the decision. It's total garbage, Jules."

"It's fine," Jules said automatically. "These things happen."

"Still garbage," Mei insisted. "You want to get a drink? Vent it out?"

Jules shook her head. "Rain check? I think I need some time to... process."

After Mei left, Jules sat in the darkening office, the glow of her laptop screen casting shadows across her desk. Outside, the city was shifting into evening—lights blinking on, people heading home to lives that weren't determined by boardroom decisions and invisible criteria.

She should go home too. Should call Sasha back. Should do something other than sit here marinating in rejection.

When she finally packed up, the office was completely empty. Her heels clicked against the polished floor as she headed toward the elevator, each step a quiet punctuation of another day spent proving herself—and still coming up short.

The elevator arrived with a soft chime. Jules stepped inside, pressed the lobby button, and leaned against the cool metal wall as the doors slid closed.

When they opened again, she wasn't in the lobby.

She was in the park across from her apartment building—the

one with the little duck pond and the bench where she sometimes ate lunch on the rare days she left the office before sunset.

Jules blinked. Looked back at the elevator. It was... gone.

In its place stood a woman.

She wore a flowing linen outfit in a soft cream color that somehow didn't show a single wrinkle. Her hair was pulled back in an elegant twist, and her eyebrows were absolutely perfect, Jules noted with a pang of completely inappropriate envy.

"Hello, Jules," the woman said, her voice calm and melodic, like she was perpetually recording a meditation app. "Hard day?"

Jules stared. She should be alarmed. Should be looking for an exit, calling for help, doing something other than noticing how this stranger's outfit resembled expensive hotel bedding.

Instead, she heard herself say, "The worst, actually."

The woman nodded, as if this were a completely normal conversation to be having in a park that Jules didn't remember walking to.

"My name is Celeste," the woman said, extending a hand. "I'm here because you're ready."

Jules didn't take the offered hand. "Ready for what, exactly?"

"To see what happens when you stop playing small," Celeste replied, withdrawing her hand without offense. "To glimpse the life where you stepped into your power years ago."

"I'm sorry," Jules said, finding her voice and her sense of self-preservation simultaneously, "but I don't know you. And I've had a really long day, so if this is some kind of sales pitch or... religious recruitment... I'm going to have to pass."

Celeste smiled serenely. "This isn't about buying or believing anything, Jules. It's about experiencing something."

She reached into a pocket of her billowing pants and pulled out a card. It was thick, cream-colored, with embossed golden lettering that caught the evening light.

TIMELINE RETREATS *FOR WHEN YOUR LIFE JUST ISN'T IT*

Jules squinted at the card. "Is this... a spa? Because I don't really have the time for—"

"It's a vacation," Celeste interrupted gently. "In a parallel life. Your life, to be exact—just with one different choice."

Jules should laugh. Should walk away. Should call her sister and tell her about the bizarre end to her already terrible day.

Instead, she found herself asking, "Which choice?"

Celeste's smile deepened. "The one where you didn't shrink. Where you demanded to be seen. Where you built a life on your own terms, not someone else's approval."

Something twisted in Jules' chest—not the sharp pain of the day's rejection, but a deeper ache. The ache of recognition. Of truth.

"That's not..." she began, then stopped. *Not what? Not possible? Not me?*

But it was her. The her she'd glimpsed in quiet moments of courage, in dreams she'd carefully folded away in favor of practical steps and careful progress.

Celeste held out the card. "One week," she said. "To see what happens when you take up the space you deserve."

Jules stared at the card, at the subtle infinity symbol in the corner, at the golden words that shouldn't make sense but somehow did.

"What's the catch?" she asked, because there was always a catch.

"No catch," Celeste replied. "Just clarity. You return to your life with whatever insights you gain. It's a glimpse, not a commitment."

Jules hesitated, then took the card. It was heavier than it looked, the paper thick and substantial between her fingers.

"How does it work?" she asked. "Do I need to... sign something?"

Celeste laughed, a sound like wind chimes. "No paperwork. You simply need to sleep. The shift happens naturally."

"That's it?" Jules asked skeptically. "I just... go to bed, and wake up in some alternate timeline where I'm—what? CEO? Astronaut? Living in Bali?"

"You'll have to see," Celeste said, her voice gently teasing. "That's rather the point."

Jules looked down at the card again. This was absurd. Completely absurd. She was a logical person, a strategic thinker. She didn't believe in... whatever this was.

And yet.

And yet, the weight of the day—of years of careful work and measured smiles and making herself *less* to make others comfortable—pressed down on her like physical gravity.

What if?

What if there was a version of her that hadn't learned to shrink?

"I don't have to decide right now, do I?" she asked.

Celeste smiled. "The offer stands. When you're ready, just hold the card before you sleep."

And then, Jules blinked and Celeste was gone. Just... gone. Like she'd never been there at all.

Jules looked around the park, at the normal people walking normal dogs, at the streetlights flickering on as evening deepened.

She looked down at the card in her hand, half expecting it to have vanished too.

But it was still there. Still heavy. Still golden.

She slipped it into her bag, next to her carefully ordered wallet and her sensibly sized emergency makeup kit.

*Ridiculous*, she told herself. *Absolutely ridiculous.*

But as she walked the short distance back to her apartment, the card seemed to burn through the leather of her bag, a small beacon of impossible possibility.

That night, after a shower and a glass of wine she barely tasted, Jules sat on the edge of her bed. The card lay on her nightstand, catching the light from her bedside lamp.

Her phone buzzed again.

> Sasha: Jules??? Hello??? Did you fall in a ditch or get the job???

She should answer. Should be responsible, reliable Jules.

Instead, she reached for the card.

It felt warm now, almost alive in her palm. She ran her thumb over the embossed lettering, the infinity symbol in the corner.

"This is crazy," she whispered to her empty bedroom.

Then she placed the card under her pillow, turned out the light, and closed her eyes.

*One week*, she thought as sleep began to claim her. *One week to be brave.*

# power suit, power life

. . .

JULES WOKE to sunlight streaming through floor-to-ceiling windows—windows that definitely did not exist in her studio apartment with its single, modest view of the building next door.

She blinked. Once. Twice.

This was not her bed. Not her cream Egyptian cotton sheets, but silky charcoal ones that felt impossibly smooth against her skin. Not her sensible Ikea frame, but something low and modern, the kind featured in design magazines she sometimes flipped through at the doctor's office.

She sat up slowly, heart hammering in her chest.

The room around her was a study in elegant minimalism—pale hardwood floors, a sleek dresser that probably cost more than her car, and an entire wall of windows showcasing a skyline she recognized as downtown, at least twenty floors up.

"What the..." she whispered, then cut herself off as the events of the previous night rushed back.

Celeste. The card. *Timeline Retreats.*

She'd actually done it. And it had... worked?

Jules swung her legs over the side of the bed, her bare feet connecting with plush carpet. On the nightstand beside her—a gorgeous piece of what looked like reclaimed wood—sat a sleek smartphone she didn't recognize and a small stack of business cards.

Carefully, she picked up the top card.

### JULES REED
*Chief Executive Officer*
*Reed & Morgan Strategic Group*

She nearly dropped it.

CEO? Of her *own company*?

And Morgan—that was a coincidence, right? It couldn't be—

"Jules?" A deep voice called from somewhere beyond the bedroom door. "Your coffee's getting cold, and you've got that nine-thirty with the Westridge team."

Jules froze.

She knew that voice.

The bedroom door swung open, and there he was—Nate Morgan. Tall, broad-shouldered, with dark hair just shy of needing a trim and deep brown eyes that had always seen a bit too much.

The same Nate who worked three doors down from her at Archer & Bloom. The same Nate who had beaten her for the junior partnership two years ago, then tried to console her with an awkward but sincere speech about corporate politics. The same Nate she'd studiously avoided ever since, because his genuine concern somehow felt worse than Adam's transparent ambition.

Except this Nate was... different. Softer around the edges. Wearing faded jeans and a chambray shirt with the sleeves rolled to expose forearms that—*focus, Jules.*

"You okay?" he asked, brow furrowing slightly. "You look like you've seen a ghost."

Jules blinked. "I'm... fine. Just... didn't sleep well."

Nate's expression softened. He crossed the room and before

Jules could process what was happening, pressed a kiss to her forehead.

"The Keller acquisition keeping you up?" he murmured, his voice a low rumble that did something entirely inappropriate to her pulse. "I told you, the numbers look solid. Stop second-guessing yourself."

Jules nodded automatically, fighting the urge to step back, to put space between herself and this impossible version of Nate Morgan.

Then she saw it—the ring on her left hand. A diamond, elegant and substantial, catching the morning light like it belonged there.

She was engaged. To Nate Morgan.

He seemed to notice her staring at the ring, and a slow, pleased smile spread across his face. "Two months and it still surprises you, huh?"

"Every time," she managed, because it seemed like the right thing to say.

Nate checked his watch—a sleek, understated timepiece that probably cost more than her monthly rent. "Shower's all yours. I've got that meeting with the development team downtown, but I'll see you tonight for dinner with Kai and Miguel?"

Jules nodded again, not trusting her voice. *Who were Kai and Miguel?*

"Perfect," Nate said, leaning in to kiss her again, this time briefly on the lips.

It was so natural, so easy, that Jules forgot to panic until he was already pulling away.

"Don't skip breakfast," he called over his shoulder as he headed for the door. "You get mean when you're hungry."

And then he was gone, leaving Jules standing in the middle of an apartment that wasn't hers, wearing a ring she hadn't wanted, living a life she didn't remember building.

She sank back onto the edge of the bed, trying to steady her breathing.

*Okay, Jules. Think. Process. Plan.*

One week, Celeste had said. She had one week in this timeline —this parallel life where, apparently, she'd made very different choices. Where she ran her own company. Where she was engaged to Nate Morgan, of all people.

She looked around the room again, searching for clues. On the dresser sat framed photos—her and Nate at what looked like a charity gala, both of them dressed impeccably in formal wear. Another of a group of people on a boat, laughing with the carefree confidence of the truly successful.

Jules stood on shaky legs and made her way to what she assumed was the closet—and gasped.

It wasn't just a closet. It was a walk-in dressing room the size of her entire apartment, lined with clothing she would never have been able to afford on her Associate Director salary. Power suits in jewel tones. Dresses with architectural details. Shoes arranged by color and style, a rainbow of heel heights and designs.

"Holy..." she breathed, running her fingers along a row of silk blouses.

This Jules—Timeline Jules—didn't shop at the mid-range department stores during end-of-season sales. This Jules didn't check price tags or calculate cost-per-wear. This Jules dressed like the executive she apparently was.

Jules selected a slate blue suit with subtle pinstriping and a silk shell in a warm copper tone. The fabric felt luxurious against her skin as she changed, and when she checked her reflection in the full-length mirror, she barely recognized herself.

Gone was the careful, conservative styling she'd cultivated at Archer & Bloom. This Jules wore her dark curls looser, more natural. Her makeup was still professional but with a bold lip color she would never have dared in her timeline. And the suit—it didn't just fit, it was clearly tailored specifically for her body, emphasizing curves she usually downplayed.

She looked... powerful.

Powerful. The word felt foreign and familiar. She remembered once standing in the mirror of the Archer & Bloom bathroom, adjusting a blazer that wasn't quite her, rehearsing lines that dulled her edges. That was the version of her who'd learned to soften ideas, to ask instead of assert, to blend in just enough. She had shrunk to fit. Now, here—she fit the room without shrinking at all.

And yet, as she stood alone in this temple of tailored success, a quiet echo stirred. There were no photos here. No shared clutter. Just immaculate racks of control and ambition.

For a moment, it felt less like stepping into a life and more like stepping onto a stage.

In the bathroom—a marble-tiled sanctuary with a rainfall shower and soaking tub—she found an array of high-end products arranged with precision. She showered quickly, trying not to get lost in the luxury of it all, and applied makeup she found in a sleek organizational system beside the sink.

By the time she emerged, fully dressed and as composed as she could manage, she felt almost like she could pull this off. Almost.

The rest of the apartment was just as impressive as the bedroom —open concept, with a gourmet kitchen and living area decorated in a style that was both minimalist and warm. Floor-to-ceiling windows showcased a panoramic view of the city from what had to be at least the twentieth floor of a luxury high-rise.

On the kitchen island, she found a travel mug of coffee—still warm—and a protein smoothie beside a note in masculine hand-writing:

*Drink both. Negotiations take energy. You've got this. —N*

Jules stared at the note, at the easy intimacy it implied. Nate knew her habits, her preferences. Nate made her coffee and left her notes and kissed her goodbye like it was the most natural thing in the world.

It was terrifying.

And...not entirely unpleasant.

She sipped the coffee—prepared exactly how she liked it, with cinnamon and just a splash of cream—and tried to formulate a plan.

Step one: Figure out what her day looked like. There had to be a calendar, a schedule, something to guide her through this unfamiliar life.

She found her phone on the counter, now fully charged. It unlocked with her fingerprint, which was both convenient and slightly unnerving. The home screen showed several missed messages and a calendar notification for "Westridge Presentation - 9:30 AM."

It was 8:17. She had just over an hour to figure out where she worked, how to get there, and what exactly a "Westridge Presentation" entailed.

She opened the calendar app and breathed a sigh of relief. Timeline Jules was organized, at least. The day was laid out in color-coded blocks, with addresses and details for each appointment.

Her inbox was pristine. No chatter, no check-ins, no emojis from coworkers asking how her day was going. Every message was about deliverables, milestones, next steps.

Efficient. Impersonal. Like everyone admired her, but no one missed her.

Reed & Morgan Strategic Group was located in the Hawthorne Tower, just ten blocks from her apartment. The Westridge presentation had detailed notes attached, complete with key talking points and expected outcomes.

This Jules didn't just have a job. She had an empire.

As she scrolled through emails—hundreds of them, all addressed with a deference she'd never experienced—Jules felt a flutter of something unfamiliar in her chest.

Not panic. Not confusion.

Excitement.

In this timeline, she wasn't passed over. She wasn't overlooked. She was in charge, respected, *valued*.

She grabbed her coffee, the sleek leather portfolio she found on the entry console, and a set of keys with an electronic fob.

Her hand trembled slightly on the door handle. Breathe. Shoulders back. Walk like you belong—even if you're just borrowing the role for a week.

Whatever timeline she was in, whatever choices her alternate self had made, Jules had one week to experience this life. To understand what happened when she claimed her space instead of making herself small.

One week to live like the CEO she'd apparently become.

She took a deep breath, squared her shoulders, and headed for the elevator.

Time to see what Jules Reed, Chief Executive Officer, was capable of.

The offices of Reed & Morgan Strategic Group occupied the entire forty-third floor of the Hawthorne Tower.

Jules stepped off the elevator into a reception area that made Archer & Bloom look like a budget motel. Sleek furnishings in warm woods and cool metals. Living green walls dotted with air plants and trailing vines. A reception desk staffed by a young man with impeccable posture and a welcoming smile.

"Good morning, Ms. Reed," he said as she approached. "Your team is set up in the Obsidian Room for the Westridge prep. Coffee service just arrived."

"Thank you..." Jules said, realizing she had no idea what his name was.

"Elijah," he supplied, without a hint of surprise or offense. "And Ms. Diaz called to confirm your lunch at Orso. She said to tell you she's bringing the preliminary mock-ups."

Jules nodded, hoping her face didn't betray her complete lack of knowledge about who Ms. Diaz was or what mock-ups she might be bringing.

"Perfect," she said, channeling the confidence of this alternate version of herself. "Please hold my calls until after the Westridge meeting."

Elijah nodded, and Jules strode past the reception desk, trying to look like she knew exactly where the "Obsidian Room" was.

The office beyond was a showcase of modern design—open work areas bathed in natural light, glass-walled conference rooms, and a few private offices tucked along the perimeter. People looked up as she passed, offering respectful nods or quiet good mornings.

She was the boss. They were *her* employees.

Jules followed the subtle signage until she found the Obsidian Room—a striking conference space with a wall of smoked glass and a table of dark wood that looked almost liquid in the morning light.

Inside, three people were arranging presentation materials and speaking in low, focused tones. They looked up as she entered, their expressions shifting subtly from concentration to attention.

"Morning, team," Jules said, hoping it was what Timeline Jules would say.

"Morning, Jules," replied a woman with a short, stylish haircut and wire-rimmed glasses. "We were just going over the final revisions to the slide deck. I incorporated your feedback on the market segmentation analysis."

"Great," Jules said, setting her portfolio on the table. "Walk me through what we've got."

Zoe launched into the pitch structure, flipping through a sleek slide deck on the built-in screen. Jules nodded, trying to follow along—but halfway through, Zoe paused.

"You still want to lead with the Q3 revenue charts?" she asked.

Jules blinked. "Of course," she said, aiming for confident. "They... set the right tone."

Zoe tilted her head. "Yesterday you said they felt too conservative. That we should open with vision."

Shit.

"Right," Jules said, recovering with a quick smile. "Good catch. Let's go with the vision slide. I'm just testing your memory."

The room chuckled politely. Zoe smiled and kept going. But Jules felt the heat rise in her cheeks. She needed to pay closer attention—she was playing a role, and these people expected the real star.

For the next forty minutes, Jules listened as her team—*her team*—outlined the proposal they'd developed for Westridge Technologies, a client that apparently represented a multi-million-dollar account. They spoke with a clarity and confidence that came from excellent leadership, discussing strategy and market positioning with an ease that made it clear this was standard operating procedure.

And the most surprising part? Jules understood it all. More than understood—she had insights, perspectives, ideas that seemed to flow naturally despite her complete unfamiliarity with the project.

It was as if some part of her—the part that belonged in this timeline—was feeding her the right words, the right questions, guiding her through a presentation she should have known nothing about.

"I think we need to emphasize the innovation pathway more," she heard herself saying. "Westridge isn't just looking for incremental improvements. They want to be seen as disruptors."

The team nodded, making notes, clearly accustomed to her direct style.

"And let's add a slide on their competitive advantage in the European market," she continued. "Bradley will ask about it, and I'd rather preempt the question."

Zoe made a note. "Good call. He always circles back to European expansion."

By the time the clients arrived, Jules felt almost comfortable in her role. The presentation flowed smoothly, with her team expertly addressing questions and Jules herself leading the discussion with a confidence she'd never experienced at Archer & Bloom.

When Bradley Westridge himself leaned across the table and said, "This is exactly why we came to you, Jules. No one else thinks like your team," she felt a rush of pride so intense it nearly took her breath away.

After the clients left, her team gathered their materials, exchanging satisfied glances.

"Nice work, everyone," Jules said. "Zoe, can you share the presentation with Morgan's development team? They'll need it for the technical specifications."

They nodded, efficient and professional, already moving on. No one lingered. No "That was amazing" or "You crushed it." Just execution.

Was this what leadership looked like now—respect without connection?

Zoe nodded. "Already on it. Nate's team has been waiting for the green light."

*Nate's team.* Of course. Reed & Morgan. They were partners in this timeline—professional and, apparently, personal.

As her team dispersed, Jules found herself alone in the Obsidian Room, staring out at a city that looked the same but felt entirely different from this height, from this position of power.

In this timeline, she wasn't just seated at the table. She owned it.

Her phone buzzed with a text:

> Nate: Heard you crushed the Westridge meeting. Never doubted you for a second. Still on for dinner tonight? Kai's excited to share the Bali photos.

Jules stared at the message, at its easy confidence and casual intimacy. In her timeline, her interactions with Nate had been strictly professional, tinged with the awkwardness of competition and her own carefully hidden resentment after losing the partnership to him.

Here, they were a team. A partnership. A... couple.

She typed back:

Jules: Thanks. And yes, dinner still works.

Simple. Safe. Noncommittal.

But as she set the phone down and gathered her materials, she couldn't help wondering:

What had this version of Jules done differently? What choice had led her here, to this corner office with her name on the door, to this partnership with Nate Morgan, to this life of confidence and authority?

And more importantly—could she learn enough in one week to take that knowledge back with her?

She straightened her already-perfect posture and headed for her office—her actual, real, corner office with floor-to-ceiling windows and a view that made her slightly dizzy.

One day down. Six to go.

Time to see what else this timeline had to offer.

# the fiancée with feelings

. . .

THE RESTAURANT WAS EXACTLY the kind of place Jules had always walked past but never entered—one of those establishments with no sign outside, just a discreet door and a host who seemed to know instantly whether you belonged there or not.

Apparently, in this timeline, she belonged.

"Ms. Reed," the host greeted her with a warm smile. "Mr. Morgan and your friends have already arrived. Right this way."

Jules followed him through the dimly lit space, past tables of well-dressed patrons engaged in quiet conversation. The décor was understated luxury—dark wood, soft lighting, the kind of atmosphere that whispered rather than shouted its exclusivity.

She spotted Nate at a corner table, his profile outlined against the ambient glow of the restaurant. He sat with a couple Jules didn't recognize—a man with a neatly trimmed beard and vibrant blue glasses, and a woman with a cloud of natural curls and statement earrings that caught the light when she moved.

Nate looked up as she approached, his expression softening in a way that made Jules's chest tighten inexplicably.

"There she is," he said, standing to greet her. His hand found the small of her back naturally, guiding her into the empty chair beside him. "The Westridge conqueror."

"News travels fast," Jules said, trying to match his easy tone.

"Only the good kind," the woman with the curls said, raising her glass in a small toast. "Kai Chen, continuing to live vicariously through your corporate badassery."

So, this was Kai—one of the names Nate had mentioned that morning.

"Please," Jules said with a smile she hoped looked natural. "You're the one who just spent three weeks in Bali. I think I'm the one living vicariously."

It was a safe guess, based on Nate's text about Bali photos, and it paid off. Kai grinned, leaning forward.

"Which is why we brought the external hard drive of doom," she said, patting her oversized bag. "Three thousand photos, carefully culled from the original eight thousand. You'll thank me later."

The bearded man—presumably Miguel—rolled his eyes fondly. "She's not exaggerating. There are twenty-seven sunset pictures from the exact same spot."

"Each one capturing a unique moment in time," Kai protested, nudging him with her elbow.

Jules felt a strange pang watching them—the easy banter, the comfortable intimacy. These were clearly close friends in this timeline, people she and Nate spent time with regularly. People who knew them as a couple, who had inside jokes and shared histories she couldn't access.

"Wine?" Nate asked, already pouring her a glass of something red and undoubtedly expensive. "They have that Bordeaux you liked at Antonio's wedding."

Jules nodded, grateful for the prompt. "Perfect."

She took a sip, letting the rich flavor ground her in the moment. Whoever Timeline Jules was, she had excellent taste in wine.

"So," Kai said, leaning forward conspiratorially, "have you found a dress yet? Because I have thoughts. Many, many thoughts."

*A dress. For the wedding. Right.*

"Still looking," Jules hedged. "You know me—thorough research phase."

Kai laughed. "You would create a decision matrix for your wedding dress."

"She has," Nate confirmed, his tone warm with affection rather than mockery. "Complete with weighted criteria and a scoring system."

"That's my girl," Miguel said, raising his glass. "Why use intuition when you can use spreadsheets?"

They all laughed, and Jules found herself joining in, surprised by how comfortable it felt. These people—strangers to her—somehow knew her, or a version of her. And they liked her. Respected her. Found her methodical nature endearing rather than robotic.

The conversation flowed easily through drinks and appetizers, with Kai sharing highlights from their trip and Miguel occasionally interjecting with drier, more practical details. Jules listened more than she spoke, gathering context, building a picture of her life in this timeline through the casual references and shared memories.

Apparently, she and Kai had been friends since business school. Miguel was Kai's husband of three years. The four of them vacationed together annually, with next year's trip already penciled in for the Amalfi Coast.

And Nate—Nate was different here. Still driven and sharp-minded, but softer around the edges. He laughed more freely, touched her with casual affection, and seemed genuinely interested in the people around him rather than what they could do for his career.

"Remember when we all went to that cooking class?" Kai was saying, gesturing with a piece of bread. "And Jules nearly set the kitchen on fire?"

"It was *not* my fault," Jules protested automatically, though she had no idea what incident they were referring to. "The recipe clearly said 'flambé.'"

"Sweetheart, it did not say 'create a towering inferno,'" Nate countered, his eyes crinkling at the corners. "The chef's eyebrows took weeks to grow back."

"You're all exaggerating," Jules said, playing along. "It was a controlled burn."

"Is that what we're calling it now?" Miguel deadpanned. "Because I distinctly remember screaming. Mostly from Nate."

"I did not scream," Nate said with mock indignation. "I expressed surprise. Vocally."

"You screamed like a Victorian lady who'd seen a mouse," Kai corrected. "And then Jules just stood there, completely calm, and said—"

"'I meant to do that,'" they all finished in unison, dissolving into laughter.

Jules felt a strange warmth spread through her chest. This was... nice. More than nice. There was an ease to this evening, to these relationships, that felt foreign to her carefully compartmentalized life back home.

Under the table, Nate's hand found hers, his thumb tracing small circles on her palm.

"You're quiet tonight," he murmured, low enough that only she could hear. "Everything okay?"

She turned to find him watching her, his dark eyes concerned and attentive in a way that made her breath catch.

"Just tired," she said. "Long day."

He nodded, but his gaze remained searching. "We can make an early night of it, if you want. Blame it on the Westridge prep."

The offer was so considerate, so lacking in any ulterior motive, that Jules felt something inside her soften.

"I'm okay," she assured him. "Really."

His smile returned, though a hint of concern lingered in his eyes. "If you say so. But the second you want to leave, just give me the signal."

"The signal?"

His brow furrowed slightly. "You know, the thing where you tap your water glass three times and then fake a phone call about a work emergency?"

Jules laughed, surprised. "That's... oddly specific."

"Well, it was your idea," he reminded her. "After that disastrous dinner with my parents last Christmas."

Before she could respond, the waiter arrived with their entrees, and the conversation shifted back to the group. But the warmth of Nate's hand against hers lingered, as did the realization that he knew her—really knew her, in ways even she didn't.

It was disconcerting. And strangely thrilling.

The apartment was quiet when they returned, the city lights twinkling beyond the wall of windows. Kai and Miguel had parted with hugs and promises of brunch next weekend, the easy affection of longtime friends.

Now, alone with Nate, Jules felt a flutter of nervous energy in her stomach.

"Nightcap?" he asked, already moving toward the kitchen. "I think we still have that Japanese whisky Kai brought back."

"Sure," Jules said, slipping off her heels and padding across the cool hardwood floor.

She watched as Nate moved around the kitchen with familiar ease, retrieving glasses and ice. He'd loosened his tie and rolled up his sleeves, revealing forearms that were lean and strong.

This domestic version of Nate was yet another revelation. In her timeline, she'd only ever seen him in the office, perfectly put together and slightly intimidating in his competence. Here, he was relaxed, approachable, and—she had to admit—unfairly attractive.

He handed her a glass, the amber liquid catching the soft light.

"To surviving dinner without a single mention of floral arrangements or cake flavors," he said, touching his glass to hers with a wry smile.

Jules sipped the whisky, letting its warmth spread through her chest. "Was that likely to happen?"

Nate laughed. "Kai has strong opinions about wedding aesthetics. I thought for sure she'd bust out her Pinterest board tonight."

Wedding. Right. They were engaged. Planning a wedding.

The reality of it hit Jules anew, and she took another sip of whisky to hide her reaction.

"You really are tired, aren't you?" Nate said, his expression softening. "You keep getting this faraway look."

Jules shook her head. "Just... processing. It's been a day."

"Westridge went well, though. Bradley called me afterward, singing your praises."

"He did?"

Nate nodded, leaning against the counter. "Said you were the only person who really understood what they're trying to build. High praise from a man who once told me my marketing strategy was 'aggressively mediocre.'"

Jules smiled. "He does have a way with words."

"That's one way to put it." Nate studied her over the rim of his glass. "But seriously, Jules. You okay? You've seemed... different today."

*Different. Because I'm literally a different Jules from a different timeline.*

"Just a lot on my mind," she said, which wasn't exactly a lie.

Nate set his glass down and crossed the small distance between them. His hands came to rest on her shoulders, warm and steadying.

"Is it the Wilson account? Because I told you, we can push the timeline if we need to. The world won't end if we deliver in March instead of February."

Jules blinked. "No, it's not that."

"The wedding, then? Because I meant what I said—City Hall and takeout works for me if all this planning is too much."

The sincerity in his voice was almost painful. This Nate—Timeline Nate—truly cared about her. Wanted her to be happy. Was willing to adjust his expectations to accommodate her needs.

It was more consideration than she'd experienced in her last three relationships combined.

"It's not the wedding," she said softly. "I promise."

He studied her face, his dark eyes intent. "Okay. But whatever it is, you know you can tell me, right? That's kind of our thing—the whole 'no BS' policy."

Jules felt a lump form in her throat. What would he say if she told him the truth? That she wasn't his Jules at all, but a visitor from another timeline? That yesterday, she barely knew him beyond professional rivalry?

"I know," she managed. "And I appreciate it."

He smiled, some of the concern leaving his expression. "Good. Because I've got your back, Reed. Always have."

And then he leaned down and kissed her.

It wasn't like the brief, affectionate peck from that morning. This was slower, deeper, a kiss between two people who knew each other's rhythms. His hand came up to cradle her jaw, thumb brushing her cheekbone in a gesture so tender it made her chest ache.

Jules froze for a millisecond before her body responded on its own, leaning into the kiss with a familiarity her conscious mind didn't possess. Her hands found his chest, feeling the solid warmth of him through his shirt.

When they broke apart, Nate's eyes were dark, his expression a mixture of affection and something more heated.

"I've been wanting to do that all day," he murmured. "Ever since you walked out of the bedroom in that blue suit."

Jules felt heat bloom in her cheeks. "The suit worked for you, huh?"

"Everything works for me when it's you," he said simply.

And oh—that was unfair. Completely unfair. How was she supposed to maintain any kind of emotional distance when he said things like that?

Before she could formulate a response, Nate's phone buzzed from his pocket. He sighed, reluctantly stepping back to check it.

"It's the Tokyo team," he said apologetically. "I need to take this. Shouldn't be more than twenty minutes."

Jules nodded, relieved and disappointed in equal measure. "Go ahead. I should get ready for bed anyway."

Nate pressed a quick kiss to her forehead before answering the call, his voice shifting into professional mode as he headed toward what she assumed was a home office.

Alone in the kitchen, Jules drained the last of her whisky, the burn in her throat a welcome distraction from the confusing tangle of emotions in her chest.

This was supposed to be a glimpse into a more confident, successful version of her life. A chance to see what happened when she claimed her power.

No one had warned her about the emotional complications. About Nate Morgan and his kind eyes and the way he seemed to genuinely care about her happiness.

She made her way to the bedroom, the events of the day settling heavy on her shoulders. In the en-suite bathroom, she found her nighttime routine laid out with the same precision as the morning —cleansers and serums arranged in order of use, a silk robe hanging from a hook beside the shower.

As she moved through the familiar motions of removing makeup and washing her face, Jules caught her reflection in the mirror.

She looked the same, mostly. Same dark eyes, same high cheek-bones, same small scar at her temple from a childhood fall. But there was something different in her expression—a confidence, a centeredness that she didn't recognize.

This Jules didn't shrink. Didn't second-guess. Didn't make herself smaller to accommodate others' comfort.

This Jules had built something. Had partnered with Nate Morgan, professionally and personally. Had carved out a life on her terms.

*How?* Jules wondered, patting her face dry with a plush towel. *What choice did you make that I didn't?*

There was no answer, of course. Just her reflection, watching her with eyes that held more questions than certainty.

Later, lying in the too-large bed with its impossibly soft sheets, Jules listened to the distant sounds of Nate's voice from the other room. His tone was patient but firm, the voice of someone used to leading, to being heard.

She wondered what it would be like to work with him rather than against him. To collaborate instead of compete. To build something together instead of fighting for the same scraps of recognition.

In her timeline, she'd written him off as another obstacle, another man who'd gotten what she deserved.

But here, in this life, they were equals. Partners.

And as Jules drifted toward sleep, one thought followed her into dreams:

What if she'd been wrong about Nate Morgan all along?

# meetings & misgivings

. . .

"THE WILSON PROPOSAL needs to be completely redone," Jules said, handing back the folder with a decisiveness that surprised even her. "This doesn't capture the essence of what they're trying to achieve."

The team assembled around the conference table—Zoe, two junior strategists whose names Jules had frantically memorized from emails, and a creative director with an impressive portfolio—exchanged glances.

"The direction seemed to align with our initial conversations," Zoe ventured, adjusting her wire-rimmed glasses. "They specifically mentioned focusing on market penetration over brand evolution."

Jules shook her head. "That's what they *said*, but it's not what they *need*. Wilson's problem isn't market reach—it's market relevance. Their entire industry is shifting toward sustainable practices, and they're clinging to outdated methods because it's comfortable."

She moved to the whiteboard—an actual whiteboard, not the sleek digital displays she'd expected in such a modern office—and began sketching a diagram.

"Their competitors are already positioning themselves as eco-conscious alternatives," she continued, drawing lines between concepts with surprising confidence. "If Wilson sticks with the same approach, they'll be obsolete within five years. What they need isn't incremental growth in their existing market—it's a complete repositioning as an industry leader in sustainability."

The room was silent for a moment, and Jules felt a flicker of doubt. Had she overstepped? Misunderstood? Was she about to reveal herself as an impostor in this timeline?

Then Zoe leaned forward, a slow smile spreading across her face. "That's... brilliant, actually. They've been so focused on short-term metrics that they're missing the bigger picture."

"Exactly," Jules said, relief washing through her. "We need to show them where the industry is headed, not just where it is now."

The creative director—Marcus, according to the nameplate in front of him—nodded thoughtfully. "I've got some concepts that could work with this approach. More future-focused, bold. It would require a complete visual rebrand, though."

"Then that's what we'll propose," Jules said. "Let's redraft with this direction in mind. I want to see initial concepts by Friday."

She capped her pen like it was a gavel, heart still thudding.

That sounded like something Timeline Jules would say, right? Cool. In control. Forward-facing.

The team nodded and took notes, but she caught a fleeting glance between two strategists—curious, maybe even impressed.

It wasn't perfection. But it was enough.

The team dispersed with a new energy, and Jules allowed herself a moment of quiet satisfaction. Whatever knowledge and instincts Timeline Jules possessed seemed to be filtering through to her—insights and perspectives she couldn't have articulated in her own timeline emerged naturally, as if they'd always been there.

Zoe lingered behind as the others filed out. "This is why I love working with you," she said, a note of genuine admiration in her voice. "You see what everyone else misses."

Jules smiled, unexpectedly touched. "Just doing my job."

"And doing it better than anyone else," Zoe countered. "There's a reason you're the boss."

As Zoe left, Jules gathered her notes, a strange warmth spreading through her chest. In her timeline, she'd never received this kind of recognition. Her insights were often overlooked, or worse, appropriated by others who spoke louder or with more assumed authority.

Here, people listened. Respected her perspective. Followed her lead.

It was intoxicating.

She made her way back to her corner office. A small collection of awards lined one shelf. Photos of various professional events dotted another. And on her desk, a single framed picture of her and Nate, their faces close together, laughing at something outside the frame.

Jules picked it up, studying their expressions. They looked... happy. Genuinely, unreservedly happy, in a way she couldn't remember feeling in a very long time.

Setting down the photo, she checked her calendar for the afternoon. A lunch with "V. Diaz" followed by internal meetings until five, then a blank evening. No mention of Nate, though she'd half-expected to see his name peppered throughout her schedule given their intertwined lives.

She was gathering her things for the lunch meeting when her phone buzzed with a notification. Not a text or an email, but a calendar reminder:

**CALL SASHA - BIRTHDAY**

Jules froze, a wave of guilt washing over her. Sasha. Her sister. Whose birthday she'd missed in her timeline because of the Mills Corporation project.

She glanced at the time—11:17. Her lunch wasn't until noon. She had time to make the call, to see what kind of relationship existed with her sister in this timeline.

Heart beating a little faster, she closed her office door and dialed Sasha's number.

The phone rang once, twice, three times. Jules was beginning to think it would go to voicemail when the line connected.

"Well, this is a surprise," came Sasha's voice, the familiar cadence laced with an unfamiliar coolness. "The CEO remembers the little people."

Jules blinked, caught off guard by the tone. "Hey, Sash. Happy birthday."

"Thanks," Sasha replied, the word clipped. "Didn't expect to hear from you, to be honest."

Jules frowned. "What? Why wouldn't I call on your birthday?"

A beat of silence. "Because you haven't for the past two years? Because the last time we spoke, you made it pretty clear that your 'high-powered life' didn't have room for family dinners and birthday brunches?"

The accusation landed like a physical blow. Jules sank into her chair, struggling to process this new reality.

"Sasha, I—"

"Look, it's fine," her sister interrupted, her voice softening slightly. "I get it. You've got your big fancy life, and I've got mine. We're just... different people now."

"We don't have to be," Jules said quietly, the words emerging before she could consider them.

Another pause. "That's... new. What brought on this sudden change of heart? Upcoming wedding making you sentimental?"

Jules closed her eyes, trying to navigate a conversation where she didn't know the history, the hurts, the boundaries. "Maybe I just miss my sister."

"Hmm," Sasha hummed, clearly skeptical but not entirely dismissive. "Well, if you're serious, you know where to find me. Same apartment, same job, same predictable life."

Jules winced. Had she really said that? What kind of person had she become in this timeline?

"I shouldn't have said that," she offered. "I'm sorry."

"Wow," Sasha said after a moment. "An apology from Jules Reed. Should I check if pigs are flying?"

"I deserve that," Jules acknowledged.

"Yeah, you kind of do." But there was the faintest hint of amusement in Sasha's voice now, a crack in the wall of cool distance.

"Maybe we could get coffee sometime," Jules suggested. "Catch up properly."

"Maybe," Sasha agreed, noncommittal but not outright refusing. "Anyway, I should go. Some of us don't get long lunch breaks."

"Right, of course," Jules said. "Happy birthday, Sash. Really."

"Thanks, Jules." A pause. "It was... nice to hear from you."

The call ended, leaving Jules staring at her phone with a sinking feeling in her stomach.

In this timeline, she and Sasha were estranged. The sister who had been her closest confidante, her unwavering support, was now a distant relation speaking to her with careful civility.

What had happened? What choices had Timeline Jules made that had damaged this relationship so fundamentally?

Before she could spiral further, a notification appeared on her screen:

**Lunch with Valentina in 20 minutes. Car waiting downstairs.**

Right. Work. The one area where this timeline seemed unequivocally better than her own. Well, her love life has improved too.

Jules gathered her portfolio and headed for the elevator, the conversation with Sasha echoing uncomfortably in her mind.

Orso was exactly the kind of restaurant where business deals were made over unnecessarily deconstructed salads and sixteen-dollar glasses of wine. Airy, minimalist, with attentive staff who seemed to materialize exactly when needed and vanish otherwise.

Valentina Diaz was already seated when Jules arrived, her sleek bob and impeccable red lipstick making her look like she'd stepped out of a high-fashion editorial. She stood as Jules approached, greeting her with the European double-kiss that always made Jules feel slightly awkward.

"Jules, darling, you look exhausted," Valentina said by way of greeting, her slight accent making even criticism sound elegant. "The Wilson project is taking its toll, yes?"

"Something like that," Jules replied, slipping into her seat. "But we've had a breakthrough this morning. New direction."

Valentina raised a perfectly shaped eyebrow. "Another pivot? The creative team will revolt."

"They'll manage," Jules said, surprised by her own assurance. "It's the right move for the client."

"Always thinking of the client," Valentina said with a small smile. "This is why we work so well together."

She pulled a sleek tablet from her bag and slid it across the table. "The mock-ups for the Archer campaign, as promised."

Jules nearly choked on her water. "Archer? As in Archer & Bloom?"

Valentina nodded, seemingly unaware of Jules' reaction. "Their rebrand is our priority for Q3. The mock-ups incorporate your feedback on the typography, though I still think the serifs are too traditional."

Jules stared at the tablet, where a completely reimagined version of her former employer's logo glowed on the screen. Bolder, more modern, with none of the conservative restraint that characterized the firm's current identity.

"We're... rebranding Archer & Bloom?" she asked, trying to keep her voice neutral.

Valentina gave her an odd look. "For the past three months, yes. Did you have another concussion during SoulCycle that I don't know about?"

Jules forced a laugh. "No, just juggling too many projects. The designs look great."

She swiped through the mock-ups, each one a sleek, contemporary interpretation that made the existing Archer & Bloom branding look stodgy and outdated by comparison.

"Diana will hate the color palette," Valentina said with a hint of satisfaction. "But that's why we're presenting three options. The middle ground is always where we intended to land."

Diana Archer. The woman who had passed over Jules three times for promotion. The woman whose firm Jules was now apparently rebranding.

"It's perfect," Jules said, genuine appreciation mixing with a petty sense of satisfaction. "They'll be thrilled."

Valentina snorted delicately. "They'll be terrified. Change always is. But you'll convince them, as you always do."

The waiter arrived to take their orders, and the conversation shifted to other clients, other projects. Jules listened and responded on autopilot, her mind churning with this new information.

In this timeline, she wasn't just successful—she was successful enough to have her former employer as a client. To be redesigning their identity. To be, essentially, their superior rather than their subordinate.

It was a delicious reversal. A validation of everything she'd felt in those moments after being passed over, when she'd wondered what might have happened if she'd walked out instead of staying, if she'd demanded more instead of accepting less.

But at what cost?

Her relationship with Sasha. Possibly other relationships she hadn't yet discovered. What else had she sacrificed on the altar of success?

"You're distracted today," Valentina observed, sipping her sparkling water. "The wedding planning is that bad?"

Jules blinked, pulled back to the present. "Just a lot on my mind."

"Well, focus on this," Valentina said, tapping the tablet. "We present to Archer next week, and I need you at your persuasive best."

"I'll be ready," Jules promised, and was surprised to find she meant it.

Whatever complex emotions this timeline stirred, there was no denying the professional satisfaction it offered. The chance to stand in front of Diana Archer not as a hopeful employee but as a successful peer—it was too perfect to resist.

As lunch concluded and Jules headed back to the office, her phone buzzed with a text.

> Nate: Need to work late tonight. Very important project requires my full attention. Possibly until 9 or 10.

Before she could respond, another text came through:

> Nate: The very important project is making you dinner. Don't be late or the soufflé will collapse and I'll be emotionally destroyed.

Jules found herself smiling at the screen, a warm feeling spreading through her chest.

> Jules: Wouldn't dream of it. What kind of monster ruins a soufflé?

His response was immediate:

> Nate: That's my girl. See you at 7. Bring only yourself and an empty stomach.

She tucked the phone away, still smiling, and was halfway back to the office before she realized she'd forgotten all about the Wilson proposal.

Her mind was on Nate. On Sasha. On the tangled web of relationships in this timeline that seemed to define her as much as her professional success.

And for the first time, she wondered if the point of this timeline glimpse wasn't just to see how she'd succeeded professionally—but to understand what that success had cost her.

The afternoon passed in a blur of meetings, emails, and strategic decisions that seemed to come to Jules with surprising ease. By the time she wrapped up her final call, the office had emptied out, the late afternoon sun casting long shadows across her desk.

She should head home. Nate was cooking. Waiting for her.

But something kept her at her desk, searching through emails, calendar entries, anything that might give her more insight into this version of her life.

Timeline Jules was organized to a fault, her digital life as meticulously maintained as her physical one. Folders for every project, archives neatly labeled, even her personal emails sorted by sender and topic.

One folder caught Jules' attention: "Sasha."

She clicked it open to find years of increasingly sporadic correspondence. Early emails were warm, chatty, full of inside jokes and shared memories. But as the dates progressed, the tone changed. Became more formal. More distant.

The most recent exchange was from nearly eight months ago:

**From: Sasha Reed**

**Subject: Mom's birthday**

*Jules,*

*Just checking if you're planning to come to Mom's birthday dinner next Saturday. I know you're busy with the merger and everything, but it would mean a lot to her. To all of us.*

*She still has that article about you from Business Insider pinned to the fridge, by the way. Right next to my community college graduation announcement from nine years ago. Balanced representation and all that.*

*Let me know.*

*- Sasha*

Jules swallowed hard as she read her own reply:

**From: Jules Reed**

**Subject: Re: Mom's birthday**

*Sasha,*

*I won't be able to make it. We're finalizing the Singapore deal that weekend and I need to be available for calls. Please give Mom my love and tell her I'll send something nice.*

*And please don't start with the passive-aggressive comparisons again. My career choices aren't a referendum on yours. We've been over this.*

*- Jules*

Cold. Dismissive. Prioritizing work over family without a second thought.

Was this who she became when she "stopped playing small"? Someone who saw family obligations as inconveniences, who dismissed her sister's feelings as mere jealousy?

Jules closed the email with a sick feeling in her stomach. She recalled Sasha's words on the phone earlier: *"You made it pretty clear that your 'high-powered life' didn't have room for family dinners and birthday brunches."*

She'd been right.

Further digging revealed similar patterns with old friends, former classmates—relationships that had withered as Jules climbed higher, achieved more, built her empire with Nate at her side.

Speaking of Nate...

Jules hesitated, then typed his name into her email search. Thousands of results appeared—work correspondence, mostly, but also personal messages filed under "N.M. Personal."

She shouldn't look. It felt invasive, reading private exchanges between two people in love, even if one of them technically was her.

But the need to understand—to see what kind of relationship they truly had—won out.

She opened the folder and clicked on a recent thread.

**From: Nate Morgan**

**Subject: Tonight**

*J,*

*I know we said no work talk at home, but I've been thinking about the Westridge approach all day. What if we positioned it as an ecosystem rather than a platform? More organic, more interconnected. It fits their sustainability angle.*

*Also, you left your black heels at my office again. That's the third pair this month. At this rate, I'll have enough to open my own boutique.*

*Love you. Even when you abandon perfectly good shoes in my workspace.*

*- N*

Her reply was equally casual, equally intimate:

**From: Jules Reed**

**Subject: Re: Tonight**

*N,*

*I like the ecosystem concept. Run it by Zoe before the meeting—she was working on something similar for the Davidson pitch.*

*And those heels were pinching. You try standing in four-inch spikes for a three-hour presentation. Consider your office my emergency shoe repository. A small price to pay for sharing your life with a woman of exceptional style and occasional foot pain.*

*Love you back. See you at home.*

*- J*

Jules stared at the screen, a confusing mix of emotions swirling through her. Their dynamic was so easy. So comfortable. Professional respect blending seamlessly with personal affection.

In her timeline, she'd barely spoken to Nate outside of necessary work interactions, and certainly never with this kind of relaxed intimacy.

What had changed? What decision point had led her here, to this life where she was both more successful and more isolated? Where she had Nate but had lost Sasha? Where she commanded respect professionally but had sacrificed personal connections?

A notification on her phone broke her reverie—a reminder to leave for home. For Nate's dinner. For the life that wasn't quite hers.

Jules shut down the computer and gathered her things, her mind still churning with everything she'd discovered. As she walked through the quiet office, she passed a wall of photos—the company history documented in professional shots of major milestones.

She paused at one—a ribbon-cutting ceremony, with a younger version of herself and Nate standing outside what appeared to be their first office. The sign behind them read simply: "Reed & Morgan."

Their names. Equal billing. Partners from the start.

Jules stared at the photo, at her own confident smile, at the way she and Nate stood shoulder to shoulder, neither one diminishing the other.

Was that the key? Not just claiming her own space, but finding someone who didn't require her to shrink in order for them to shine?

The evening light caught on her engagement ring as she shifted, sending prisms dancing across the glass of the photo frame.

One decision. One different choice.

But which one?

# the price of winning

. . .

THE APARTMENT SMELLED LIKE GARLIC, herbs, and something decadent baking in the oven. Soft jazz played from hidden speakers, and the lights were dimmed to a warm, intimate glow.

Jules stepped out of her heels by the door, letting her tired feet sink into the plush area rug. "Nate?"

"In the kitchen," he called back. "No peeking until I say so!"

She smiled despite herself, setting down her bag and padding toward the kitchen in her stocking feet. She stopped at the threshold as instructed, taking in the domestic scene before her.

Nate stood at the stove, his back to her, sleeves rolled up and a dish towel tossed over one shoulder. He'd changed from his work clothes into jeans and a soft henley that emphasized the breadth of his shoulders. A bottle of wine breathed on the counter beside two glasses, and the table was set with what appeared to be their good dishes.

"Can I look now?" she asked, an unexpected lightness in her chest.

He turned, spatula in hand, his expression brightening. "Technically you're already looking, but yes, you can come in. Just don't judge the mess."

There was barely any mess—just the organized chaos of someone who actually knew their way around a kitchen. Whatever Nate was cooking looked and smelled incredible.

"What's the occasion?" Jules asked, moving to the kitchen island.

Nate raised an eyebrow. "Do I need an occasion to cook for my fiancée?"

The word still sent a little jolt through her. Fiancée. She was Nate Morgan's fiancée. They were getting married. Building a life together.

"I suppose not," she said, accepting the glass of wine he poured for her. "But this looks fancy enough to be a celebration."

"Well," he said, returning to the stove to stir something that simmered tantalizingly, "maybe I am celebrating a little."

"What are we celebrating?"

He glanced over his shoulder, his expression softening. "Three years ago today was the first time you told me you loved me."

Jules nearly choked on her wine. "It was?"

"Mmhmm," he hummed, seemingly unperturbed by her surprise. "After the Johnson presentation. You were exhausted and delirious from that seventy-two-hour work sprint, and you said—and I quote—'I'm in love with you, you infuriating perfectionist, and I'm too tired to pretend otherwise.'"

He turned fully to face her, his eyes warm with the memory. "And then you fell asleep on my couch while I ordered celebratory Thai food that you didn't wake up to eat."

"Very romantic," Jules managed, struggling to imagine herself making such a blunt declaration.

"It was perfect," Nate said simply. "Because it was real. And because it was you."

Something tight and warm unfurled in Jules' chest. In her timeline, no one had ever looked at her the way Nate was looking at her now—like she was both a miracle and a familiar comfort.

"So," he continued, "butternut squash risotto, crusty bread, and chocolate soufflé for dessert. Assuming I don't mess up the timing."

"It sounds perfect," Jules said, and meant it.

Nate grinned. "Good. Now go change into something comfortable and I'll open another bottle. We're celebrating properly tonight."

Dinner was, in a word, incredible.

The risotto was creamy and rich, the wine paired perfectly, and the soufflé—which Nate had anxiously watched rise in the oven like an expectant father—was a decadent finale that melted on her tongue.

But what surprised Jules most wasn't the food. It was the conversation.

Nate was... interesting. Thoughtful. Genuinely funny in a dry, understated way she'd never appreciated in her limited interactions with him in her own timeline.

He told stories she hadn't heard before, like his disastrous first attempt at starting a business when he was twenty-three.

"Wait," Jules interrupted, setting down her wine glass. "You tried to start a personalized dog food delivery service?"

Nate nodded, unembarrassed. "Bark Bites. Custom nutrition for your canine companion."

"That's..."

"A terrible idea?" he supplied with a grin. "Yes, it absolutely was. Turns out most people are fine with just buying kibble from the store. Who knew?"

Jules laughed, genuinely delighted by this unexpected tidbit. "So, what happened?"

"I burned through my savings, realized I knew nothing about dog nutrition or logistics, and crawled back to my entry-level consulting job with my tail between my legs." He shrugged. "Best failure of my life."

"How so?"

"Because it taught me that a good business needs more than a clever name and enthusiasm. It needs a solid foundation, a real value proposition, and ideally, a co-founder who'll tell you when your ideas are stupid."

His eyes met hers across the table, warm and sincere. "That's why we work so well together, you know. You never let me get away with the easy answer."

Jules felt her cheeks warm, and not just from the wine. "I find that hard to believe. You're one of the most insightful people I've ever met."

It wasn't even a lie. In the few days she'd spent in this timeline, she'd seen enough of Nate's work to recognize his genuine talent.

"I have good instincts," he acknowledged. "But you have vision. You see the whole board when everyone else is just looking at the piece in front of them."

The compliment was so specific, so thoughtful, that Jules didn't know how to respond. In her timeline, praise was rare and usually generic—"good job" or "nice work" tossed out like obligatory treats.

This was different. This was someone who saw her, really saw her, and valued what he saw.

"Thank you," she said simply.

Nate smiled, then began clearing their plates. "No need to thank me for stating facts. Now, shall we take our wine to the couch? I think we've earned a comfortable surface after that meal."

The living room was as elegantly appointed as the rest of the apartment, with a plush sectional that seemed designed for luxurious lounging. Jules sank into it with a contented sigh, kicking off her slippers and tucking her feet beneath her.

Nate joined her, close enough that she could feel the warmth of him but not so close that it felt presumptuous. He'd dimmed the lights further, the city skyline beyond their windows now a glittering tapestry against the night.

"Tell me about your day," he said, turning to face her. "And not the sanitized version. The real one."

Jules hesitated. What could she say? That she'd spent the day navigating a life she didn't recognize? That she'd discovered she was estranged from her sister and had no idea how to fix it?

"It was... complicated," she settled on. "I spoke to Sasha."

Nate's eyebrows rose in genuine surprise. "Wow. How did that go?"

"Not great," Jules admitted. "I think I really hurt her, Nate. And I don't know how to make it right."

His expression softened. "You did what you thought was necessary at the time."

"Did I?" Jules asked, the question more genuine than he could possibly know. "Or did I just get so focused on winning that I forgot what I was fighting for?"

Nate studied her for a long moment, his dark eyes thoughtful. "Where is this coming from, Jules? You've never second-guessed your choices before."

She looked down at her wine, swirling it gently in the glass. "Maybe I should have."

A soft silence fell between them, not uncomfortable but weighted with unspoken thoughts.

"You know," Nate said finally, "when we started Reed & Morgan, you made me promise something. Do you remember what it was?"

Jules shook her head, both genuinely curious and buying time.

"You made me promise to tell you if you ever became the kind of boss you hated at Archer & Bloom. The kind who stepped on others to get ahead."

He reached out, his hand covering hers on the couch between them. "I've never had to keep that promise, Jules. Not once. You've always been ambitious, yes. Driven, absolutely. But never at the expense of others."

Jules frowned, thinking of Sasha, of the emails, of the relationships that had clearly withered. "I don't think that's true. I think I've hurt people. Maybe not intentionally, but still."

Nate considered this, his thumb tracing small circles on the back of her hand. "There's a difference between hurting people by making necessary choices and hurting them because you don't care. You've always cared, Jules. Sometimes too much."

"What do you mean?" Jules asked, genuinely curious about insights into herself she couldn't access.

"You carry the weight of every decision," he said quietly. "Second-guess yourself when you have to make tough calls. I've watched you lose sleep over choices that were ultimately right but still painful for someone involved."

Jules felt something tighten in her chest. "Like what?"

Nate was quiet for a moment, as if deciding whether to share something difficult. "Like when we restructured last spring. You spent weeks finding alternative solutions before we had to let anyone go. And even then, you made sure everyone landed somewhere better."

Jules nodded, not because she remembered but because she could feel the truth of it—this version of herself who succeeded without losing her humanity.

"But Sasha," Jules said softly. "My own sister..."

Nate's expression grew more serious. "That's different. And complicated. You know it wasn't just about your career. It was about the things she said about us. About me."

Jules blinked, genuinely confused. "What did she say?"

A shadow passed over Nate's face. "That I was the reason you changed. That I'd turned you into someone your family didn't recognize. That we were 'toxic power couple' material."

Jules winced. That didn't sound like Sasha at all—her sister had always been her most loyal supporter, her fiercest defender.

"When was this?" she asked carefully.

"After we announced our engagement," Nate said. "She cornered me at your parents' place and gave me quite the speech about how I'd changed you, how you used to be warmer, more present, more... I don't know, pliable? She implied I was the one who made you 'ruthless,' as she called it."

He shook his head, old hurt flickering in his eyes. "As if you weren't the one who pitched Reed & Morgan in the first place. As if you weren't the one who stayed up for three days straight writing our business plan. As if you weren't already the most brilliant strategist I'd ever met before we even became partners."

Jules absorbed this, trying to reconcile it with the Sasha she knew. Her sister could be fierce, yes, but never cruel. Never unfair.

"Maybe she was just worried about me," Jules suggested. "About us moving too fast."

Nate's brow furrowed. "Jules, we'd been working together for four years before we got involved personally. We lived together for another two before I proposed. That's hardly too fast."

Six years? They'd been a couple for six years in this timeline?

"I just mean..." Jules fumbled for the right words. "Maybe she felt like she was losing me. To the business. To you. To this whole life we've built."

Nate was quiet for a moment, considering this. "Maybe," he allowed. "But she didn't have to make it about me being some kind of villain who corrupted you."

"You're right," Jules said, meaning it. Whatever had happened with Sasha, blaming Nate wasn't fair. "I'm sorry she said those things."

His expression softened. "You don't need to apologize. It was a long time ago."

"Still," Jules insisted. "You didn't deserve that."

Nate set down his wine glass and took both her hands in his. "Look, Jules. Families are complicated. I've never expected you to cut Sasha out of your life. That was your choice, and I've respected it. But if you want to try to mend things with her... I support that too."

The sincerity in his voice, the genuine care in his eyes—it made something twist painfully in Jules' chest. This man, who she'd barely known in her timeline, who she'd dismissed as just another obstacle in her path, was offering her understanding and support without hesitation.

"Thank you," she said, her voice barely above a whisper.

He smiled, his hands squeezing hers gently. "That's what partners do, remember? We have each other's backs. Always."

Partners. The word resonated through her, carrying new meaning. Not just business partners, though they were clearly that. Not just romantic partners, though the evidence of their relationship surrounded her.

True partners. Equals who lifted each other instead of competing. Who saw strength as something to celebrate rather than something to fear or control.

Before she could overthink it, Jules leaned forward and kissed him. Not the cautious, responding kiss of the night before, but something more deliberate. More honest.

Nate made a soft sound of surprise before his hand came up to cradle her face, his touch gentle but sure. The kiss deepened, and Jules felt herself melting into it, into him, into the warmth and certainty he offered.

When they finally broke apart, Nate's eyes were dark, his expression a mixture of desire and tenderness that made her breath catch.

"What was that for?" he asked, voice low.

"For being you," Jules said simply. "For seeing me."

He smiled, tucking a strand of hair behind her ear. "Always have. From the first day you marched into that meeting at Archer & Bloom and told Diana her entire campaign strategy was backward."

Jules blinked. "I did what?"

Nate laughed. "You don't remember? You were barely six

months into the job, and you completely dismantled her approach in front of the entire team. I'd never seen anyone so brilliantly, strategically correct before."

"And you weren't... intimidated?"

"Intimidated?" He looked genuinely puzzled. "I was impressed. Everyone else was trying to blend in, to say the right things to get ahead. But you? You were focused on doing the right work, saying the necessary things, even if they weren't popular."

His hand found hers again, fingers interlacing with casual intimacy. "That's when I knew I wanted to work with you someday. Not because you were the loudest or the most aggressive, but because you were the clearest. The most honest."

Jules tried to imagine it—herself, junior strategist, challenging Diana Archer in front of the entire team. It seemed impossible. In her timeline, she'd been careful, restrained, always conscious of overstepping.

But in this timeline...

"What happened after that?" she asked, genuinely curious.

Nate smiled. "Diana was furious, of course. But the client loved your approach. Implemented it exactly as you'd outlined. The campaign exceeded every metric."

"And then?"

"And then you were quietly removed from client-facing roles for three months," he said with a hint of old anger. "Standard punishment for making the boss look bad, even when you're right. Especially when you're right."

Jules nodded slowly. This sounded more like the Archer & Bloom she knew.

"That's when I started talking to you about leaving," Nate continued. "About starting something where good work would be rewarded, not punished. Where we could build a culture that valued clarity over conformity."

"And I agreed?" Jules asked before she could stop herself.

Nate gave her an odd look. "Eventually. After they passed you over for the Reynolds account even though everyone knew you'd developed the winning strategy."

The Reynolds account. In her timeline, that had gone to... Adam. Her first major disappointment at Archer & Bloom.

"Right," she said. "Of course."

Nate studied her face, a slight furrow appearing between his brows. "You're different tonight."

Jules felt a flicker of panic. "Different how?"

"More... reflective," he said after a moment. "Usually when we talk about the early days, you get fired up all over again. Ready to take on the world."

He reached out, brushing his thumb across her cheekbone in a gesture so tender it made her chest ache. "But tonight, you seem almost... sad."

"Not sad," Jules corrected gently. "Just... realizing what's important."

Nate's expression softened. "And what's that?"

She held his gaze, finding it easier than she'd expected. "This. Us. The people who matter."

Something shifted in his eyes—a warmth, a deepening. "Jules Reed, are you going soft on me?"

"Never," she promised with a small smile. "Just... recalibrating."

He leaned forward, pressing his forehead against hers. "I like it. Recalibrate all you want."

They stayed like that for a long moment, connected, close, sharing the same air. Jules closed her eyes, allowing herself to sink into the intimacy of the moment.

This was what she'd been missing in her timeline. Not just professional success or recognition, but this—connection. Partnership. Someone who saw her strength as beautiful rather than threatening.

Someone who made space for her because he wanted to stand beside her, not above or below.

When Nate kissed her again, Jules didn't hesitate. Didn't overthink. Just welcomed the warmth, the belonging, the quiet certainty that this—*he*—was what had been missing all along.

Later, much later, as they lay tangled together in the soft sheets of their shared bed, Nate's breathing deep and even beside her, Jules stared at the ceiling and wondered if she could find the strength to make that same choice when she returned to her own life.

Because for the first time since arriving in this alternate reality, Jules was certain of one thing: she didn't want to go back to being overlooked. To being small. To being alone.

She wanted this—the success, yes, but more than that, the partnership. The balance. The life built on her terms, with someone who celebrated rather than diminished her.

She turned on her side, watching Nate's profile in the dim light filtering through the windows. His features were relaxed in sleep, vulnerable in a way he never was when awake.

Six days left in this timeline.

Six days to understand what she'd done differently.

Six days to learn how to be brave enough to claim this life for herself.

# success ≠ satisfaction

. . .

JULES WOKE to an empty bed and the smell of coffee brewing. Sunlight streamed through the partially open curtains, casting the room in a warm glow that made even waking up feel luxurious.

For a moment, she didn't move, just absorbed the sensations around her: the impossibly soft sheets, the lingering warmth where Nate had slept beside her, the distant sounds of movement from somewhere else in the apartment.

Last night had been... unexpected. Intimate in ways that went beyond the physical. She'd seen a side of Nate—of herself—that had changed her understanding of this timeline completely.

This wasn't just a glimpse of professional success. It was a window into what partnership could truly mean.

The bedroom door opened quietly, and Nate appeared with two steaming mugs. He'd already showered, his hair damp and his lower half covered only by a towel wrapped around his waist. Jules found herself appreciating the view without embarrassment.

"Morning," he said, voice still rough with sleep despite his showered state. "Thought you might need this."

He handed her a mug of coffee—prepared exactly how she liked it, she noticed—and sat on the edge of the bed beside her.

"Thanks," she murmured, taking a grateful sip. "What time is it?"

"Just after seven," he replied. "We don't have to be in until nine today, remember? The team's recovering from the Westridge push."

Jules nodded, though she hadn't remembered any such thing. The considerate gesture—giving their team a later start after a major project—seemed perfectly in character for the leaders they appeared to be in this timeline.

"How did you sleep?" Nate asked, his eyes soft with something that made Jules' chest tighten.

"Well," she said honestly. Better than she had in years, actually, wrapped in the security of Nate's arms and the luxury of this life they'd built.

"Good." He leaned forward to press a kiss to her forehead—casual, intimate, the gesture of someone who had performed it a thousand times before. "I'm going to make breakfast. Preferences?"

"Surprise me," Jules said, surprising herself with the easy trust in her voice.

Nate grinned. "Dangerous words. What if I surprise you with my famous cereal and milk combination?"

"I'll take my chances," she replied, smiling over the rim of her mug.

He laughed, the sound warm and genuine, and stood to leave. At the doorway, he paused, glancing back at her with an expression that was part wonder, part familiar contentment.

"What?" Jules asked, suddenly self-conscious.

"Nothing," Nate said, shaking his head slightly. "Just... I like this version of you. Relaxed. Present."

Before she could respond, he was gone, leaving Jules to contemplate his words as she sipped her coffee.

*This version of you.*

The irony wasn't lost on her.

By the time Jules emerged from the shower, dressed in a deep burgundy dress she'd found in the closet, Nate had prepared a breakfast that put his "cereal and milk" joke to shame.

The kitchen island held a spread of sliced fruit, yogurt, granola, and what appeared to be freshly baked scones.

"When did you have time to bake?" Jules asked, genuinely impressed.

Nate looked up from where he was plating something at the stove. "I didn't. These are from that bakery around the corner. I may have sneaked out while you were sleeping."

"You went out just for scones?"

He shrugged, a small smile playing at his lips. "You had a rough day yesterday. Seemed like a scone kind of morning."

The casual thoughtfulness of the gesture caught Jules off guard. How many times had she dragged herself to the office after a difficult day, forcing herself through the motions with nothing but vending machine coffee and sheer determination to sustain her?

Here, in this timeline, rough days were met with understanding. With support. With someone who noticed when she needed a little extra care.

"Thank you," she said, the words inadequate for the warmth spreading through her chest.

Nate set a plate in front of her—eggs perfectly scrambled with chives and goat cheese. "It's just breakfast, Jules. No need to look at me like I've reinvented romance."

But there was pleased color rising in his cheeks, and Jules found herself charmed by it. By him. By this whole domestic scene she'd never imagined herself wanting or needing.

They ate together at the kitchen island, discussing the day ahead between bites of food and sips of coffee. Nate had a meeting with their development team about the Westridge technical specifications. Jules had a lunch with a potential client followed by internal reviews for the Wilson rebrand.

It was... normal. Comfortable. The rhythm of two people whose lives were thoroughly intertwined.

"By the way," Nate said as they were clearing the dishes, "I meant to ask—do you have plans this weekend? Because I was thinking we might drive up to the lake house. Get some fresh air, clear our heads before the Wilson presentation next week."

"Lake house?" Jules echoed before she could stop herself.

Nate gave her an odd look. "Yes, the lake house. That place we bought last year? About two hours north? Scene of many mosquito bites and at least one unfortunate attempt at paddleboarding?"

"Right," Jules recovered quickly. "Of course. The lake house sounds perfect."

Nate studied her for a moment longer, that same slight furrow between his brows that appeared whenever she said something unexpected. "Are you sure you're okay, Jules? You've been... I don't know, a little off these past couple of days."

Jules busied herself rinsing a plate, avoiding his eyes. "Just tired. The Westridge deal took a lot out of me."

"Hmm," Nate hummed, not sounding entirely convinced. "Well, if there's something else going on, you know you can talk to me, right? That's kind of our whole thing—no bullshit, remember?"

She looked up then, meeting his concerned gaze. "I know. And I appreciate it. I'm just... processing some things."

It wasn't even a lie.

Nate nodded slowly. "Okay. Processing is allowed. Mandatory, even. Just don't process alone if you don't have to."

He pressed a kiss to her temple as he passed, heading to the bedroom to finish getting ready. Jules stayed in the kitchen, hands braced on the counter, trying to steady her breathing.

This was getting dangerous. Not just the easy domesticity, the comfortable routine they'd established. Not just the physical attraction, which was undeniable.

No, what was truly dangerous was how quickly she was coming to rely on Nate's presence. His support. His unwavering belief in her.

What would happen when the week ended? When she returned to her timeline, to a life where Nate Morgan was just another colleague, another competitor? Where they had no history, no connection, no shared understanding?

The thought left a hollow feeling in her chest.

Five days left. Just five days to understand what made this timeline different. To learn what she needed to take back with her.

Five days to prepare for the possibility that, when she returned, Nate wouldn't look at her the way he did here—with warmth, with admiration, with love.

Five days before she lost something she was starting to want more than she'd ever thought possible.

Reed & Morgan Strategic Group buzzed with the focused energy of a company in its prime. As Jules moved through the office, she noticed details she'd missed in the initial overwhelm—the thoughtful design elements, the comfortable collaborative spaces, the general atmosphere of creativity and purpose.

This wasn't a place where people competed for recognition or hoarded opportunities. This was a culture built on mutual respect and collective achievement.

In her office, a fresh stack of briefs awaited her review, each one accompanied by clear notes from the team members who'd prepared them. Jules settled at her desk, ready to immerse herself in the work that came so naturally to her in this timeline.

A soft knock interrupted her concentration. She looked up to find Zoe standing in the doorway, tablet in hand.

"Got a minute?" Zoe asked. "I have the revised approach for Wilson."

"Of course," Jules said, gesturing to the chair across from her desk. "Walk me through it."

For the next thirty minutes, they dove deep into strategy, with Jules finding herself contributing insights and perspectives that seemed to emerge from some well of knowledge she didn't consciously possess. It was like muscle memory—her body knew how to do things her mind didn't remember learning.

As they wrapped up, Zoe lingered, an uncharacteristic hesitation in her usual efficient manner.

"Is everything okay?" Jules asked.

Zoe adjusted her glasses—a nervous gesture Jules had picked up on even in her short time here. "Actually, I wanted to thank you."

"For what?"

"For the advice you gave me last month. About the Simpson account."

Jules nodded, hoping her expression didn't betray her complete lack of memory regarding any Simpson account.

"I was ready to play it safe," Zoe continued. "Go with the conventional approach because I was afraid of pushback. But you said something that really stuck with me."

"What did I say?" Jules asked, genuinely curious to hear what wisdom her alternate self had imparted.

"You said, 'The work that scares you is usually the work that matters.'" Zoe smiled, a hint of admiration in her eyes. "You were right. They loved the bolder approach. The CMO specifically mentioned it in their feedback."

The work that scares you is usually the work that matters. It sounded like something she might have said if she'd had the confidence, the security to believe it.

"I'm glad it worked out," Jules said warmly. "Your instincts are strong, Zoe. You should trust them more often."

Zoe ducked her head, pleased by the praise. "Coming from you, that means a lot."

After Zoe left, Jules found herself turning the phrase over in her mind. The work that scares you is usually the work that matters.

Had that been the difference in this timeline? Had she chosen to do the scary work, to take the bigger risks, to trust her instincts even when they led her away from the safe path?

Her computer chimed with a calendar reminder: lunch with a potential client at noon. Jules gathered her notes, tucked them into her portfolio, and headed out.

As she passed through the main workspace, she noticed Nate in one of the glass-walled conference rooms, deep in discussion with a team gathered around a table covered in diagrams and mock-ups. He gestured animatedly, his expression focused but open, clearly inviting input from the group.

He looked up as she passed, his serious expression breaking into a warm smile when he spotted her. He gave her a small nod— not quite a wave, but definitely an acknowledgment. A connection.

Jules nodded back, a flutter of warmth in her chest.

This was what partnership looked like. Not competing for the same spotlight, but illuminating different aspects of the same vision.

It was beautiful.

And increasingly, terrifyingly, something she couldn't imagine living without.

The lunch meeting went smoothly, with Jules finding herself perfectly capable of discussing services and approaches she objectively knew nothing about. The potential client—a sustainability-focused tech startup with ambitious goals—seemed impressed by her insights and the firm's portfolio.

By the time she returned to the office, Jules was riding the confidence high that came from successfully navigating yet another aspect of this borrowed life.

She was on her way to her office when she spotted a familiar figure through the glass walls of the company cafe—a petite woman with a cloud of curly hair and statement earrings. Kai.

Acting on impulse, Jules diverted her path and entered the cafe. Kai looked up from her laptop, surprise and pleasure lighting her features.

"Jules! Fancy seeing you in the middle of the day," she said warmly. "Usually, we need the jaws of life to extract you from your office between the hours of nine and six."

Jules smiled, sliding into the chair opposite her friend. "I'm practicing this radical new concept called 'taking breaks.' Very revolutionary."

Kai laughed. "Nate's influence, no doubt. That man has been trying to get you to experience work-life balance for years."

"He's persistent," Jules agreed, curious about this dynamic. "Has he always been that way? So... balanced?"

Kai gave her an odd look. "Pretty much, yeah. I mean, he works hard—you both do—but he's always had that whole 'work to live, not live to work' philosophy. Why?"

Jules shrugged, trying to seem casual. "Just thinking about how we approach things differently sometimes."

"Opposites attract and all that," Kai said, closing her laptop to give Jules her full attention. "Though you're not as different as you think. You're both stubborn as hell, for one thing."

"I am not stubborn," Jules protested automatically.

Kai's eyebrows shot up. "Says the woman who once spent three days straight restructuring an entire campaign because, and I quote, 'It's not right yet and I'd rather die than present work that's merely adequate.'"

Jules winced. That did sound like something she'd say.

"Fair point," she conceded. "I can be... determined."

"That's one word for it." Kai took a sip of her tea, studying Jules over the rim of her mug. "So, what's really on your mind? Because the Jules Reed I know doesn't take spontaneous coffee breaks to discuss personality traits."

There was something about Kai's direct approach that Jules found refreshing. In her timeline, she didn't have many close friends—acquaintances, yes, professional contacts, certainly, but few people she could be truly vulnerable with.

Here, it seemed, she had Kai. And perhaps that was a resource worth utilizing.

"Can I ask you something?" Jules said, leaning forward slightly. "About me and Nate?"

"Ooh, intrigue," Kai replied, mimicking her posture. "Ask away."

"When did you know we were right for each other? That it wasn't just... professional compatibility or physical attraction?"

Kai's expression softened, becoming more thoughtful. "That's actually a good question."

She tapped her long nails against the table, considering. "I think it was after that disaster with the Henderson account, remember? When the client pulled out at the last minute and you lost that massive commission you'd been counting on?"

Jules nodded as if she remembered.

"Nate showed up at your place with takeout and a bottle of tequila," Kai continued. "But instead of just letting you wallow, which is what most guys would do, he brought his laptop and stayed up all night with you, rebuilding your pitch deck for other clients. He said—and this is the part that got me—he said, 'Your ideas are too good to waste just because Henderson's an idiot.'"

Kai smiled at the memory. "He didn't try to fix your feelings or tell you it would be okay. He acknowledged the loss and then helped you repurpose the work you were proud of. That's when I knew he got you—really got you—in a way most people don't."

The story landed with unexpected weight. It was such a small moment, in some ways—not grand or dramatic, just deeply understanding.

"And what about me?" Jules asked quietly. "When did you know I was serious about him?"

Kai laughed. "Oh, that was obvious from day one. You've never looked at anyone the way you look at Nate. Like he's a puzzle you can't quite solve but are thoroughly enjoying trying to figure out."

"That doesn't sound very romantic," Jules observed with a small smile.

"It is for you," Kai countered. "For someone else, romance might be flowers and poetry. For Jules Reed, it's intellectual fascination and respect."

She reached across the table, briefly touching Jules' hand. "You found someone who challenges you without trying to change you. Do you know how rare that is? Especially for women like us who don't fit neatly into society's little boxes?"

Jules felt something catch in her throat. "Women like us?"

"Smart, ambitious, occasionally terrifying," Kai clarified with a wink. "The ones who get called 'difficult' when we're just being direct."

That resonated deeply. How many times had Jules modulated her tone, softened her opinions, made herself smaller to avoid that very label?

"Nate never found you difficult," Kai continued, as if reading her thoughts. "He found you fascinating. Still does, judging by the way he looks at you."

Jules nodded, absorbing this. "Thanks, Kai. For the insight."

"Anytime," Kai replied. "Though I'm curious—what brought this on? You two seem solid as ever."

"Just... reflecting," Jules said, which wasn't untrue. "Sometimes it's good to remember why we choose the people we choose."

Kai studied her for a moment longer, then nodded. "Well, if you need an official reminder, I've got about six thousand photos of you two making disgusting heart-eyes at each other over the years. Very well-documented love story."

Jules laughed. "I'll keep that in mind."

As she walked back to her office, Jules felt a curious mixture of emotions churning within her. The picture Kai had painted—of a relationship built on mutual respect, intellectual admiration, and genuine understanding—was so far from anything she'd experienced in her own timeline.

In her world, dating had always felt like a series of compromises, of making herself more palatable, less intimidating, less... herself.

But here, with Nate, it seemed she'd found someone who valued exactly the parts of her that others had found challenging. Who saw her ambition as a feature, not a flaw.

It was a revelation. And increasingly, a complication.

Because what would happen when she had to leave this timeline behind? When she returned to a world where Nate Morgan was just a colleague who'd beaten her for a promotion? Where they had no history, no connection, no foundation of shared respect and understanding?

The thought left a hollow feeling in her chest.

The afternoon blurred into a series of meetings, reviews, and decisions that Jules navigated with increasing confidence. By the time she wrapped up her final call of the day, the office had emptied out, leaving her alone with her thoughts in the quiet of her corner office.

She was gathering her things to leave when her phone buzzed with a text.

> Nate: Still at the office? Come to the roof when you're done. I have something to show you.

The roof? Jules frowned slightly, but her curiosity was piqued. She replied with a simple **On my way** and headed for the elevator.

The top floor of the building housed a small executive lounge that led to a rooftop terrace—a perk of leasing the penthouse suite. As Jules pushed through the glass doors to the outdoor space, the early evening air greeted her, cool but not cold, carrying the scent of the city and something else... something floral?

She followed the stone path around a landscaped corner and stopped, surprised by the scene before her.

Nate stood beside a small table set for two, complete with candles and a bottle of wine already opened to breathe. String lights had been wrapped around the neighboring planters, casting a warm, intimate glow over the setting.

"What is this?" Jules asked, genuinely stunned.

Nate smiled, a touch of uncertainty in his expression. "Surprise rooftop dinner? I thought we could use a change of scenery."

He gestured to a large white box sitting on a nearby bench. "Food's from Antonio's. All your favorites."

Jules approached slowly, taking in the effort, the thought that had gone into this impromptu date night. "You did all this... why?"

Nate's smile faltered slightly. "Because you've seemed a little... I don't know, distant lately? I thought maybe we needed some time just for us. Away from the apartment, away from the office, but still... ours."

The simple sincerity of it made her chest ache. This man—this version of Nate Morgan—paid attention. Noticed when something was off. And instead of pulling away or becoming defensive, he created space for connection.

"It's perfect," Jules said softly, meaning it.

Relief flickered across his features. He pulled out a chair for her, an old-fashioned gesture that somehow didn't feel patronizing coming from him.

"Wine?" he offered, already reaching for the bottle.

Jules nodded, settling into her seat and watching as he poured two glasses with practiced ease. The city spread out around them, a tapestry of lights against the darkening sky. It was beautiful. Intimate. Impossibly romantic.

"So," Nate said, taking his own seat, "I have a theory."

Jules raised an eyebrow. "About?"

"About what's been going on with you this week."

Her heart stuttered. Had he somehow figured it out? Realized she wasn't *his* Jules at all, but an impostor from another timeline?

"And what's your theory?" she asked, trying to keep her voice steady.

Nate took a sip of his wine, studying her over the rim of his glass. "I think you're having second thoughts."

"About?"

"About us. The wedding. All of it."

Jules stared at him, genuinely surprised. "What? No, Nate, that's not—"

He held up a hand, his expression gentle. "Let me finish. Please?"

She nodded, heart racing.

"You've been different this week," he continued. "More distant, yes, but also more... present, in an odd way. Like you're seeing everything for the first time. Questioning things. Me. Us."

He set down his glass, leaning forward slightly. "And that's okay, Jules. It really is. Big commitments should be questioned. Examined. It's how we know they're real."

Jules didn't know what to say. He wasn't wrong, exactly—she was seeing everything with new eyes, questioning the reality she'd stepped into. But not because she doubted it. Because she was beginning to want it too much.

"I'm not having second thoughts," she said finally, the words feeling heavy with truth despite the strange circumstances. "If anything, I'm more certain than ever."

Nate's expression softened with visible relief. "Yeah?"

"Yeah," Jules confirmed. "I've just been... reflecting. On us. On how we got here."

"Any particular reason?"

She hesitated, then decided on a version of the truth. "I had a dream the other night. That we never met. That I stayed at Archer & Bloom, kept trying to prove myself to people who would never see me. It felt so real, and so... empty."

Nate reached across the table, taking her hand in his. "But that's not what happened."

"No," Jules agreed softly. "It's not. But it could have been. If things had gone differently. If I'd made different choices."

"Such as?"

"If I hadn't spoken up in that meeting with Diana," she suggested, drawing on what he'd told her the night before. "If I'd stayed quiet, played it safe."

Nate considered this, his thumb tracing small circles on the back of her hand. "I don't think you could have, Jules. Not for long. It's not in your nature to stay small when you see something that needs to be said."

"You think so?"

"I know so," he said with quiet certainty. "It's one of the first things I admired about you. Your clarity. Your willingness to stand in your truth, even when it was uncomfortable."

He smiled, a touch of nostalgia in his expression. "You remember what you said to me, that day I suggested we leave Archer & Bloom and start our own firm?"

Jules shook her head, desperately curious.

"You said, 'I'm tired of asking for a seat at a table where I've already earned the right to sit.' And I thought—yes. That's it exactly."

The words resonated through her, striking a chord so deep she could almost feel it physically. Wasn't that precisely what she'd been doing in her timeline? Asking permission to occupy space she'd already earned? Waiting for recognition instead of claiming it?

"I said that?" she asked softly.

"You did," Nate confirmed. "And then you outlined your vision for what eventually became Reed & Morgan. I was sold within ten minutes."

"Just like that?"

"Just like that." His gaze was warm, certain. "Some decisions are easy, Jules. Partnering with you—professionally, personally—has been the easiest choice I've ever made."

Something twisted in Jules' chest—a pang of longing so acute it was almost painful. In her timeline, nothing had been easy. Every step forward had been a battle, every achievement qualified by doubt or dismissal.

Here, she'd found a partnership that amplified her strengths rather than diminishing them. A relationship that celebrated her ambition rather than being threatened by it.

"You okay?" Nate asked, noticing her silence.

Jules nodded, blinking back unexpected moisture in her eyes. "Yes. Just... grateful. For you. For us."

He smiled, squeezing her hand gently. "Me too. Every day."

As they sat on that rooftop, sharing wine and pasta and stories of their journey together, Jules felt something shifting inside her. A realization. A clarity.

In her timeline, she'd been so focused on proving her worth, on fighting for recognition, that she'd missed something crucial: the power of aligning herself with people who already saw her value. Who didn't need convincing. Who wanted to build with her, not compete against her.

She'd been so busy trying to win seats at the wrong tables that she hadn't considered the possibility of building her own.

And that, perhaps, was the key difference in this timeline. Not just that she'd spoken up in that meeting with Diana. Not just that she'd claimed her space more boldly.

But that she'd recognized when it was time to create a new space entirely. With the right person at her side.

As the city lights twinkled around them and Nate recounted the story of their first client pitch—a disaster by all accounts, but one they'd laughed about afterward over cheap beer in her tiny apartment—Jules felt the weight of the realization settle over her.

Success wasn't about winning within a broken system.

It was about having the courage to envision and create something better.

And she was running out of time to figure out how to take that knowledge back with her.

# no title worth this

. . .

JULES STOOD in front of her closet—her timeline closet—staring at rows of garments that represented a life she hadn't built but was beginning to covet. Power suits in jewel tones. Dresses that commanded attention without apology. Shoes that added height she didn't need to apologize for.

Four days left in this timeline.

Four days to understand what she needed to take back with her.

Four days until she lost Nate.

The thought sent a sharp pang through her chest, one she couldn't ignore or dismiss. In less than a week, she'd gone from barely knowing him to... what? Not love, surely. That would be absurd. But something. Something real. Something that mattered.

She selected a sapphire blue suit with architectural details at the shoulders—power-dressing that didn't pretend to be anything else—and laid it on the bed.

"The lake house is confirmed for the weekend," Nate called from the bathroom, his voice slightly muffled. "I added groceries to our delivery order. Anything specific you want me to add?"

Jules froze for a moment. The lake house. The weekend. A

romantic getaway with a man who thought she was his fiancée, who had years of shared history with a version of her that wasn't her at all.

"No, I'm sure whatever you ordered is perfect," she called back, hating the slight tremor in her voice.

Nate appeared in the doorway, towel around his waist, hair still damp. "You okay? You look a little pale."

Jules nodded too quickly. "Fine. Just... thinking about the Wilson presentation next week."

It was a convenient excuse. The timeline was rapidly filling her head with details about the Wilson account—their conservative leadership, their resistance to change, the major repositioning strategy she was supposed to pitch next Tuesday.

Nate studied her face, not entirely convinced. "We've got this, Jules. The team's aligned, the strategy is solid, and your pitch skills are legendary. Wilson will sign before you reach slide ten."

His confidence in her was so unwavering, so genuine. Not like the hollow reassurances she'd received in her timeline—the "you'll get 'em next time" platitudes after each disappointment.

"I know," she said, forcing a smile. "Pre-presentation jitters, that's all."

Nate crossed the room and pressed a kiss to her forehead, casual and tender. "Want me to take point on this one? I'm happy to lead if you're not feeling it."

The offer was so sincere, so free of any power play or ulterior motive, that Jules felt something in her chest twist painfully.

"No," she said, reaching up to touch his cheek briefly. "It's my project. I'll see it through."

He smiled, pleased by her resolve. "That's my girl."

As he returned to the bathroom, Jules sank onto the edge of the bed, a heavy feeling settling in her stomach.

This was getting too complicated. Too real. She was beginning to rely on the partnership they shared, the easy give and take, the unwavering support. What would happen when she returned to her timeline and it was all gone?

She reached for her phone, needing a distraction from her spiraling thoughts, and found a notification she'd missed the night before.

**Reminder: Brunch with Kai & Miguel tomorrow, 11 AM at Milo's**

Another social obligation. Another performance as Timeline Jules. Another opportunity to fall deeper into this life that wasn't truly hers.

She set the phone down and covered her face with her hands, taking a deep, steadying breath. She needed to get a grip. To remember that this was temporary. A glimpse, not a permanent relocation.

But as she heard Nate humming in the bathroom—some obscure indie song he'd probably played for her a dozen times in this timeline—Jules couldn't help but wonder: what if it could be permanent? What if she could stay here, in this life, with this version of Nate who knew her, appreciated her, supported her in ways she'd never experienced before?

The thought was seductive. Dangerous.

And completely against the rules.

Reed & Morgan was unusually quiet when Jules arrived, most of the team engaged in focused work at their desks or in small huddles throughout the space. She made her way to her office, nodding to those who looked up as she passed.

Her desk was impeccably organized, as always, with the day's priorities neatly laid out in her own handwriting. A stack of briefs for review. A draft of the Wilson presentation. And a small envelope that hadn't been there the day before.

Jules picked it up curiously. It was unmarked, just a simple cream-colored envelope sealed with a drop of wax impressed with a familiar symbol: the infinity loop of Timeline Retreats.

Her heart beat faster as she carefully broke the seal and withdrew a single card.

### THREE DAYS REMAINING

*THE GLIMPSE CONCLUDES AT MIDNIGHT ON THE SEVENTH DAY.*
*CHOOSE WISELY.*

Choose? What choice was there to make? Celeste had said this was temporary—a glimpse, not a permanent relocation. Had she been mistaken? Was there a way to stay?

And if there was... would she take it?

Jules tucked the card back into the envelope and slipped it into her bag, her mind churning with possibilities. The thought of staying in this timeline—of keeping this life, this career, this relationship with Nate—was dangerously appealing.

But what about her real life? Her real timeline? The Jules who belonged there?

Before she could spiral further into these unsettling questions, her phone buzzed with a meeting reminder. She had five minutes to get to the Onyx Room for a strategy session on the Wilson presentation.

Professional Jules took over, pushing the timeline complications aside for the moment. She gathered her materials and headed for the meeting, determination in every step.

The strategy session was productive, with the team building on Jules' repositioning concept for Wilson with enthusiasm and insight. She led the discussion with a confidence that felt both foreign and familiar, drawing out the best ideas from each team member and weaving them into a cohesive approach.

"This is strong," Zoe said as they wrapped up, her expression thoughtful. "But Wilson's board is notoriously risk-averse. They're going to push back hard on such a dramatic repositioning."

"Let them," Jules replied, surprising herself with her certainty. "Our job isn't to tell them what they want to hear. It's to tell them what they need to know."

The team exchanged glances—not doubtful, but impressed.

"That's why she's the boss," someone murmured appreciatively.

As they filed out, Nate caught her eye from across the room where he'd been observing quietly. He gave her a small nod—acknowledgment, approval, partnership in a single gesture.

Jules nodded back, that now-familiar warmth spreading through her chest.

This was what she'd always wanted, wasn't it? Recognition. Respect. The freedom to lead on her own terms.

So why did it suddenly feel incomplete?

The day passed in a blur of meetings, calls, and strategic decisions. By late afternoon, Jules found herself alone in her office, staring out at the city skyline as the sun began its slow descent.

Tomorrow was the weekend. The lake house. Two days alone with Nate in what was undoubtedly a romantic setting, playing the role of his loving fiancée while knowing that in just a few days, she'd be gone.

The thought left her feeling hollow.

A soft knock at her door broke her reverie. She turned to find Nate leaning against the doorframe, jacket slung over one shoulder, tie already loosened.

"Hey," he said, his voice warm. "Ready to call it a day? Traffic's going to be brutal if we don't leave soon."

Jules nodded, gathering her things on autopilot. "Just finishing up a few things."

"Anything I can help with?"

She shook her head, managing a small smile. "Nothing urgent. I'll meet you at the elevator in five?"

Nate studied her for a moment, that now-familiar concern flickering in his eyes. "Take your time. I'll wait."

After he left, Jules sat at her desk, trying to steady her racing thoughts. This was becoming unsustainable—the constant pretense, the guilt, the growing attachment to a life and a man that weren't truly hers to claim.

She needed to talk to someone. Someone who would understand.

Without overthinking it, she picked up her phone and dialed Sasha's number.

It rang several times before her sister answered, surprise evident in her voice. "Jules?"

"Hi, Sash," Jules said, her throat suddenly tight. "Do you... do you have a minute?"

A pause. "Sure. Everything okay?"

"Not really," Jules admitted, the words spilling out before she could reconsider. "I know we haven't been close lately, and that's my fault, but I could really use my sister right now."

The silence that followed seemed to stretch for an eternity.

"Where are you?" Sasha finally asked, her tone softer.

"At the office."

"Nate with you?"

Jules frowned slightly at the edge in Sasha's voice when she mentioned Nate. "No, he's waiting for me downstairs. We're supposed to be heading to the lake house for the weekend."

Another pause. "Do you want to go?"

It was such a simple question, but it hit Jules with unexpected force. Did she want to go? Did she want to spend two more days deepening her connection to a man she'd have to leave behind?

"I don't know," she whispered.

Sasha sighed, a sound both familiar and strange. "Look, Jules, I don't pretend to understand your life choices these days. But if you're asking for my advice? Don't do things that make you say 'I don't know' in that voice."

"What voice?"

"The small one," Sasha said simply. "The one you used to use before... everything."

Before everything. Before this timeline. Before Reed & Morgan. Before Nate.

"I've missed you, Sash," Jules said, the words emerging from some deep, honest place within her.

"I've missed you too," Sasha replied after a moment. "The real you, I mean. Not Corporate Jules who's too busy for family dinners."

The pointed comment stung, but Jules couldn't deny its truth—at least in this timeline.

"I'm sorry," she said, meaning it. "For whatever happened between us. For the things I said or didn't say. For... disappearing."

Sasha was quiet for so long that Jules wondered if she'd hung up.

"Did something happen?" she finally asked. "You sound... different."

"Let's just say I've had some perspective shifts lately," Jules said carefully. "Made me realize what's important. Who's important."

"And what have you realized?" Sasha pressed, a hint of her old directness returning.

Jules closed her eyes, leaning back in her chair. "That success doesn't mean much if you don't have people to share it with. People who knew you before the corner office and the power suits."

"Well," Sasha said, a smile evident in her voice now, "that's the most un-Jules-like thing you've said in years. Maybe ever."

"Maybe I'm growing," Jules suggested with a small laugh.

"Maybe you are," Sasha agreed, sounding cautiously hopeful. "So, what are you going to do about the lake house?"

Jules sighed, the question bringing her back to her immediate dilemma. "I don't know. I really don't."

"Do you love him?" Sasha asked bluntly.

The question caught Jules off guard. Did she love Nate? This version of Nate who she'd known for less than a week?

"It's... complicated," she hedged.

"It always is," Sasha replied. "But that doesn't answer my question."

Jules stared out at the city skyline, the colors of sunset painting the glass buildings in pinks and golds. "I could," she admitted softly. "Love him, I mean. If things were different."

"Different how?"

How could she possibly explain that she was from another time-line? That she had only days left before she returned to a world where Nate Morgan was just a colleague, not the partner who knew her coffee order and left her encouraging notes and looked at her like she was both a challenge and a gift?

"Just... different circumstances," Jules said inadequately.

Sasha made a small, frustrated sound. "Jules, I love you, but you're being cryptic as hell right now."

"I know. I'm sorry."

"Don't be sorry. Be honest. With yourself, if not with me."

The simple directive struck a chord. Honesty. When was the last time Jules had been truly honest with herself? About what she wanted, what she needed, what she was willing to sacrifice?

"I think..." she began slowly, "I think I need some time alone. To figure things out."

"Then take it," Sasha said simply. "Nate will understand if he's half the guy you claim he is."

Jules smiled faintly. "When did you get so wise?"

"Always been wise, sis. You've just been too busy to notice."

The gentle teasing felt like a lifeline—a connection to something real and grounding in the midst of all this timeline confusion.

"Thanks, Sash," Jules said softly. "For listening. For... being you."

"Anytime," Sasha replied, her voice warming. "And Jules? Whatever you decide about the weekend, about Nate, about... whatever's going on with you right now? Just make sure it's what *you* want. Not what you think you should want."

After they hung up, Jules sat in the quiet of her office, Sasha's words echoing in her mind.

*Make sure it's what you want. Not what you think you should want.*

What did she want?

The corner office? Yes, but not at any cost.

The successful company? Yes, but not if it meant losing the people who mattered.

Nate? Yes. God, yes. But not this Nate—not the one who belonged to another Jules, whose history and connection were built with someone else.

She wanted... she wanted the possibility of finding her own Nate. Of building her own path to success. Of creating a life that included ambition and connection, professional achievement and personal fulfillment.

And she couldn't do that here, in a timeline she'd borrowed but not earned.

With sudden clarity, Jules knew what she had to do.

Nate was waiting by the elevator, scrolling through something on his phone, when Jules approached. He looked up, his expression brightening when he saw her.

"There you are," he said warmly. "Ready for a weekend of mediocre fishing and excellent wine?"

Jules took a deep breath. "Actually, Nate, I need to talk to you."

His smile faltered slightly at her serious tone. "Sure. What's up?"

"Not here," she said, glancing around at the few employees still working. "Can we go somewhere private?"

Concern flickered in his eyes, but he nodded. "Of course. Roof again?"

A few minutes later, they stood on the rooftop terrace where they'd had dinner the night before. The setting sun cast long shadows across the space, the city beginning to light up as dusk approached.

"What's going on, Jules?" Nate asked, his voice gentle but direct. "You've been... different all week. And now you look like you're about to deliver bad news."

Jules wrapped her arms around herself, suddenly cold despite the mild evening. "I can't go to the lake house this weekend."

Nate's brow furrowed. "Okay... Is it work? Because whatever it is can wait until Monday."

"It's not work," Jules said, shaking her head. "It's... me. I need some time. Alone."

She watched as understanding dawned in his eyes, followed quickly by concern, then something like resignation.

"I see," he said quietly. "Is this about the wedding? Because if you need more time—"

"It's not about the wedding," Jules interrupted, hating the pain she was causing but knowing it was necessary. "It's about... everything. I need to step back and figure out what I really want."

Nate was silent for a long moment, his expression carefully controlled. "And you don't know if that includes me."

It wasn't a question.

"I don't know if it includes... this version of me," Jules said, the words feeling wholly inadequate. "The CEO, the fiancée, the woman who seems to have it all figured out."

Nate took a step closer, his eyes searching hers. "Jules, everyone has doubts. Everyone questions their path sometimes. It doesn't mean you have to blow up your whole life."

"I'm not," she said, the irony of the statement not lost on her. "I'm just... pressing pause. Just for a few days."

"Where will you go?"

Jules had already thought this through. "A hotel. Just for the weekend. I need some space to think, to... recalibrate."

Nate studied her face, his expression a mixture of confusion and concern. "This isn't like you, Jules. The impulsive decisions, the sudden need for 'space.' If something's wrong, just tell me. We can figure it out together. That's what we do."

The earnest plea nearly broke her resolve. How could she explain that she wasn't his Jules at all? That she was a visitor, a temporary placeholder, who had stumbled into loving the life and the man that belonged to someone else?

"I know," she said, her voice catching. "And I'm sorry. But this is something I need to do alone."

Nate took a step back, his shoulders straightening as he processed her decision. "Okay. If that's what you need, I respect it. But Jules?"

"Yes?"

"Don't leave me in the dark," he said simply. "Whatever you're going through, whatever you're figuring out—I'm still here. Still on your team."

The quiet certainty in his voice, the unwavering support even in the face of her pulling away—it was everything she'd never had in her own timeline. Everything she didn't know she could have.

"Thank you," she whispered, blinking back sudden tears.

He nodded once, his expression softening despite the hurt evident in his eyes. "Call me when you're ready to talk. I'll be here."

As he turned to leave, Jules felt a sudden, overwhelming urge to call him back. To tell him everything. To ask if maybe, just maybe, when she returned to her timeline, he might give her a chance to become the woman he could love.

But she stayed silent, watching as he disappeared through the rooftop doors, taking with him a piece of her heart she hadn't realized she'd given away.

The hotel room was sleek and impersonal, a far cry from the warm, lived-in apartment she'd shared with Nate. Jules set her overnight bag on the pristine duvet and sank into the desk chair, emotionally exhausted.

She'd done it. Created space. Distance. Room to think without the constant reminder of what she stood to lose when the timeline reset.

But now, alone with her thoughts, the reality of her situation pressed in more acutely than ever.

Three days left.

Three days, and then she'd be back in her windowless office at Archer & Bloom, passed over for promotion, alone.

The thought sent a wave of panic through her. She'd glimpsed what was possible now—not just professional success, but partnership. Connection. A life built on her terms, with someone who valued her strength rather than being threatened by it.

How could she go back to settling for less?

Her phone buzzed with a text.

> Nate: Just checking if you arrived safely. No pressure to respond. Just want to know you're okay.

Even now, even hurt and confused by her abrupt withdrawal, he was thinking of her wellbeing.

> Jules: I'm safe. Thank you for asking.

She hesitated, then added:

> Jules: I'm sorry for how this happened. You deserve better.

His response came quickly:

> Nate: You don't need to apologize for needing time, Jules. Just be safe. And when you're ready to talk, I'm here.

Jules set the phone down, a lump forming in her throat. How had she gotten so lucky—and so unlucky—all at once? To find this kind of understanding, this kind of partnership, only to know it wasn't truly hers to keep?

She moved to the window, looking out at the city lights twinkling against the night sky. Somewhere out there, Nate was probably at their apartment, confused and hurt by her sudden need for distance. Somewhere, Sasha was perhaps wondering about their unexpected conversation earlier. And somewhere, the real Jules of this timeline was... where? Living her life, unaware that a visitor had stepped into her world, fallen for her fiancé, and complicated everything?

The cream-colored envelope still rested in her bag, its message both a promise and a threat: **Three Days Remaining.**

Three days to what? To understand? To decide? To say goodbye?

Jules returned to the desk and reached for the hotel stationery— simple notepaper with the hotel's logo embossed at the top. She picked up a pen and began to write.

*Dear Sasha,*

*I know this letter will seem strange coming after years of distance, but I need to tell you something important:*

*I'm sorry.*

*I'm sorry for letting success change me in ways that hurt you. I'm sorry for choosing professional* achievement over family connection. I'm sorry for the arrogant things I said and the important moments I missed.

You were right—I did change. But not because of Nate, or Reed + Morgan, or any external factor. I changed because I forgot what really matters. I got so caught up in proving my worth that I lost sight of the people who already knew my value.

You're my sister. My first friend. My most honest mirror. And I've missed you more than I allowed myself to admit.

I don't know if you'll believe this apology. I don't know if you'll want to try again. But I need you to know that I see now what I couldn't see before—no title, no corner office, no professional achievement is worth losing the people who truly matter.

If you're willing, I'd like to try again. To be sisters again. To rebuild what I broke.

With love and hope,

Jules

She read the letter over twice, then carefully folded it and placed it in an envelope. She didn't have Sasha's address in this timeline, but she could mail it tomorrow after getting it from the contact list on her phone.

It was a small thing, perhaps. A gesture that might arrive after she'd already left this timeline. But it felt important—necessary—to leave something behind. Some healing, some acknowledgment of what truly mattered.

As she prepared for bed, Jules found herself thinking about

what she would take back with her when the glimpse ended. Not material things, obviously. But lessons. Insights. Courage.

In this timeline, she hadn't just claimed her power—she'd defined it on her own terms. She hadn't fought for scraps at someone else's table; she'd built her own. And she hadn't done it alone. She'd found a partner who amplified her strengths rather than diminishing them.

Those were the lessons worth taking home.

That, and the knowledge that Nate Morgan might be someone worth knowing better in her own timeline. Not as a borrowed fiancée with years of shared history, but as a potential ally. A possible friend. Maybe, someday, something more.

But first, she needed to create her own path. To make her own bold choices. To become the kind of woman who didn't need to borrow someone else's life to feel worthy of love and success.

As sleep claimed her, Jules held that thought close: she didn't need to be Timeline Jules to deserve what Timeline Jules had built.

She just needed to be brave enough to build it for herself.

The morning brought clarity Jules hadn't expected. She woke early, the hotel room bathed in the soft glow of dawn, her mind unusually settled given the emotional turbulence of the previous day.

She knew what she needed to do.

After a quick shower and coffee from the in-room machine, she sat at the desk and reached for her phone. She hesitated only briefly before dialing.

"Jules?" Celeste's voice was calm and unsurprised, as if she'd been expecting the call. "I was wondering when I'd hear from you."

"I want to go back," Jules said without preamble. "To my time-line. Now."

A brief pause. "The glimpse isn't complete yet. You still have three days."

"I don't need them," Jules replied with certainty. "I've seen what I needed to see. Learned what I needed to learn."

"And what's that?" Celeste asked, genuine curiosity in her tone.

Jules took a deep breath. "That success isn't about winning in a broken system. It's about having the courage to create something better. And that partnership—real partnership—doesn't diminish power. It amplifies it."

"Impressive insights," Celeste acknowledged. "But why the rush? Afraid of what else you might discover if you stay?"

The question was pointed, almost provocative. And entirely accurate.

"Yes," Jules admitted. "I'm afraid of how much harder it will be to leave if I stay longer. Afraid of hurting Nate more than I already have. Afraid of... loving a life I can't keep."

Celeste was quiet for a moment. "And you're certain? No regrets about cutting the glimpse short?"

"The only regret would be staying and making it harder to leave," Jules said firmly. "I know what I need to do now. In my own timeline. With my own choices."

Another pause, longer this time. "Very well," Celeste said finally. "Return to your hotel room this evening. Place the card I sent you under your pillow. The shift will occur naturally, as before."

"Thank you," Jules said, relief washing through her.

"Before you go," Celeste added, "may I ask what you plan to do when you return?"

Jules smiled faintly. "Create my own table. And maybe... invite Nate to sit at it."

Celeste's laugh was like wind chimes. "I look forward to seeing how that unfolds."

After hanging up, Jules felt lighter, more purposeful. She had one day left in this timeline—one day to tie up loose ends, to say goodbye in her way, to prepare for her return.

First, she needed to mail Sasha's letter. Then, perhaps more difficult, she needed to write one to Nate.

Not a goodbye, exactly. But an explanation. As much of one as she could offer without revealing the impossible truth.

By noon, she had checked out of the hotel, Sasha's letter safely in the mail and Nate's carefully composed in her bag. She took a cab to the apartment—their apartment—knowing Nate would be at the lake house by now. He'd texted earlier to say he was going anyway, to clear his head, and would return Sunday evening.

The apartment was quiet, empty without his presence. Jules moved through it slowly, taking in details she wanted to remember: the coffee maker he'd set to her preferences, the books they apparently shared on the living room shelves, the framed photo of them laughing at some event, faces close, eyes only for each other.

She placed her letter on the kitchen island where he would find it upon his return. Then, before she could second-guess herself, she slipped off her engagement ring and set it beside the envelope.

It felt like a betrayal, in a way. But also like honesty. This ring belonged to another Jules—the one who had built this life, who had earned Nate's love, who would return when the glimpse was complete.

Not her. Not yet.

With one last look around the apartment—at the life she was choosing to leave behind—Jules gathered her overnight bag and left, closing the door quietly behind her.

Her final hours in this timeline would be spent not at Reed & Morgan, not at the apartment, but in the park across from her building. The same park where she had met Celeste, where this journey had begun.

It seemed fitting that it should end there too.

As evening approached, Jules found a quiet bench and settled in, watching as the city transitioned from day to night. Professionals hurried home, couples strolled hand in hand, families gathered children and belongings as the sky deepened to indigo.

She felt strangely peaceful. Not regretful, though there was sadness in leaving this glimpse behind. But ready. Ready to return to her timeline with new purpose, new clarity, new courage.

When the streetlights flickered on, Jules knew it was time. She returned to the hotel room she'd re-booked for the night, set her bag down, and pulled out the cream-colored envelope.

She had chosen. Not to stay in a borrowed life, no matter how appealing. But to return and build her own, with the lessons she'd learned and the courage she'd found.

As instructed, she placed the card under her pillow and lay down, still fully dressed, on top of the hotel duvet.

"Thank you," she whispered to the empty room, to Celeste, to the universe that had granted her this strange, transformative glimpse.

Then she closed her eyes and waited for sleep to claim her.

For the journey home to begin.

# this time, she picks herself

. . .

JULES WOKE to the familiar sound of her alarm—the gentle chime she'd chosen because it was less jarring than the default buzz. Her eyes opened to a ceiling she recognized immediately: the slightly uneven paint job she'd been meaning to fix, the small water stain in the corner from the time the upstairs neighbor's bathtub had overflowed.

Her ceiling. Her apartment. Her timeline.

She sat up slowly, taking in the familiar surroundings. The modest queen bed with its practical gray duvet. The IKEA dresser she'd assembled herself three years ago. The small window that looked out at the building across the street rather than a panoramic city view.

Home.

Not the luxury high-rise with floor-to-ceiling windows. Not the designer clothes and corner office. Not the life where she was CEO of her own company and engaged to Nate Morgan.

But her life. Real. Imperfect. Full of possibilities not yet realized.

Jules reached for her phone on the nightstand, checking the date. It was the morning after her meeting with Celeste in the park

—as if no time had passed at all in this timeline while she'd been away.

Friday. The day she was supposed to give Diana her decision about the Associate Director role.

The role that was a consolation prize. The role that would keep her at a table where she'd never truly have a voice.

Jules set the phone down and got out of bed, moving to her closet with renewed purpose. She pushed past the safe, conservative suits she typically wore to the office, reaching for something at the back—a suit in deep burgundy that she'd bought on impulse last year but never had the courage to wear.

Today was a day for courage.

As she dressed, Jules considered what lay ahead. The conversation with Diana. The decision she'd already made, though Diana didn't know it yet. The first step on a new path that would be entirely her own.

Not a borrowed path from Timeline Jules. Not the exact same journey. But one informed by what she'd learned, by what she'd seen was possible.

She studied her reflection in the bathroom mirror as she applied her makeup with more confidence than usual, adding a subtle but definite red lip. The woman who stared back at her wasn't Timeline Jules with her easy authority and corner office. But she wasn't the same Jules who'd been passed over three times, either.

This was a new Jules. One who knew her worth and was ready to claim it.

Her phone buzzed with a text.

> Sasha: Any news from yesterday's meeting? Did they FINALLY recognize your genius?

Jules smiled, warmth spreading through her chest at the familiar, supportive message. In this timeline, she and Sasha were still close. Still each other's biggest champions. That was something

Timeline Jules had lost—something this Jules wouldn't take for granted.

> Jules: Meeting went as expected. But I have a plan. Brunch this weekend? I have some big ideas to run by you.

Sasha's response was immediate:

> Sasha: Intriguing! Sunday at Mabel's? 11am? I want ALL the details.

Jules confirmed the plan, then tucked her phone into her bag. She had one stop to make before heading to the office.

The coffee shop wasn't particularly trendy or upscale—just a reliable local place with decent espresso and pastries that weren't mass-produced. Jules ordered her usual latte, then, on impulse, added a second order.

"Can I get a large Americano, extra shot, room for cream?"

She didn't know if it was Nate's usual order in this timeline. But it had been his preference in the other one, and it seemed like a place to start.

Drinks in hand, Jules made her way to the office, her heart beating a little faster with each step. She was early—deliberately so. She wanted to be settled and centered before the conversation with Diana.

The lobby of Archer & Bloom was sleek and corporate, all glass and chrome and quiet efficiency. Jules nodded to the security guard as she badged in, then took the elevator to the seventeenth floor.

The office was still mostly empty at this hour, just a few early birds getting a jump on the day. Jules moved through the space with purpose, heading not to her own office but to one three doors down.

Nate's door was ajar, light spilling from within. Jules hesitated for just a moment, then knocked softly.

He looked up from his computer, surprise registering on his features when he saw her. "Jules? You're in early."

In this timeline, their interactions had been limited since he'd beaten her for the junior partnership two years ago. Professional, civil, but distant—more from her side than his, she now realized. She'd been so focused on her resentment that she'd never considered he might have been a potential ally rather than just another obstacle.

"Thought I'd get a jump on the day," she said, offering what she hoped was a friendly smile. "Brought you coffee."

Confusion flickered across his face as she extended the cup, but he recovered quickly. "Thanks. That's... unexpected."

"Good unexpected, I hope," Jules said, finding herself genuinely curious about his response.

Nate took a sip, his eyebrows rising slightly. "Americano with an extra shot. How did you know?"

Jules shrugged, a small smile playing at her lips. "Lucky guess."

He studied her over the rim of his cup, something like interest warming his dark eyes. "Well, thank you. What brings you by my office? Besides random acts of caffeine kindness."

This was the tricky part. In the other timeline, she and Nate had connected after standing up to Diana together. But that history didn't exist here. Not yet.

"Actually," Jules said, deciding on honesty, "I wanted to ask your advice about something."

Nate gestured to the chair across from his desk. "I'm all ears."

Jules settled into the seat, setting her own coffee on the edge of his desk. "Diana offered me the Associate Director position yesterday."

"Ah," Nate nodded, his expression carefully neutral. "Congratulations?"

The slight questioning tone told Jules everything she needed to know. He wasn't sure if this was good news—if she considered it a victory or another disappointment.

"It's not what I wanted," she admitted. "It's an execution role, not leadership. A way to keep me busy without giving me any real influence."

Nate's eyebrows rose slightly, perhaps surprised by her candor. "That's... direct."

"I'm tired of not being direct," Jules said simply. "I've spent years trying to prove my worth to people who have no intention of truly seeing it. And I'm done."

Interest flickered in Nate's eyes. "What are you going to do?"

This was the moment. The first concrete step on her new path.

"I'm going to leave," Jules said, the words feeling right as she spoke them. "Start something new. Something that reflects my vision, not someone else's limitations."

Nate leaned back in his chair, studying her with new intensity. "Your own firm?"

Jules nodded. "I have ideas, strategies, approaches that never get traction here because they don't fit the conservative Archer & Bloom model. But I believe in them. And I think there's a market for a different kind of strategic consulting."

"Bold move," Nate said, but there was admiration in his tone rather than skepticism. "Starting from scratch isn't easy."

"The best things rarely are," Jules replied, echoing words she'd heard in another timeline.

A small smile curved Nate's lip. "True enough."

Jules took a deep breath, summoning courage for the next part. "Actually, that's partly why I wanted to talk to you."

"Oh?"

"I've seen your work, Nate. The Westmore campaign. The

Davidson rebrand. You have a perspective that's wasted here, confined to Archer & Bloom's formula."

Nate's expression shifted, something like surprise and cautious interest mingling in his features. "What exactly are you suggesting, Jules?"

Here it was. The moment of truth. The first real divergence from her cautious, safe approach to her career and her life.

"I'm suggesting," Jules said, meeting his gaze directly, "that we should talk. About possibilities. About what we could build if we weren't constrained by someone else's vision."

Nate stared at her, clearly trying to process this unexpected turn. "Are you... proposing a partnership?"

"I'm proposing a conversation," Jules clarified. "No commitments. Just... exploration. Two people with complementary skills and similar frustrations seeing if there might be a better way forward."

For a long moment, Nate said nothing, just studied her with an intensity that might have made the old Jules uncomfortable. But this Jules—the one who had glimpsed what partnership could truly mean—held his gaze steadily.

"Why me?" he finally asked. "We've barely spoken in the past two years. Since..."

"Since you got the partnership instead of me," Jules finished for him. "I know. And I'll be honest—I resented that. For a long time."

"And now?"

Jules considered her answer carefully. "Now I realize that fighting over scraps at someone else's table isn't the path to real success. For either of us."

Something shifted in Nate's expression—a recognition, perhaps. A resonance with words she hadn't yet said but somehow understood.

"When did you come to this realization?" he asked, genuine curiosity in his voice.

Jules smiled. "Let's just say I've had a perspective shift recently. Seen things... differently."

Nate nodded slowly, taking another sip of his coffee. "So. A conversation."

"Yes," Jules confirmed. "Maybe dinner next week? Neutral territory, no pressure. Just... possibilities."

The smile that spread across Nate's face then was something Jules would remember later—the first glimpse of the warmth she knew existed beneath his professional exterior.

"I'd like that," he said simply.

"Good," Jules replied, standing to leave. "I'll text you details."

At the door, she paused, looking back at him. "And Nate? Thank you. For hearing me out."

"Anytime, Jules," he said, and she could almost believe he meant it.

As she walked to her own office, Jules felt a lightness in her step that had been missing for years. This wasn't the same as the other timeline. She and Nate weren't partners yet, weren't anything beyond colleagues with a tentative new connection.

But it was a beginning. A real one, built on her own courage, not borrowed from a glimpse of what might be.

And for now, that was enough.

"Jules," Diana greeted her with practiced warmth as Jules entered her office later that morning. "Have you had a chance to consider our offer?"

Jules took a seat in the chair across from Diana's imposing desk, her burgundy suit a quiet statement against the conservative gray and navy that dominated the Archer & Bloom aesthetic.

"I have," Jules replied, her voice steady and clear. "And I appreciate the consideration. But I'm going to have to decline."

Diana's perfectly shaped eyebrows rose slightly. "I see. May I ask why? If it's a matter of compensation—"

"It's not about the money," Jules interrupted gently but firmly. "It's about alignment. My vision for strategic consulting doesn't align with the Archer & Bloom approach. And rather than try to force that fit, I think it's better for both of us if I pursue my vision elsewhere."

Diana's expression shifted from surprise to something more calculating. "You're leaving the firm?"

"Yes," Jules confirmed. "I'll submit my formal resignation today, of course. And I'm happy to help with the transition over the next two weeks."

"This is... unexpected," Diana said, clearly recalibrating. "May I ask where you're going?"

Jules smiled. "I'm starting my own strategic consultancy. One that focuses on forward-thinking approaches rather than incremental improvements to existing models."

She didn't mention Nate. That conversation was too new, too tentative to share. And regardless of whether he ultimately joined her venture, this decision was hers alone.

Diana's lips pressed into a thin line. "I see. Well, while I'm disappointed, I respect your decision. I'll have HR prepare the necessary paperwork."

"Thank you," Jules said, rising to leave. "And Diana? I appreciate the opportunities Archer & Bloom has provided. They've been valuable stepping stones on my path."

It was gracious without being submissive. Appreciative without compromising her position. The kind of exit she would have been too intimidated to execute before her glimpse into another timeline.

Diana nodded, surprise at Jules' composure evident in her expression. "Good luck, Jules. The consulting world is... competitive."

"I'm counting on it," Jules replied with a small smile, then turned and walked out of the office.

As the door closed behind her, Jules felt a weight lift from her shoulders. No more fighting for recognition in a system designed to withhold it. No more making herself smaller to fit someone else's expectations.

From now on, she would create her own table. Set her own terms. Build something that reflected her vision, not someone else's limitations.

And if a certain dark-eyed strategist with unexpectedly good coffee preferences decided to join her? So much the better.

But this time, she wasn't waiting for anyone else to validate her path. This time, she was claiming her space from the start.

"You did WHAT?"

Sasha's voice rose in pitch, drawing glances from nearby tables in the crowded brunch spot. It was Sunday morning, two days after Jules had resigned from Archer & Bloom, and the reality of her decision was still sinking in.

"Quit," Jules repeated calmly, stirring her latte. "Effective two weeks from Friday."

"To start your own firm," Sasha clarified, wide-eyed. "Without a client base. Or startup capital. Or, apparently, any concern for minor details like paying rent."

Jules laughed. "I have savings. And a business plan. And three potential clients who've already expressed interest in following me once I'm established."

"Holy shit," Sasha breathed, sitting back in her chair. "Who are you and what have you done with my risk-averse sister?"

"Let's just say I had a revelation," Jules replied with a small smile. "Life's too short to keep trying to win in a system designed for me to fail."

Sasha studied her across the table, something like admiration mingling with concern in her expression. "I mean, I've been telling you Archer & Bloom didn't deserve you for years. But I never thought you'd actually leave."

"I should have done it sooner," Jules admitted. "After the first time they passed me over for promotion. But I was too afraid of failing, of losing what little security I had."

"And now?"

Jules considered the question, thinking about what she'd learned—about herself, about partnership, about creating something rather than just fighting for scraps.

"Now I'd rather risk failure pursuing my own vision than guarantee mediocrity pursuing someone else's."

Sasha's eyes widened further. "Okay, seriously. You've changed. Like, overnight."

Jules smiled. "Not overnight. Just... finally seeing things clearly."

"Well, I'm for it," Sasha declared, raising her mimosa. "To my sister, the future CEO of... wait, what are you calling this venture?"

Jules hadn't even considered a name yet. In the other timeline, it had been Reed & Morgan. But this was a new path, one that might or might not include Nate.

"I don't know yet," she admitted. "Still figuring that out."

"What about 'Reed Strategies'?" Sasha suggested. "Simple. Strong. Very you."

Jules considered it, rolling the name around in her mind. "Maybe. We'll see."

"We'll see? Is there... someone else involved?" Sasha's intuition was, as always, unnervingly accurate.

Jules hesitated. "Possibly. I've invited someone to discuss potential partnership. But it's very preliminary."

"Anyone I know?" Sasha pressed, curiosity sparkling in her eyes.

"Nate Morgan," Jules admitted. "He's a strategist at Archer & Bloom. Brilliant, actually, but underutilized in the current structure."

Sasha sat back, eyebrows raised. "Nate Morgan. The guy who got the promotion instead of you two years ago? That Nate Morgan?"

"The very one."

"And now you want to be business partners? That's... unexpected."

Jules smiled. "Sometimes the best partnerships start in the most unlikely places."

"Partnership," Sasha repeated, a speculative gleam in her eye. "Just... business partnership? Or...?"

"Professional collaboration," Jules clarified, though she couldn't quite suppress the slight warmth in her cheeks. "Nothing more. At least, not yet."

"Not yet," Sasha echoed, grinning now. "Well, well, well. My sister, the risk-taker in both business and personal life. I never thought I'd see the day."

Jules laughed, shaking her head. "Don't get ahead of yourself. We haven't even had our first meeting yet."

"But you're having dinner with him," Sasha pointed out. "That's more than a meeting."

"It's a professional discussion in a relaxed setting," Jules insisted, though she couldn't quite suppress her smile. "That's all."

"Mmhmm," Sasha hummed skeptically. "Whatever you say. Just remember, I expect to be maid of honor when the time comes."

"You're impossible," Jules said, but there was affection in her voice.

As they continued their brunch, conversation flowing easily between them, Jules felt a deep gratitude for this relationship—the solid foundation of sisterhood that had weathered so many changes and challenges over the years.

In the alternate timeline, she'd lost this connection. Sacrificed it on the altar of professional achievement. It had been one of the hardest lessons of her glimpse—that success meant nothing without the people who mattered most to share it with.

That was one mistake she wouldn't repeat, no matter what path her new venture took.

The restaurant Nate had suggested for their dinner meeting was neither too formal nor too casual—a thoughtfully designed space with good food and ambient noise levels that allowed for actual conversation. Jules arrived a few minutes early, choosing a table in a quiet corner away from the main traffic flow.

She'd put thought into her outfit—professional but not corporate, a deep blue dress that conveyed confidence without the armor-like quality of her usual suits. Her hair was loose around her shoulders rather than pulled back in its typical severe style.

Small changes, perhaps. But meaningful ones.

Nate arrived precisely on time, scanning the restaurant briefly before his gaze landed on her. The smile that spread across his face as he approached sent an unexpected flutter through Jules' chest.

"Jules," he greeted her, sliding into the seat across from her. "You look... different."

"Different good or different concerning?" she asked, a hint of teasing in her tone.

His smile widened. "Definitely good. The corporate shell seems to be cracking already."

"Turns out resignation is good for the complexion," she replied lightly.

"I can see that," he agreed, a spark of something like admiration in his eyes. "How does it feel? Freedom?"

Jules considered the question seriously. "Terrifying. Exhilarating. Right."

Nate nodded, understanding in his expression. "The best decisions usually feel that way."

Their conversation paused as the waiter approached, taking

their drink orders and leaving menus. When they were alone again, Nate leaned forward slightly.

"So. This new venture of yours. Tell me more."

For the next hour, over shared appetizers and entrees, Jules outlined her vision—not the exact Reed & Morgan she'd glimpsed in the other timeline, but something uniquely her own. A consultancy focused on forward-thinking strategies, on helping clients position themselves for future markets rather than just current ones.

Nate listened intently, asking thoughtful questions, offering insights that complemented rather than challenged her approach. Their discussion flowed with an ease that surprised her—though perhaps it shouldn't have, given what she'd seen of their potential dynamic in the other timeline.

"Your vision is compelling," Nate said as they lingered over coffee. "You're right about the gap in the market. Most firms are so focused on immediate results that they miss the bigger picture."

"Exactly," Jules agreed, warming to his understanding. "Short-term gains at the expense of long-term positioning. It's shortsighted and ultimately self-defeating."

Nate nodded, then seemed to hesitate before asking, "Why me, Jules? Why now? We've both been at Archer & Bloom for years. What changed?"

It was the question she'd been expecting—the one she couldn't answer fully without sounding like she'd lost her mind. How could she explain that she'd seen what they could build together in another timeline? That she knew, with a certainty that defied rational explanation, that they would be stronger together than apart?

"I've been watching your work," she said instead, which wasn't untrue. "The Westmore approach. The Davidson rebrand. You see patterns others miss. Think in systems, not just singular campaigns."

She took a sip of her coffee, gathering her thoughts. "As for why now... let's just say I had a moment of clarity. Realized I was fighting for recognition in a system that was never designed to give it freely. And that I'd rather build something new than keep pushing against those limitations."

Nate studied her, quiet contemplation in his dark eyes. "And you think we'd work well together? Despite our... history?"

"Because of it, maybe," Jules suggested. "We've both seen the same flaws from different perspectives. Both been limited by the same structures. Imagine what we could create without those constraints."

He nodded slowly, a small smile playing at his lips. "It's an interesting proposition."

"Just interesting?" Jules prompted, surprised by her own boldness.

"Compelling," Nate amended. "Risky. Potentially brilliant."

"But?"

"No but," he said, surprising her. "Just... I'd want equal partnership. True collaboration. Not just bringing my client list to your vision."

Jules felt a smile spread across her face—genuine, unguarded. "I wouldn't have it any other way."

Nate's expression warmed. "In that case... I think we should continue this conversation. Maybe with financial projections and a more formal business plan next time?"

"Already working on it," Jules assured him. "I can have a draft to you by Wednesday."

"Efficient," he noted with approval. "I like that."

As they settled the bill—splitting it equally, a small but symbolic gesture—Jules felt a sense of alignment she'd never experienced in her professional life before. Not competition. Not compromise. But true complementary vision.

Outside the restaurant, the evening air was cool and pleasant. They paused on the sidewalk, that slightly awkward moment at the end of a meeting that wasn't quite business but wasn't quite personal either.

"This was good," Nate said, his gaze warm as it met hers. "Unexpected, but good."

"I'm glad you thought so," Jules replied, surprised by the flutter of nerves in her stomach. "To be continued, then?"

"Definitely," he agreed. Then, he said with a small smile, "You know, Jules, I always thought you and I could do great things together. If we weren't always positioned as competitors."

The simple statement landed with unexpected weight. Had he been thinking that all along? Even in this timeline, where they'd barely spoken beyond professional necessity?

"Well," she said, finding her voice, "looks like we'll finally get to test that theory."

His smile deepened. "Looking forward to it."

As they parted ways—Nate heading toward the subway, Jules opting to walk the few blocks to her apartment—she felt a lightness in her step that had nothing to do with timeline glimpses or borrowed success.

This was real. Her choice. Her path. Her courage.

And whether or not it led to exactly the same place she'd glimpsed in the other timeline, it was unquestionably leading somewhere better than where she'd been.


Three months later, Jules stood in the empty space that would soon become the offices of Reed & Morgan Strategic Group. Sunlight streamed through large windows, illuminating the potential of the open floor plan. It wasn't the sleek penthouse suite of the other timeline—not yet—but it was a solid beginning. A foundation to build upon.

"What do you think?" Nate asked, coming to stand beside her. "Can you see it?"

Jules smiled, looking around at the bare walls and unfinished floors. "Absolutely. This is perfect."

In the weeks since their initial dinner, their partnership had evolved with surprising speed and certainty. Financial projections had led to business plans, which had led to formal partnership agreements. They'd secured their first three clients—two who had followed Jules from Archer & Bloom, and one who had worked with Nate on a previous campaign.

It wasn't the instant success of the alternate timeline. But it was real. Earned. Theirs.

"We should celebrate," Nate suggested, his shoulder brushing against hers as they surveyed their future office. "Sign the lease, then dinner?"

Jules turned to look at him, struck once again by how easily they'd fallen into sync. Their working dynamic was everything she'd hoped for—challenging without being combative, supportive without being smothering. They pushed each other to think bigger, to be bolder, to reach further than either would have alone.

And somewhere along the way, something else had begun to develop between them. Something neither of them had named yet, but that hung in the air during late night strategy sessions and lingered in brief touches when they exchanged documents or coffee cups.

"Dinner sounds perfect," she agreed. "Landlord said she'd meet us at four with the final paperwork."

Nate checked his watch. "That gives us two hours to finalize the floor plan. I still think the conference room should be by the windows."

"And I still think natural light is wasted on client meetings when we could have it for our daily workspace," Jules countered, the familiar debate resuming comfortably between them.

As they moved through the space, discussing layout options and design elements, Jules felt a deep sense of satisfaction settle over her. This was what she'd glimpsed in the other timeline—not just professional success, but partnership. Balance. The power of two perspectives aligned toward a shared vision.

She hadn't needed to borrow someone else's life to achieve it. She'd just needed the courage to claim her own space, to invite the right person to join her, to build something new from the ground up.

Later, as they signed the lease that made Reed & Morgan official, Jules caught Nate watching her with a warm expression she was beginning to recognize.

"What?" she asked, signing her name with a flourish.

"Nothing," he said, shaking his head slightly. "Just... when you walked into my office with that coffee three months ago, I never imagined we'd end up here."

Jules smiled, thinking of all he didn't know—couldn't know—about the journey that had led her to that moment. "Life is full of unexpected turns."

"The best ones usually are," he agreed, taking the pen she offered and adding his signature beside hers.

As they left the building—their building now—the late afternoon sun cast long shadows across the sidewalk. Nate's hand brushed against hers, a question in the gesture.

Jules answered by twining her fingers with his, the contact sending a now-familiar warmth through her chest.

This wasn't the end of her story. It wasn't even the middle. It was just the beginning—a beginning she'd claimed for herself, built on courage and clarity and the lessons learned from a glimpse of what could be.

She didn't know exactly where this path would lead. If she and Nate would eventually share more than just a business partnership. If Reed & Morgan would grow into the success she'd seen in the other timeline.

But she knew this: she'd never again make herself small to fit someone else's expectations. Never again wait for permission to claim her space. Never again measure her worth by someone else's recognition.

This time, she'd picked herself.

And that made all the difference.

The End

# rain, tea, and other avoidance tactics

. . .

NORA BYRNE DID NOT BELIEVE in sentiment before noon. Especially not on a Thursday, especially not in the rain, and especially not when her tea tasted off and her last customer had been a tourist asking if she "did commissions of people's pets but, like, as angels."

It was 11:42 a.m. and raining just hard enough to count as an excuse for everything she wasn't doing.

She flipped the "Open" sign on her gallery door to "Back at 1" even though she knew she wouldn't be. The foot traffic on this given Thursday was dismal anyway—three browsers, one serious looker who'd left without buying, and Mrs. Chen from the flower shop next door dropping off wilted daisies she thought Nora might "find inspiring."

Nora had smiled. Said thank you. Waited until Mrs. Chen left before dumping them in the trash.

She was very good at smiling and waiting.

The gallery was small enough that she could see everything from the counter—eight easels displaying local artists' work, her own paintings relegated to the back corner where the lighting made everything look like it was apologizing for existing. Clean white walls. Polished concrete floors. The kind of sterile perfection that said, "serious art space", but whispered, "emotionally unavailable."

She made herself a fresh cup of tea that she wouldn't drink and stared at the corner where her sketchbook sat unopened. The last thing she'd attempted was a line drawing of a fern that looked like it had been through a breakup and lost custody of the soil.

As she reached for her cup, the late morning light shifted strangely—not cloudy, exactly, but softer, like someone had adjusted the saturation on the world. She blinked, and it returned to normal.

The bell above the door chimed.

Nora looked up, already arranging her face into Professional Gallery Owner Expression #3: interested but not desperate.

A man in his sixties stepped in, shaking rain from a paint-splattered jacket. She recognized him—Franklin, a retired art teacher who came in monthly to browse and never bought anything but always had opinions.

"Nora, my dear," he said, approaching the counter with the confidence of someone who'd never met a silence he couldn't fill. "Terrible weather for foot traffic. How are the sales?"

"Fine," she lied smoothly. "Steady."

Franklin nodded knowingly, then gestured toward her corner. "Any new work from you? It's been months since I've seen anything fresh."

Nora's smile tightened. "I'm in a... research phase."

"Ah." Franklin's expression shifted to that particular blend of pity and encouragement that made her want to crawl under the counter. "You know, when I was teaching, I always told my students—the work finds you when you stop hiding from it."

"Mm," Nora said, which was her standard response to unsolicited advice.

Franklin wandered toward a landscape painting, squinting at it like it might reveal secrets. "You remind me of myself after my divorce. Couldn't paint for nearly two years. Kept organizing my brushes instead."

Nora glanced at her pristinely organized supplies. Color-coded. Arranged by size. Categorized by hostility.

"I should let you browse," she said, already backing toward the storage room.

"Take care of yourself, dear," Franklin called after her. "Art waits, but inspiration doesn't."

The storage room was barely larger than a closet, crammed with frames and shipping supplies and the portfolio she kept meaning to sort through. She closed the door and leaned against it, breathing shallow.

Routine was safer. Predictable. Brush teeth. Brew tea. Open gallery. Smile at customers. Deflect concern. Close gallery. Repeat.

There had been a time when she'd felt her hands buzz at the thought of color. When inspiration came like a sunbeam, sudden and warm and impossible to ignore. Now, it came like mail, infrequently, and feeling less like a letter and more like an unavoidable bill. She rubbed the back of her neck and moved to the back corner, where a dusty portfolio leaned against the wall like it was tired of waiting. Out of habit—or masochism—she flipped it open.

There he was.

Julian. Not in photo form, but in ink and memory. A sketch of him from years ago—loose strokes, half-finished. His eyes laughing, mouth mid-thought, the way he used to look when he was about to say something that would make her simultaneously want to kiss him and throw paint at his head.

She'd drawn this the night after they'd spent hours in her cramped studio apartment, debating whether Van Gogh was a genius or just really good at being dramatic. Julian had fallen asleep on her paint-stained couch, and she'd sketched him in the pre-dawn light, all soft lines and possibility.

She hadn't seen him in three years.

She'd meant to throw this out a dozen times.

She hadn't.

Her breath caught in her throat as she touched the page lightly, like it might fade if she pressed too hard. The paper was yellowed now, the edges soft with age, but the lines were still there. Still him. And for just a moment, the infinity symbol doodle in the corner—one she didn't remember adding—seemed to shimmer.

Franklin's voice drifted from the main gallery: "I'll be going now, dear. Think about what I said."

The bell chimed. The door closed.

Silence settled back around her.

Nora stared at the sketch, at Julian's half-smile, at the version of herself who'd been brave enough to capture someone she cared about on paper. Who'd trusted her hands to hold something precious.

A soft knock startled her from the memory.

She exited the storage room.

No one was there.

Just the rain. She went to the door. And a cream-colored envelope on the ground outside the door, oddly dry for the weather.

Nora opened it slowly. No address. No name.

Just a card. Thick stock. Gold lettering that seemed to shimmer when she tilted it.

### Timeline Retreats

*For when your life just isn't it.*

She frowned, turning it over. Nothing but a tiny, looping infinity symbol in the corner, delicate as a signature.

Was this... spam? A wellness retreat? Some Pinterest-branded cult selling expensive meditation and overpriced crystals?

She looked back at the sketch. Julian's face. That smile that used to make her believe in things like forever and maybe.

And for a moment—just a breath—she let herself wonder.

What if?

What if she'd been braver that night? What if she'd woken him up, told him how she felt, and risked the friendship for something more? What if she hadn't spent the last three years perfecting the art of emotional distance?

What if she still remembered how to want things?

The rain picked up, drumming against the gallery windows. The light shifted gray and soft, the kind that made everything look like watercolor.

Nora slipped the card between the pages of the portfolio, next to Julian's sketch.

Then closed it.

But she didn't put it back into storage.

The next afternoon crawled by with the enthusiasm of a sedated sloth.

Two browsers. One woman who spent twenty minutes photographing paintings for "inspiration" without buying anything. A teenager who tracked mud across the floor and asked if Nora sold "anything, like, happy."

By four-thirty, the rain had settled into a persistent drizzle, and Nora was fighting the urge to close early. Again.

She was wiping down the counter for the third time when Mrs. Chen appeared in the doorway, shaking droplets from her bright yellow umbrella.

"Nora, honey," she called, bustling in with the determined cheer of someone who refused to let weather dictate her mood. "I brought you some soup."

She held up a thermos decorated with dancing sunflowers—aggressively cheerful, like Mrs. Chen herself.

"You didn't have to—" Nora started.

"Nonsense. You look thin. And sad. Thin and sad is no way to sell art." Mrs. Chen set the thermos on the counter and studied Nora with the intensity of someone who'd raised five children and could spot emotional distress from three blocks away. "When's the last time you created something?"

"I'm between projects," Nora said, the lie smooth as river stone from overuse.

Mrs. Chen made a skeptical noise. "Between projects for six months? That's not between, honey. That's stuck."

Nora opened her mouth to deflect, but Mrs. Chen was already moving, circling the gallery like she was conducting an inspection.

"You know," Mrs. Chen said, pausing in front of a particularly vibrant abstract piece, "my grandson David is taking art classes at the community center. The teacher says he has 'natural talent,' whatever that means. I think he just likes making messes." She turned back to Nora. "You should teach. You'd be good with kids. Patient."

"I'm not really teacher material," Nora said quickly.

"Why not?"

The question was simple. Direct. The kind that shouldn't have felt like a trap but somehow did.

"I just... I prefer working alone," Nora said.

Mrs. Chen's expression softened. "Alone is safe. But safe doesn't make art. Safe makes... this." She gestured around the pristine gallery. "Pretty. Clean. Empty."

Nora felt something sharp twist in her chest. "It's not empty. I represent twelve local artists."

"I'm not talking about the walls, honey."

The words hung in the air like smoke. Mrs. Chen's expression wasn't unkind, but it was knowing in a way that made Nora want to hide behind the counter.

"Try the soup," Mrs. Chen said gently. "It's got healing powers. Or at least enough salt to make you feel something."

She patted Nora's hand—brief, warm, maternal—and headed for the door.

"Mrs. Chen?" Nora called after her.

"Yes, honey?"

"Thank you. For the soup. And... for checking on me."

Mrs. Chen smiled, the kind that reached her eyes and made the rainy afternoon feel a little less gray. "That's what neighbors do. We look out for each other."

After she left, Nora stood alone with the thermos and the weight of being seen by someone who cared enough to bring soup on a rainy Thursday.

She unscrewed the cap. The smell rose up—ginger, garlic, something rich and nourishing—made her realize she hadn't eaten since yesterday.

When was the last time someone had taken care of her? Really taken care of her, not just polite concern or professional courtesy, but actual, intentional kindness?

She couldn't remember.

That realization sat heavier than she'd expected.

The bell above the gallery door jingled—a delicate chime that usually meant tourists or teenagers wanting shelter and pretending to like art.

But when Nora turned, the room was empty.

No footsteps. No wind. Just the echo of a door that hadn't been opened.

She stepped outside, scanning the sidewalk.

The street glistened, empty of pedestrians. The streetlamp blinked its usual one-two rhythm. Across the road, the bakery was still lit up, warm and golden and full of cinnamon, like it always was. No one had passed through her door. But something shimmered—*not light, not quite shadow*.

Back inside, another card lay on the counter like it had always belonged there.

This one was different. Same cream stock, same gold lettering, but the message had changed:

**Sometimes the door opens for you.**

*Are you ready to walk through?*

She should throw it away. Should laugh it off as an elaborate prank or guerrilla marketing campaign.

Instead, she slid it into the drawer with her dried-up brushes and unopened birthday cards from her mother, next to the first one.

She moved to close up early. Again. Another blank day in the books.

But her hand brushed a drawer she rarely opened—the flat file where her older work lived. Pieces from art school. From the year she almost moved to Montreal for a fellowship. From when Julian had sat in her kitchen and offered critiques in the form of metaphors and homemade cookies.

She didn't mean to open it.

But she did.

And there it was: the painting.

Not the sketch from earlier. This one was older. Messier. An early self-portrait—her face half-shadowed, one eye unfinished, the whole thing pulsing with indecision and raw want.

It was the last thing she'd painted the night before Julian graduated and moved to Portland. The night she'd almost told him she loved him. The night she'd chosen safety over truth.

The painting was aggressive in its honesty. Unfinished in all the right ways. It made her stomach ache—not because it was bad, but because it was hers. The version of her that used to feel first and fix later. Who painted like her hands were trying to outrun her fear.

She stood there for a long time, her fingers curled at her sides, breathing shallow and strange.

Then, almost against her will, she whispered, "What did I do with her?"

She didn't expect an answer.

Which made the voice behind her even more jarring.

"You left her here. Neatly shelved between your unopened watercolors and that terrifyingly organized brush caddy."

Nora whirled.

A woman stood in the gallery—linen-draped, sunlit despite the storm outside. Calm in the way cliffs are calm: still, but older than weather. Her hair was silver-streaked, pulled back in a way that suggested she'd never worried about being photogenic. Her eyes were the color of sea glass.

Nora's heart stuttered.

"Who are you? How did you get in?" The woman's smile was small and certain. "I'm Celeste. I'm simply someone who believes you've got more to paint. And maybe more to feel."

She moved closer, not threatening but inevitable, like a tide.

"The door was open," she said simply.

"No, it wasn't. I locked—"

"Not that door."

Celeste placed another card on the counter. Identical to the others, but this one had something new. A date. Tomorrow. And the words: *One week. One heart reopened.*

Nora stared. "This is insane. You can't just—"

"I'm not doing anything," Celestesaid gently. "I'm simply offering."

"Offering what?"

"A glimpse," Celeste said. "Into the life where you didn't choose fear."

She gestured to the self-portrait still lying open in the drawer. "The woman who painted that—she made different choices."

"What kind of choices?"

She tilted her head. "You're surrounded by beauty—just not your own."

Nora's voice came out softer than she intended. "I haven't touched a brush in months."

Celeste's smile deepened. "And still, the art waits."

She stepped closer to the portrait. "What if you could spend a week with the version of yourself who never stopped creating? Who chose love over fear?"

The questions hit like arrows, each one finding its mark.

"I don't think I'm brave enough," Nora whispered.

Celeste smiled like she'd been waiting for that exact admission.

"You don't need to be brave," she said. "Just curious."

She handed Nora the card again—this time with a flicker of light beneath the infinity symbol. Almost a pulse.

"If you want to go," Celeste said, stepping back like stage fog, "just sleep. Preferably with your heart a little open this time."

And then, as softly as she'd arrived, she vanished.

Not dramatically. Not with smoke or mirrors. She simply... wasn't there anymore.

Nora stood in the silence, holding the card.

Card in one hand.

Hope in the other.

The rain had stopped, she realized. Sunlight slanted through the gallery windows, painting everything gold.

And for the first time in longer than she dared admit... Nora didn't feel entirely gray.

Just a little soft around the edges.

Like maybe she still remembered how to be warm.

She looked down at the self-portrait one more time. At the woman who'd been brave enough to paint her own longing.

Then she carefully closed the drawer.

But she kept the card.

# i woke up like this
# (terrified but flawless)

. . .

NORA'S FIRST THOUGHT WAS: *My bedroom ceiling is all wrong.*

It wasn't cracked plaster with a hint of mildew. It was wood—whitewashed, beamed, the kind found in coastal home magazines she didn't let herself buy.

Her second thought: *Something smells like rosemary and possibility.*

She sat up slowly, heart hammering.

The bed was enormous, soft as a cloud myth, wrapped in linen that whispered wealth but felt like comfort. Sunlight poured through wide windows framed in gauzy curtains, casting gold across polished floors that definitely weren't hers.

This wasn't her apartment.

She swung her legs over the side and froze.

Her nails were coral. Neat. Elegant. Suspiciously cheerful—as if someone had painted them while humming optimism.

The robe she wore was dove gray and draped like it had opinions about architecture. She didn't own anything this soft. Or this... *hopeful.*

The room was beautiful in the way real artists lived—not

staged, but lived-in. Canvases leaned against walls. Paint-stained clothes hung on a hook beside the door. Her sketchbook lay open on a side table, and across one page—

A watercolor of a window she'd only seen in dreams.

A breeze lifted the curtains. Outside: a garden blooming in impossible abundance. Beyond that, water—lake or sea—shimmering with morning light.

And on the easel in the corner?

A portrait.

Unfinished.

Of her.

But not as she was. As she had been. Eyes wide, shoulders relaxed, smiling like she meant it.

She took one step closer—and paused at a sound from down the hall.

Humming.

Low. Familiar. A man's voice threading through the scent of brewing coffee.

The kettle whistled.

And suddenly, impossibly—

"Tea or coffee, Nor?"

Like it was the most natural thing in the world.

Like they did this every day.

Like he loved her.

Nora's breath caught, and the world—sunlight, tea, art, *him*— spun slightly, sweetly off-kilter.

The kitchen smelled like cinnamon and citrus and something warm she couldn't name. Like memory, or safety in a skillet.

Nora followed the humming down the hall barefoot, fingers brushing the painted doorframe. It was chipped in a charming way

—lived-in, loved-in. The kind of imperfection she'd never let herself own.

Julian stood at the stove, humming something jazzy while scrambling eggs with the casual competence of someone who'd never questioned his right to take up space. He wore a faded t-shirt that clung exactly where it should and pajama pants patterned with tiny sketch pencils.

He looked like Julian.

But more... present. Settled into his own skin like he'd never doubted he belonged.

He turned before she could bolt.

The smile that spread across his face was sunshine and recognition and home.

"Morning," he said, like he'd said it a thousand times before. "Sleep okay?"

She opened her mouth. Closed it. Tried again. "I think I might be having an existential crisis before breakfast."

He laughed—rich, low, the sound curling around her ribs like smoke. "Good. You were out cold. I almost sketched you, but the eggs called and I couldn't find my soft pencils."

"Tragic," she said automatically.

"You always say that when I threaten to draw you sleeping. It's practically tradition."

*Tradition.* The word hung between them, loaded with history she couldn't access.

He plated something golden—toast with honey and sliced pear —and slid it across the counter like an offering.

Then leaned in and kissed her temple.

Quick. Casual.

Devastating.

Because it felt like memory carved into her bones.

She smiled—awkward, trembly—but he didn't seem to notice. Just brushed paint from her hair with the fondness of someone who'd learned to love her mess.

"You've got cerulean blue behind your ear," he said. "Guess that landscape finally fought back."

She blinked. "Landscape?"

He nodded toward the living room. "You started it after dinner last night. Said the light was 'calling you names' and you had to answer."

"I... did?"

Julian grinned, pouring tea into a mug that read: *Artist at Work. Interrupt at Your Own Risk.*

"That's the Nora I know. Feisty at midnight, philosophical by breakfast."

He handed her the mug, and when their fingers brushed, she felt it everywhere.

"Did I make this?" she asked, staring at the threatening ceramic.

"Yeah, last spring. Said it was for emergencies only."

"Does this count as an emergency?" she asked before thinking.

He tilted his head, eyes warm with mischief. "If it doesn't, I'm very disappointed in us."

She laughed despite herself—then caught it, surprised by the sound. When was the last time she'd laughed without bracing for the crash? Without waiting for the universe to notice she was happy and correct it?

But Julian didn't seem to notice her momentary panic. Just bumped her hip with his—lightly, like punctuation—and she found herself leaning in instead of pulling away.

And for one terrifying, beautiful moment, she thought: *Maybe I could stay.*

After breakfast, Julian kissed her cheek and headed out to "grab fresh bread and eavesdrop on the old poets at the café"—a phrase he tossed over his shoulder like it was perfectly ordinary.

Apparently, it was.

Nora wandered the house like someone learning to breathe underwater.

Everything was light and space, and color. Books stacked on windowsills. Pottery glazed in blues and greens scattered across shelves. Plants cascading from macramé hangers like the house had decided to garden itself.

In the bathroom—robin's-egg blue vanity, clawfoot tub, trailing vines—she caught her reflection and froze.

The woman in the mirror looked like her.

But softer. Lighter. Hair loose and wavy, eyes bright with something that might've been joy. No makeup, paint smudged on one cheek, wearing the kind of smile that suggested she'd just come back from laughing.

Nora reached for the glass.

Her reflection didn't move.

She stepped closer, heart hammering.

The other Nora tilted her head—curious, calm. Then mouthed it slowly, like it was a name: *You, if you stayed.*

The air went still—no sound, no breeze, just that strange hush that happened sometimes in dreams, right before something important.

Nora's voice cracked. "I don't know how to be her."

The reflection placed a hand to the glass. Nora mirrored it.

They touched through the barrier, and she heard—felt—a whisper inside her ribs: *You're not broken. Just bruised.*

Tears welled, sudden and sharp.

When she blinked, the mirror showed only her again. Wide-eyed, uncertain, real.

But softer around the edges.

Like maybe this place was teaching her how to be gentle with herself.

• • •

The studio was attached to the house through a glass-walled breezeway lined with succulents.

Nora found it by following the scent of turpentine and lemon oil.

She should've been horrified.

The wide-planked floors were spattered in paint—blues and ochres and cadmium yellow dried into abstract maps. Jars of brushes sat in old teacups and mason jars. Canvases crowded every surface, some finished, others half-born, all pulsing with life.

Instead of chaos, she felt... *relief.*

Like walking into a room that had been waiting for her to come home.

Paintings lined the walls—some clearly hers, others joint efforts, a few she didn't recognize but felt in her bones. One canvas held intertwined hands under rain. Another was pure light captured somehow in pigment and hope.

She'd painted joy here. Actually painted it.

Julian was crouched beside a large canvas on the floor, sleeves rolled, charcoal smudged on his cheek like he'd leaned too close to something important.

He looked up when she entered.

"There she is. I was about to send a search party."

"Just... exploring," she said, still taking it in.

"You always do this. Walk in like you've never been here before. Like the light surprises you."

"It does," she said honestly.

He didn't question it. Just stood and offered her a brush, handle worn smooth from use.

"Want to finish this one? You said last night it was ready to speak."

She took the brush, and it fit her hand like coming home.

They worked in easy silence—paint mixing, jazz crackling from an old radio, their movements complementing like dancers who'd learned each other's rhythms.

Then, mid-stroke, he leaned in and kissed the top of her head.

Soft. Certain. Like he'd done it a thousand times and planned to do it a thousand more.

Nora froze.

Because it felt like history.

History she didn't remember earning.

The panic hit sharp and sudden—*what if she messed this up? What if she couldn't be the woman he loved? What if happiness was just another thing she'd find a way to break?*

"You okay?" he asked, noticing her stillness.

She nodded too quickly. "Just... concentrating."

But when he stepped behind her to reach for ultramarine blue, his chest brushing her back, she had to grip the easel to stay steady.

Julian moved around her like he knew her geography. Like he'd mapped every freckle and learned to love the way she held her breath when she painted something true.

She didn't know how to want someone this openly.

Didn't know how to be wanted back.

But here, in this sun-soaked studio with paint on her fingers and jazz in the air, she was starting to remember.

"Perfect," Julian murmured, stepping back to study their work.

He wasn't looking at the painting.

He was looking at her.

And for the first time in years, Nora didn't flinch away from being seen.

She just painted another stroke and let herself be loved.

# paint-splattered
# chemistry

. . .

THE MURAL WAS HIDEOUS.

Not in an artistic way. In a "what happens when you let seven-year-olds vote on color schemes" way.

Nora stood in the town square, paintbrush dripping electric lime, staring at what could only be described as a rainbow having an emotional breakdown across the side of Miller's Hardware Store.

"It's... vibrant," said a voice behind her.

She turned to find Julian approaching with two coffee cups and the expression of someone trying very hard not to laugh.

"Vibrant is one word for it," Nora said. "Retina-searing is another."

"I teach a children's art class and this is a collective work. The kids are very proud of it."

Julian handed her a cup—oat milk latte, extra shot, cinnamon—exactly how she liked it, though she couldn't remember telling him. "Mrs. Henley specifically requested 'more purple in the sky area.'"

Nora gestured at the wall, where purple clouds drifted through what appeared to be a lime-green aurora borealis. "I think we've achieved maximum purple."

"Could use more yellow," piped up a small voice.

They both turned. Emma, age six, stood with paint-covered hands and the confidence of someone who'd never met a color she didn't like.

"More yellow where?" Nora asked, crouching to Emma's level.

"Everywhere," Emma said seriously. "Yellow is happy."

Julian caught Nora's eye and grinned. "The artistic director has spoken."

"Fine," Nora sighed, loading her brush with cadmium yellow. "But if anyone complains about this looking like a unicorn exploded, I'm blaming you."

"Deal," Julian said, already adding yellow highlights to a purple tree that defied several laws of botany.

An hour later, the mural had evolved from hideous to magnificently chaotic.

Emma had recruited three more children, all of whom had Strong Opinions about where the yellow should go. Julian had somehow convinced Mrs. Henley that the lime-green sky was "reminiscent of early Rothko, but more optimistic."

Nora was adding yellow polka dots to a blue elephant (Emma's request) when she felt eyes on her.

She looked up to find Julian watching her with that expression again—the one that made her feel like she was being studied for a portrait she'd never agreed to pose for.

"What?" she asked, self-consciously wiping paint from her cheek.

"Nothing. You're just..." He stepped closer, reaching out to tuck a paint-streaked curl behind her ear. "You're in your element. Happy."

The word hung between them like something precious and fragile.

"I am," she said, surprised by how true it sounded.

"Good," he murmured, thumb brushing her jawline. "I love watching you create things."

Before she could overthink it—before the panic could set in—he kissed her.

Not the careful temple kisses from this morning. This was real. Soft but certain, tasting like coffee and possibility.

Her knees nearly buckled. She almost pulled back—almost said "this isn't mine"—but then he kissed her again, and she let herself forget the rules.

When they broke apart, Nora felt dizzy.

"Public display of affection!" Emma announced loudly. "Gross!"

Julian laughed, not moving away. "Sorry, Em. Couldn't help myself."

"Ew," Emma said, but she was grinning. "Are you getting married?"

Nora's heart stopped.

"Not today," Julian said easily, squeezing Nora's hand. "But thanks for the reminder."

*Reminder?*

Emma skipped off to terrorize the purple elephant with more yellow, leaving Nora staring at Julian.

"Reminder?" she managed.

His brow furrowed slightly. "The wedding planning meeting? Tomorrow? With your sister?"

Nora blinked. "My... sister?"

Julian's expression shifted to concern. "Nora, are you feeling okay? You've been off all day. Did you hit your head on something?"

"I'm fine," she said quickly. "Just... distracted by all the yellow."

But she wasn't fine. Because apparently, in this life, she had a sister. And they were planning a wedding. Her wedding. To Julian.

And she had absolutely no memory of any of it.

The grocery store was a minefield of casual intimacy.

Julian pushed the cart while Nora wandered the aisles in a daze, trying to act like she knew what they needed for tomorrow's mysterious book club.

"Cheese," Julian said, consulting a list written in her handwriting. "You specifically wrote 'good cheese, not the sad cheese.'"

"Right," Nora said faintly. "Anti-sad cheese."

In the wine aisle, an elderly woman with silver hair and paint-stained fingernails waved at them.

"Nora, dear! How's the mural coming?"

"Colorfully," Nora replied, which seemed to satisfy her.

"And Julian, tell your mother I found that book she was looking for. The one about the woman who talks to plants."

"Will do, Mrs. Patterson," Julian said warmly.

Everyone knew them. Everyone had opinions about their life, their wedding, and their choice of pasta sauce (apparently they were Team Marinara, which Julian defended with surprising passion).

By the time they reached checkout, Nora felt like she was drowning in other people's assumptions about who she was.

"You okay?" Julian asked as they loaded groceries into the car. "You look pale."

"Just overwhelmed," she said, which wasn't a lie.

He stopped what he was doing and looked at her—really looked.

"Hey," he said softly, reaching for her hand. "What's going on? And don't say 'nothing.' I can tell when you're spiraling."

The kindness in his voice nearly undid her.

"What if..." she started, then stopped. How could she explain that she felt like an impostor in her own life? "What if I'm not who you think I am?"

Julian's expression softened. He cupped her face gently, thumbs brushing her cheeks.

"Nora," he said. "I know exactly who you are. You're the woman who cries at dog videos but pretends it's allergies. Who organizes her paints by emotional intensity. Who once spent three hours convincing Mrs. Henley that the hardware store needed a mural because 'art is democracy in action.'"

Each detail hit like a small revelation.

"You're the person who makes me want to be better," he continued. "Not perfect. Just... more myself. And if you're having pre-wedding jitters, that's normal. But don't doubt this. Don't doubt us."

Before she could respond, he kissed her forehead and went back to loading groceries.

Leaving Nora standing there, her heart full and breaking at the same time.

Because he was so sure. So certain of their story.

And she was just a visitor, stealing moments that belonged to someone else.

That evening, they cooked dinner together in their sun-filled kitchen.

Julian chopped vegetables with the precision of someone who actually read cooking magazines. Nora stirred risotto and tried not to think about how domestic this felt, how right.

"So," Julian said, not looking up from his cutting board, "want to talk about what's really bothering you?"

Nora's spoon paused mid-stir. "I told you, I'm just—"

"Overwhelmed. I know. But this isn't normal overwhelmed. This is 'I don't recognize my own life' overwhelmed."

She turned to face him, surprised by his directness.

"Am I that obvious?"

"Only to me," he said, setting down his knife. "You get this look when you're trying to solve a problem you can't paint your way out of."

He moved closer, not crowding but close enough that she could smell his soap—something clean and cedar-scented.

"Talk to me," he said simply.

Nora stared at him—this man who knew her tells, who brought her exactly the right coffee, who kissed her like he'd been doing it forever.

"What if," she said carefully, "you woke up one day and everyone expected you to be someone you weren't sure you could be?"

Julian considered this. "Like an imposter?"

"Something like that."

"Then I'd probably panic for a while," he said. "And then I'd remember that the people who love me aren't loving some perfect version. They're loving me, mess and all."

He reached out, tucking that perpetually wayward curl behind her ear.

"You don't have to be perfect, Nora. You just have to be here."

The words hit deeper than they should have.

Because she wasn't sure she could be. Here, present, real.

Not when this whole life felt borrowed.

But when Julian smiled at her—patient, understanding, completely hers—she wanted to try.

Even if it was just for now.

Even if she was lying to everyone, including herself.

She kissed him—harder than she meant to, full of confusion, guilt, and the awful ache of wanting something that didn't belong to her.

When they broke apart, he looked dazed.

"What was that for?"

"For being patient with me," she said. "For knowing me better than I know myself sometimes."

"Always," he said simply.

And God help her, she believed him.

# identity theft, but make it existential

. . .

THE SISTER I never had arrived at nine sharp with a binder the size of a small aircraft carrier and the organizational energy of someone who'd alphabetized her spice rack for fun.

"Traffic was murder," she announced, sweeping into the kitchen like she owned it. "But I brought mimosas and a color-coded timeline for the next six weeks."

Nora stared.

The woman was her height, her build, her nose—but polished to a shine that suggested regular spa visits and a retirement fund. Her hair was professionally highlighted, her manicure fresh, and she wore the kind of confidence that came from never doubting your place in the world.

"Nora?" Julian's voice came from behind her. "You remember Claire, right? Your sister?"

*Claire.*

The name felt foreign on her tongue, like a word from a language she'd never learned.

"Of course," Nora said weakly. "Hi, Claire."

Claire paused mid-binder-extraction, studying Nora with sharp blue eyes—their mother's eyes, apparently.

"You look terrible," she said with sisterly bluntness. "Are you sleeping? Eating? Julian, is she eating?"

"She's been painting a lot," Julian said diplomatically.

"Stress painting," Claire diagnosed, pulling out a chair. "I brought B vitamins. And a backup wedding dress, because knowing you, you've probably spilled paint on the first one."

Nora's mouth went dry. "Backup dress?"

"The Vera Wang," Claire said patiently. "The one we picked out last month? The one you cried over because it made you look like 'a goddess who'd learned to waltz'?"

Nothing. Not even a flicker of recognition.

Julian was watching her again, that concerned crease between his brows deepening.

"Maybe we should postpone the planning session," he suggested gently. "Nora's been—"

"Nonsense," Claire interrupted, already spreading papers across the kitchen table. "We're six weeks out. The caterer needs final numbers, the florist is threatening to substitute peonies for garden roses, and don't get me started on the band situation."

She looked up at Nora expectantly. "Please tell me you remember the band situation."

Nora looked helplessly at Julian, who mouthed: *They broke up.*

"They... broke up?" Nora ventured.

"See?" Claire said, vindicated. "This is exactly why I made backup plans. Option A is the string quartet from the country club. Option B is that acoustic duo you liked from the farmers market. Option C is a DJ, but over my dead body."

For the next hour, Claire systematically dismantled and reconstructed a wedding that Nora had apparently been planning for months. Flower arrangements were debated. Seating charts were revised. Menu options were discussed with the intensity of a UN peace negotiation.

Nora nodded and smiled and tried to look invested while her stomach churned with each new detail.

Because this wasn't just Julian's life she was borrowing.

She'd stolen an entire family.

"You're being weird," Claire announced after Julian left to pick up lunch.

They were alone at the kitchen table, surrounded by the detritus of wedding planning—fabric swatches, venue photos, a timeline that looked like it required military precision to execute.

"I'm not being weird," Nora protested.

"You are. You've agreed to everything I've suggested without a single argument. Yesterday you would have fought me on the napkin color."

Claire leaned back in her chair, studying Nora like a particularly puzzling crossword. She tilted her head. "Did you hit your head or have some kind of midlife breakdown and forget to tell me?"

"I'm fine," Nora said quickly.

"Then what's going on? Pre-wedding jitters? Cold feet? Having second thoughts about Julian?"

"No!" Nora said too quickly. "Julian's... Julian's perfect."

"Then what?"

How could she explain? *Hi, I'm not actually your sister. I'm a sad woman from another timeline who borrowed your Nora's life and fell in love with her fiancé.*

"I just..." Nora fumbled for words. "Sometimes I feel like I don't deserve this. Any of this."

Claire's expression softened. She reached across the table and took Nora's hand.

"Nora," she said gently. "You've been planning this wedding

since you were twelve. You used to make me play bride and groom with your stuffed animals."

A memory that wasn't hers. A childhood that belonged to someone else.

"You deserve to be happy," Claire continued. "You deserve Julian. You deserve the art studio, the house, the ridiculous mural that's making Mrs. Henley famous on TikTok."

"TikTok?"

"Emma posted a video of you painting the elephant. You're viral, apparently. #MuralMom is trending."

Nora blinked. "I'm a hashtag?"

"You're a lot of things," Claire said, squeezing her hand. "But undeserving isn't one of them."

The kindness in her voice was worse than an accusation. Because Claire—this sister she'd never had—was defending her to herself.

And she was lying to all of them.

After Claire left (with promises to "fix the band situation" and threatened to "stage an intervention" if Nora didn't start eating more vegetables), Nora escaped to the studio.

She needed to paint. Needed to move her hands and quiet her mind and maybe make sense of the emotional tornado currently demolishing her from the inside.

But when she sat down in front of the easel, she froze.

She didn't recognize her own brushstrokes.

They were bold. Joyful. Unafraid. The woman who'd painted these canvases had never second-guessed her right to take up space, had never apologized for the brightness of her colors or the audacity of her joy.

Nora hadn't felt any of those things since... well since never.

A soft sound made her turn.

A woman sat on the paint-splattered stool by the window—linen-draped, serene, completely out of place in the chaos of creation.

Celeste.

"Hello, Nora," she said calmly. "How are you settling in?"

Nora's heart hammered. "What are you doing here?"

"Checking in. This is usually when visitors start to... struggle."

"I'm not struggling."

Celeste raised an eyebrow. "You lied to your sister about remembering your own wedding plans. You're having an identity crisis in a borrowed life. And you kissed a man who thinks he knows you while feeling like a fraud."

Each word hit like a dart finding its target.

"That's not struggling," Celeste continued mildly. "That's drowning."

Nora sank onto a stool, suddenly exhausted. "She has a sister. A whole family. A life full of people who love her."

"Yes."

"And I'm stealing it."

"Are you?" Celeste asked. "Or are you living it?"

"There's a difference?"

Celeste stood, moving to examine a half-finished canvas—a landscape full of impossible colors and wild joy.

"This life exists because another version of you chose it," she said. "Chose to stay open after heartbreak. Chose to trust love when it finally came. Chose to create instead of hiding."

She turned to face Nora. "The question is: what would you choose?"

Nora stared at her. "What do you mean?"

"I mean," Celeste said gently, "this doesn't have to be temporary."

The air in the studio went very still.

"What?"

"You could stay. Permanently. This life could be yours."

Nora's breath caught. "But what about... the other me? The one who built this?"

Celeste's expression was carefully neutral. "She would... transition. To another possibility. Another path."

"You mean she'd disappear."

"I mean she'd find a different story."

The words hung between them like smoke.

Nora looked around the studio—at the canvases full of light, the brushes worn smooth with use, the easel where she and Julian had painted together just yesterday.

"I could stay," she whispered.

"You could," Celeste confirmed. "If that's what you choose."

"And Julian would never know?"

"He'd know the woman he fell in love with. The one sitting in front of me right now."

Nora's hands trembled. Because the offer was everything she'd never dared to want. Love. Art. A sister who brought mimosas and fought about napkin colors. A man who kissed her like she was precious.

A life where she mattered.

"How long do I have to decide?" she asked.

Celeste smiled, sad and knowing. "You're already deciding. Every moment you choose to stay, every kiss you don't pull away from, every time you let yourself believe this could be real."

She moved toward the door, pausing in the threshold.

"The heart doesn't wait for permission, Nora. It just loves. The question is whether you're brave enough to let it."

And then she was gone, leaving Nora alone with her paint and her choices and the terrible, wonderful possibility that she could keep this life.

If she was willing to take it from someone else.

Julian found her an hour later, sitting on the studio floor with paint in her hair and tears on her cheeks.

"Hey," he said softly, settling beside her. "What's wrong?"

She looked at him—this man who'd somehow become the center of a life she'd never lived—and felt her heart break a little more.

"Do you ever wonder if you're living the wrong life?" she asked.

He considered this seriously. "Sometimes. Usually, when I'm stuck in traffic or trying to assemble IKEA furniture."

That pulled a watery laugh from her.

"But then," he continued, reaching out to wipe paint from her temple, "I come home to you. And everything feels right again."

"What if I'm not who you think I am?"

"Then I'd love whoever you actually are," he said simply. "That's how this works, Nora. I don't love you because you're perfect. I love you because you're you."

He leaned in, pressing his forehead to hers.

"Weird, paint-covered, occasionally existential you." He paused, voice softening. "And even if you changed, I'd still know how to find you."

She closed her eyes, memorizing the moment. The weight of his head against hers. The smell of cedar and coffee. The absolute certainty in his voice when he said he loved her.

Even if the "her" he loved was someone else entirely.

"I love you too," she whispered.

And for the first time since she'd arrived, she meant it completely.

Which was exactly the problem.

# mirror, mirror, heart aflutter

. . .

NORA COULDN'T SLEEP.

She lay in the perfect bed with its perfect sheets, listening to Julian's steady breathing beside her, and felt like she was drowning in silk and guilt.

Every time she closed her eyes, she saw Claire's face. The easy way she'd said, *"You deserve to be happy."* The casual intimacy of shared childhood memories that weren't hers. The wedding binder full of dreams that belonged to someone else.

At three a.m., she gave up and slipped from the room.

The house was different in the dark—softer shadows, deeper silences. She padded to the kitchen and made tea she wouldn't drink, just needing the ritual of normalcy.

But when she turned around, cup in hand, her reflection in the window stopped her cold.

Not because it was her reflection.

Because it wasn't.

The woman in the glass had the same face, the same wild hair, but her eyes were different. Calmer. More settled. She wore a paint-stained nightgown instead of the silk pajamas Nora had found in the drawer.

The other Nora.

The real one.

Her mouth moved silently: *We need to talk.*

Nora's teacup slipped from nerveless fingers, shattering against the kitchen tiles.

The bathroom mirror was waiting for her.

Not the cheerful robin's-egg vanity from before. This time, the glass was dark, reflecting candlelight that seemed to come from somewhere else entirely.

The other Nora sat on what looked like a simple wooden stool, hands folded in her lap. She looked... tired. Not broken, but worn in the way of someone who'd been carrying something heavy for too long.

"You're staying," she said. Not a question.

Nora pressed her palms against the glass. "I don't know. Maybe. I—"

"You love him."

The words hit like a physical blow. "I didn't mean to."

"I know." The other Nora's smile was sad but not unkind. "It's impossible not to, isn't it? He makes you feel like the best version of yourself."

Nora nodded, throat tight.

"But here's the thing," the other Nora continued, leaning forward. "I am the best version of yourself. I'm who you became when you chose love over fear. When you stayed open instead of closing down. When you picked up a brush instead of organizing your paints into neat, untouchable rows."

"I know," Nora whispered.

"Do you?" The other Nora tilted her head. "Because if you stay, I disappear. Not just from this timeline—from everywhere. Every choice I made, every moment of joy I found, every painting I created. Gone."

The mirror seemed to pulse with each word.

"And Claire?" the other Nora continued. "She doesn't have another sister. She gets a stranger wearing my face, pretending to remember birthdays and inside jokes and the time we got food poisoning from that sketchy sushi place and swore we'd never tell Mom."

Each detail was a knife twist.

"Julian doesn't get to keep loving me," she said softly. "He gets to love someone who'll always be partly pretending. Someone who'll never quite know all the stories, all the history, all the small moments that made us... us."

Nora's vision blurred. "Then what am I supposed to do? Go back to being nothing? Go back to hiding?"

"You were never nothing." The other Nora's voice was fierce now. "You just forgot how to see yourself clearly."

She stood, moving closer to the glass. "I didn't become this version by magic, Nora. I became her by choosing, again and again, to be brave. To try. To fail and try again."

"I don't know how."

"Yes, you do. You've been doing it all week. Every time you painted with him, every time you let yourself laugh, every time you didn't pull away when he kissed you—that was you being brave."

The other Nora placed her hand against the glass. "You don't need my life. You just need to stop being afraid of your own."

Nora mirrored the gesture, their palms separated only by the impossible barrier of choice and consequence.

"What if I can't do it alone?" Nora asked.

"Who says you have to be alone?"

The mirror shimmered.

And suddenly, Nora could see through to the other side—not just the other Nora, but the space beyond. A different studio. Simpler, smaller, but filled with the same golden light. And there, barely visible in the corner, a familiar silhouette bent over a canvas.

Julian.

But not her Julian. This one was older, softer around the edges. Gray at his temples. Paint under his fingernails.

There was a small scar on his left hand—faint but familiar. She remembered the night he'd sliced it opening on a stubborn jar of gesso and insisted it was a "battle wound in the name of art."

And when he looked up, sensing something, his eyes held a different kind of love—quieter, deeper, earned through years of small moments and shared struggles.

Nora's breath caught. "How do you know?"

"Because love doesn't just exist in one place, Nora. It echoes. It finds a way."

The vision faded, leaving only the mirror and two women who shared a face but not a fate.

"I have to go back," Nora said, the words tasting like loss and rightness in equal measure.

"Yes," the other Nora agreed. "You do."

"Will I remember this? Any of this?"

"The love? Yes. The lesson? I hope so." The other Nora smiled, and for the first time, it reached her eyes. "The specific details? Probably not. But you'll remember how it felt to be brave. To be seen. To believe you deserved good things."

She stepped back from the glass. "That's enough. That's everything."

The mirror began to dim, the connection wavering like a candle in the wind.

"Thank you," Nora whispered.

"Thank you," the other Nora replied. "For giving me back my life."

And then she was gone, leaving Nora alone with her reflection —tired, paint-stained, real.

But somehow, finally, enough.

She found Julian in the kitchen, crouched beside the broken teacup with a dustpan and the careful movements of someone trying not to wake a sleeping house.

"I heard the crash," he said without looking up. "Couldn't sleep either?"

"Something like that."

He glanced at her then, taking in her pale face and red-rimmed eyes. "You okay?"

She wanted to lie. Wanted to pretend everything was fine, that she wasn't about to break both their hearts for the sake of someone else's happiness.

Instead, she said, "I need to tell you something."

He set down the dustpan, giving her his full attention.

"This is going to sound crazy," she began.

"Try me."

So she did.

She told him about the gallery, about Celeste, about waking up in a life that felt like a dream. She told him about the mirror, about the other Nora, about the choice she had to make.

She expected him to laugh. To call her delusional. To suggest therapy or medication or a nice long vacation somewhere without mysterious linen-clad women offering impossible gifts.

Instead, he listened.

When she finished, the kitchen was quiet except for the hum of the refrigerator and the distant sound of rain beginning to fall.

"Well," Julian said finally. "That explains why you've been looking at me like you're trying to memorize my face."

She blinked. "You believe me?"

"I believe that something changed. I believe that you're struggling with something bigger than wedding jitters." He moved closer, not crowding but close enough that she could see the flecks of gold in his brown eyes. "And I believe that you love me enough to tell me the truth, even when it hurts."

"Julian—"

"Let me finish." His voice was gentle but firm. "I also believe that whoever you are—wherever you came from—you're still the woman I fell in love with. Maybe not the same history, but the same heart."

Tears spilled over then, hot and unstoppable.

"I have to go back," she whispered.

"I know."

"And you'll forget me."

"Maybe. Or maybe I'll just remember you differently." He reached up, cupping her face in his hands. "Maybe I'll remember you as the woman who taught me that love doesn't have to make sense to be real."

He kissed her then—soft, careful, like he was trying to press the memory into her skin.

When they broke apart, she could taste salt on her lips.

"How do I do this?" she asked. "How do I leave you?"

"The same way you found me," he said simply. "With courage."

Outside, the rain picked up, drumming against the windows with the insistence of a world waiting for her to choose.

"Will you be okay?" she asked.

Julian smiled, sad but genuine. "I'll be fine. And so will you."

"How can you be sure?"

"Because," he said, brushing a tear from her cheek, "you're braver than you think. You always have been."

They sat together until dawn, not talking much, just breathing the same air and memorizing each other's presence.

When the first light crept through the kitchen windows, Julian made coffee with the careful precision of someone trying to make an ordinary moment last.

"I should go," Nora said, though every cell in her body rebelled against the words.

"Should," Julian agreed. "But not yet."

"Not yet."

He handed her a mug—not the threatening ceramic from before, but something simple and white and clean.

"For the road," he said.

They drank in silence, watching the world wake up outside their windows. Birds calling to each other. Light slowly painting the garden gold. The ordinary miracle of another day beginning.

"I'm going to miss this," Nora said.

"Me too."

When she finally stood to leave, Julian caught her hand.

"Hey," he said. "When you get back to your timeline? Be kind to yourself. And maybe... maybe give the guy a chance."

"What guy?"

Julian's smile was mystery and mischief and goodbye. "You'll know him when you see him."

She kissed him one last time—quick, fierce, final.

Then she walked away, leaving her heart in a kitchen that had never been hers and carrying the memory of love like a compass pointing home.

The rain had stopped, but the world still glittered with possibility.

She walked into the quiet morning, heart still aching but her hands finally open—ready to make something new.

# one last painting

### . . .

NORA WOKE to the sound of her old ceiling fan.

Not the gentle creak of weathered wood beams, but the familiar groan of aging plaster settling against cheap drywall. Her eyes opened to water stains shaped like storm clouds and the persistent drip from the upstairs neighbor's bathroom that no amount of complaining had ever fixed.

Home.

She lay still for a long moment, cataloging the differences. The scratchy sheets that smelled like discount fabric softener instead of sea salt and possibility. The narrow window that showed the brick wall and fire escape instead of gardens blooming with impossible abundance. The silence—not peaceful, but hollow, like an echo chamber for disappointment.

Her hands moved to her nails, expecting coral polish and finding only chipped clear coat. The silk pajamas were gone, replaced by an old t-shirt from a 5K run she'd never finished and flannel pants with a hole near the left knee.

She sat up slowly, her body protesting in ways it hadn't in the other timeline. Her back ached from the cheap mattress. Her neck was stiff. Even her skin felt different—duller, like someone had adjusted the saturation on the world and forgotten to change it back.

The apartment was exactly as she'd left it. Tidy to the point of sterility. Books arranged by height instead of affection. The easel in the corner still covered by a paint-spattered sheet like a shrouded corpse.

But something felt wrong.

Not just the absence of Julian and Claire and the house full of light. Something in her chest sat differently now, like furniture that had been moved and not quite put back in place.

She padded to the bathroom and stared at her reflection.

Same face. Same tired eyes. Same mouth that had forgotten how to want things.

But underneath it all, something new. A restlessness. A knowledge of what was possible that made her current life feel like a costume she'd outgrown.

She touched the glass, half-expecting to see the other Nora staring back.

Only her own reflection looked back—hollow-eyed, paint-free, alone.

The gallery felt like a tomb.

Nora stood in the doorway, keys heavy in her hand, staring at the space that had once been her sanctuary and now felt like a monument to all the chances she'd never taken.

*The heart doesn't wait for permission,* she thought suddenly, Celeste's words echoing in her mind like a half-remembered song. *It just loves.*

The pristine white walls mocked her. The carefully arranged brushes—still sorted by hostility—seemed to judge her from their caddy. Even the light was wrong, fluorescent and harsh instead of the golden warmth that had bathed everything in the other timeline.

She moved through the space like a ghost, touching surfaces that felt foreign under her fingers. The counter where Mrs. Chen had left soup. The corner where her portfolio waited, still closed, still hiding Julian's sketch beneath layers of dust and regret.

When she opened it, his face looked back at her—young, laughing, mid-thought. The same eyes that had watched her paint with such tenderness just hours ago. Or lifetimes ago. Or never at all.

Her chest clenched.

She'd kissed this mouth. Had felt these hands brush paint from her hair. Had watched this face soften with love for a version of her that deserved it.

Now it was just ink on paper. A memory of something that had never really been hers.

She traced the edge of the sketch with one finger, careful not to smudge the lines that were all she had left of him.

"I'm sorry," she whispered to the empty gallery. To Julian. To the other Nora. To herself.

Sorry for borrowing what wasn't hers. Sorry for leaving. Sorry for not being brave enough to earn her own version of that love.

Sorry for coming back to a life that no longer fit.

She tried to paint.

Three times.

The first attempt lasted fifteen minutes before she gave up, staring at a canvas that looked like someone had sneezed color onto it without purpose or passion.

The second time, she managed to mix a blue that almost captured the color of Julian's eyes. She dipped her brush into the color—so rich it hurt—and for one second, her hand moved without thinking, tracing the curve of a collarbone she hadn't seen since waking up.

She remembered Julian's hands over hers, guiding her brush in that sun-drenched studio, whispering, "Let it speak before you try to fix it."

The memory hit like a physical blow. Her hand trembled, and the brushstroke went wild, streaking blue across the canvas like a scar.

Now, the canvas stared back at her—silent, stubborn, blank except for that one desperate mark.

She set down the brush and stepped away, her hands shaking.

The third time, she didn't even pick up a brush. Just sat on the stool in front of the easel and cried—messy, gulping sobs that echoed off the gallery walls like accusations.

Because she could feel it slipping away.

The confidence. The joy. The sense of being someone worth loving.

Already, the memories were softening at the edges. The exact shade of the kitchen walls. The sound of Julian's laugh. The way the light felt different when she painted with purpose instead of obligation.

She was losing the other Nora's gifts as surely as if they'd been borrowed clothes she'd had to return.

By afternoon, she'd convinced herself it had all been a dream. A stress-induced hallucination brought on by too much isolation and too little human connection. The mind's way of showing her what she wanted so desperately that she'd invented an entire alternate reality to house it.

That made more sense than timeline magic.

That made everything easier to bear.

Mrs. Chen appeared at four-thirty with another thermos and the determined expression of someone who refused to be ignored.

"You look worse," she announced, bustling through the door without invitation. "Thin and sad and now haunted. That's not an improvement."

Nora managed a weak smile. "Good to see you too, Mrs. Chen."

"Don't sass me. Sit. Eat." She thrust the thermos at Nora with the authority of someone who'd spent decades forcing nutrition into reluctant recipients. "It's chicken noodle this time. With extra ginger for whatever's making you look like you've seen ghosts."

The kindness hit Nora like a physical blow. Such a small gesture —soup on a difficult day—but it reminded her of other kindnesses. Claire's mimosas and backup wedding dresses. Julian's careful way of making coffee exactly how she liked it.

People who cared enough to notice when she was struggling.

People she'd never really had.

Mrs. Chen paused by the open portfolio, squinting at Julian's sketch. "Handsome. Looks like he'd ruin your life gently."

Nora gave a brittle laugh. "He was... kind."

"They usually are, the ones you never quite forget." Mrs. Chen settled into the chair across from her, studying Nora with sharp eyes. "Lost love?"

"Something like that."

"Ah." Mrs. Chen nodded knowingly. "I had one of those. Before Mr. Chen. Beautiful boy who wrote me poems and left town the day after graduation. Broke my heart so thoroughly I thought I'd never recover."

She sipped thoughtfully from her own small cup. "But heartbreak teaches you things. Makes you know the difference between love that feeds you and love that starves you. When Mr. Chen came along—quieter, steadier—I almost missed him because he didn't write poems."

"Did you regret it? Not going with the poet?"

Mrs. Chen smiled. "For about ten years. Then Mr. Chen started leaving me little notes in my lunchbox. Not poems—grocery lists, mostly. But written with such care, such attention to what I needed..." She shrugged. "Poetry comes in many forms, honey."

"Mrs. Chen," Nora said, her voice cracking slightly. "Do you have any siblings?"

Mrs. Chen looked surprised by the question. "Three sisters. All younger, all louder, all convinced they know better than me about everything." Her expression softened. "Why?"

"I was just wondering what it felt like. Having a family who knew you that well."

"Awful most of the time," Mrs. Chen said cheerfully. "They call me every week to argue about recipes and tell me I'm doing my hair wrong. But when my husband died, they all showed up with casseroles and bad advice and refused to leave until I was eating again."

She studied Nora with sharp eyes. "You thinking about reaching out to yours?"

Nora blinked back sudden tears. "I don't... I don't have any. Siblings, I mean."

"Ah." Mrs. Chen nodded like this explained everything. "Well, family isn't just blood, honey. Sometimes it's the people who bring you soup when you look like death warmed over."

She patted Nora's hand like she always didbriefly, but warm, real—and headed for the door.

"Eat the soup," she called over her shoulder. "And maybe think about calling someone. Anyone. Being alone too much makes people strange."

After she left, Nora sat with the thermos and tried not to think about Claire's laugh or the way Julian had hummed while making breakfast or how it felt to be part of something larger than herself.

Instead, she opened her laptop and scrolled through old emails from her mother—brief, functional updates about weather and doctor's appointments and grocery store encounters with former neighbors.

No wedding planning. No shared memories. No sisterly arguments about napkin colors.

Just the careful politeness of people who loved each other from a distance and had forgotten how to bridge the gap.

The absence of what she'd never had felt sharper now.

Like losing something she'd only borrowed but had learned to need.

The man arrived just as she was closing up.

Nora was turning the sign from "Open" to "Closed" when movement on the street caught her eye. Someone walking slowly past the gallery windows, pausing to look at the paintings displayed in the front.

She couldn't see his face clearly through the glass—just a silhouette backlit by streetlamps. Tall, lean, wearing a jacket that had seen better seasons. His posture was familiar in a way that made her chest tighten.

For a moment, she was certain she was hallucinating.

The stress of the day, the emotional whiplash of returning to a life that no longer fit—it had finally broken something in her brain. She was seeing Julian because she wanted to see him, because some part of her couldn't accept that he belonged to another timeline entirely.

But then the man moved closer to the window, and she could see his face more clearly.

Not Julian.

But something about the eyes...

He hesitated at the door, hand raised as if to knock, then seemed to notice the "Closed" sign. His shoulders dropped slightly in disappointment.

Nora found herself at the door before she'd made a conscious decision to move. Her hand hovered over the lock.

*Don't be afraid,* she told herself. *What's the worst that could happen?*

She opened the door.

"We're closed," she said softly. "But if you were looking for something specific..."

The man turned, and she saw him clearly for the first time.

He was older than she'd expected, in that kind of rugged, quiet way that suggested he read more than he talked. Laugh lines bracketed his mouth, and his hair—dark but streaked with gray—curled slightly at the collar of his coat, like it hadn't been cut in a while. His clothes were soft and worn, like he'd stepped out of a slow morning, not a fast-paced life.

There was nothing familiar about him, and yet—something about his presence felt steady. Grounded. Like a hush before inspiration.

Not Julian. Not even close.

But when he smiled, something inside her stirred anyway.

"I was just..." he began, then paused, studying her face with an intensity that made her breath catch. "This might sound strange, but I know this sounds insane, but... have we met before? I swear I've dreamed your face."

Nora's heart stopped.

Then started again, faster.

"I don't think so," she managed. "But... would you like to come in anyway?"

He smiled then—nothing like Julian's smile—this one was crooked, boyish, unguarded, but something close enough to make her believe in possibility again.

"I'd like that very much."

As he stepped through the doorway, Nora caught a scent that was almost familiar—cedar and coffee and something clean that made her think of fresh starts.

"I'm Nora," she said, extending her hand.

"Victor," he replied, taking it gently.

He held her hand for a moment longer than necessary, and she felt something spark—not recognition exactly, but resonance. Like a tuning fork finding its match.

"And I have the strangest feeling," he continued, "that we were supposed to meet."

Outside, the first snow of the season began to fall, dusting the gallery windows with something that looked almost like magic.

# becoming in
# brushstrokes

. . .

THE KEY still stuck in the lock, like it always did.

Nora jiggled it twice, muttered something unprintable under her breath, and finally shoved the gallery door open with a familiar creak and a gust of dust-scented air.

But this time, she didn't mind the resistance.

This time, she was fighting back.

She stood in the doorway for a long moment, seeing the space not as it was—sterile, cautious, apologetic—but as it could be. The morning light slanted through the front windows differently now, or maybe she was looking with different eyes. Either way, possibility hummed in the air like a song she was finally ready to hear.

Victor had stayed until nearly midnight, talking about art and light and the strange way inspiration struck when you weren't looking for it. He'd examined every piece in the gallery with the careful attention of someone who understood that creating required courage, that showing your work to the world was an act of faith.

"You have an interesting perspective," he'd said, pausing in front of a small watercolor she'd painted years ago and forgotten.

"There's honesty here. Vulnerability. Most people are afraid to be this... present."

"I used to be braver," she'd admitted.

"You still are," he'd replied simply. "You just forgot for a while."

When he'd finally left—with promises to return, to bring his own sketchbook, to show her the community art center where he taught classes on weekends—Nora had stood alone in her gallery and felt something she hadn't experienced in years.

Hope.

Not the desperate, grasping kind that clung to impossible dreams, but the quiet, steady kind that planted seeds and tended them patiently.

Now, in the morning light, she got to work.

The first thing she did was move the easel back to the center of the room.

Not hidden in a corner where it wouldn't offend anyone, but right in the middle of the space where people could see it. Where they could watch her work, if they wanted. Where she could stop hiding behind other people's courage.

The second thing she did was open all the windows.

Fresh air poured in, carrying the scent of autumn leaves and possibility. The gallery exhaled, releasing months of careful sterility.

The third thing she did was breathe.

Deep, intentional breaths that filled her lungs and reminded her body what it felt like to take up space.

Then she got to work.

She dusted shelves with the efficiency of someone who'd spent too long organizing her life instead of living it. She rearranged paintings, grouping them by emotion rather than size, creating conversations between pieces instead of mere displays.

She unearthed supplies from forgotten corners—brushes that remembered her touch, paints that still held their vibrancy, canvases that had been waiting patiently for her to be ready again.

And when she found the flat file—the one with her older pieces—she didn't hesitate.

She pulled out the self-portrait.

The one with the half-shadowed face and the hunger in her eyes. The one that had scared her with its honesty, its raw want.

Looking at it now, she could see what the other Nora had seen. Not failure, but attempt. Not imperfection, but truth.

This woman in the painting wasn't broken.

She was becoming.

Nora hung it on the gallery wall—right in the front where anyone walking by could see it.

Below it, she placed a small white card with three words in her own handwriting:

**In progress. Always.**

She stepped back, studying the effect.

The painting looked different here, in its proper place. Confident. Unapologetic. Ready to start conversations instead of avoiding them.

Like the woman who'd painted it.

Victor returned on Tuesday with coffee and a sketchbook worn soft with use.

"I brought reinforcements," he said, holding up a paper bag that smelled like cinnamon and possibility. "And I was hoping you might show me how you see light."

"How I see light?"

"In your paintings," he clarified, setting the coffee on the counter with careful reverence. "There's something about the way you capture it that feels... alive. Like it has weight."

Nora felt heat rise in her cheeks. "I'm not sure I know what I'm doing half the time."

"The best artists never do," Victor said, pulling up a stool beside her easel. "That's what makes it art instead of illustration."

They spent the morning painting together—not the desperate, borrowed intimacy she'd shared with Julian, but something new. Tentative but real. Two people learning each other's creative language, finding rhythm in the spaces between brushstrokes.

Victor painted like he talked—thoughtfully, with quiet conviction. His work had a gentleness to it that reminded her of Mrs. Chen's thoughtful soup stop ins, of comfort given without expectation of return.

"You're holding back," he observed, watching her hesitate over a color choice.

"I don't want to ruin it."

"Ruin what? The painting or the moment?"

The question caught her off guard. "Both?"

Victor set down his brush and turned to face her fully. "Nora, what's the worst thing that could happen if you painted exactly what you're feeling?"

She considered this. "Someone might see it. And judge it. And think I'm... too much."

"And what if they think you're exactly enough?"

The words hit like a small revelation. Like permission she'd been waiting years to receive.

She picked up her brush.

And painted what she was feeling.

The piece that emerged over the following days wasn't pretty.

It was wild, messy, full of contradictions, and impossible colors. A self-portrait, but not the careful, shadowed one from years past. This one was blazing, uncompromising. A woman mid-transformation, caught between who she'd been and who she was becoming.

Victor watched it develop with the kind of attention that felt like prayer.

"It's fierce," he said on Friday, when she finally set down her brush and stepped back.

"It's honest," she replied.

"Same thing."

Other people began to notice too. Mrs. Chen stopped by daily now, ostensibly to check on Nora's eating habits but really to see what new wildness had emerged on the canvas.

"You're different," she announced on Thursday, studying both Nora and the painting with equal intensity. "Louder. In a good way."

Franklin, the retired art teacher, lingered longer during his weekly visits, asking questions about technique and inspiration with the kind of respect he'd never shown her careful, safe work.

"This has teeth," he said approvingly. "Like you've finally stopped hiding."

Even strangers began wandering in, drawn by something they couldn't quite name. A young woman with paint-stained fingernails spent an hour studying the self-portrait, then asked if Nora taught classes.

"I don't," Nora said automatically, then paused. "But I'm thinking about starting."

The idea took root slowly, like wildflowers in sidewalk cracks.

A class. Real people, learning to see color the way she saw it. Learning to be brave with their brushes, to stop apologizing for taking up space on the canvas.

"I think you should," Victor said when she mentioned it. "I think you have something important to teach."

"Like what?"

"Like how to paint with your whole heart," he said simply. "How to be seen without flinching."

The class started small.

Five students in the first week—Mrs. Chen's grandson, David (who had, in fact, inherited artistic talent along with strong opinions), two college students looking for a creative outlet, a recently retired teacher, and Victor.

"I'm not here as a student," he clarified on that first Tuesday evening. "I'm here as moral support. And because I like watching you teach."

Nora felt her cheeks warm. "I have no idea what I'm doing."

"Perfect," said the retired teacher, a woman named Joan with silver hair and a mischievous smile. "The best learning happens when everyone's figuring it out together."

By the third week, word had spread. The class had grown to twelve, then fifteen. People hungry for permission to create imperfectly, to embrace the mess and beauty of making something with their own hands.

Nora perched on the edge of a stool during Thursday's session, holding a brush like a conductor's baton as she watched her students work.

"Emma," she said, approaching one of the college students who was frowning at her canvas. "Why did you pick that color?"

The girl looked up from a blob of ultramarine she'd just applied with obvious frustration. "I don't know. It felt... sad. But in a good way? Does that make sense?"

Nora grinned. "That makes perfect sense. Then that's exactly what it is."

"But it doesn't look like anything."

"It doesn't have to look like anything but feeling," Nora said gently. "Color can be emotion made visible. Let it be sad. Let it be blue. Let it be exactly what your heart needs it to be."

Emma's frown softened. She dipped her brush again, this time with purpose instead of apology.

Across the room, Mrs. Chen's grandson was adding violent streaks of orange to what had started as a landscape. "It's supposed to be a sunset," he said defensively when he caught Nora watching.

"Sunsets can be angry," Nora replied. "Especially if they have something to say."

Joan laughed from her spot by the window. "You're corrupting us, dear. Making us all dangerous with our brushes."

"Good," Nora said, moving between easels like a gentle storm. "Art should be a little dangerous. If it doesn't scare you, you're not trying hard enough."

She found herself saying things she didn't know she knew:

"Color doesn't have to be realistic to be true."

"Your first instinct is usually right. Trust it."

"Art isn't about being good enough. It's about being honest enough."

Watching her students discover their own voices, seeing the moment when someone stopped apologizing for their brushstrokes and started celebrating them—it filled something in Nora that she hadn't realized was empty.

This was what the other timeline had been trying to teach her.

Not that she needed a different life, but that she needed to live the one she had more bravely.

The letter arrived on a Tuesday, mixed in with the usual pile of bills and gallery supply catalogs.

Her name and address were written in careful script on cream-colored paper that felt expensive beneath her fingers. No return address, just a small infinity symbol pressed into the sealing wax.

Nora's heart stopped.

Inside, a single sheet of paper and four words in Celeste's elegant handwriting:

**You chose well. -C**

Below that, a photograph.

Not of the timeline she'd visited, but of something else. A wedding—small, intimate, held in a garden exploding with impossible colors. The bride wore paint-stained sneakers beneath her dress and laughed with her whole body while the groom spun her in circles beneath fairy lights.

Their faces were blurred, motion-caught, but Nora could see enough.

The other Nora and her Julian, celebrating a love they'd earned through choice and courage and the daily decision to stay open.

Happy.

Complete.

Together in the timeline where they belonged.

Nora traced the edge of the photograph with one careful finger, then slipped it into the frame beside her easel. Not as a reminder of what she'd lost, but as proof of what was possible when you stopped being afraid of your own heart.

She wasn't the Nora who wore silk pajamas and said yes easily to love that fell from the sky like magic. She was the Nora who came back. Who tried again. Who taught people to be messy and brave and real. Who earned her happiness one honest brushstroke at a time.

That Nora was enough.

More than enough.

She lingered in the gallery long after her students left that Thursday, the scent of turpentine and possibility thick in the air. Brushes soaked in mason jars. Easels stood at attention like soldiers waiting for their next battle. Paint tubes lay scattered across tables like evidence of beautiful chaos.

The original self-portrait hung quietly in its place of honor, no longer demanding an apology. Just presence.

*I'm still here,* she thought, looking at the woman in the painting —half-shadowed, hungry, unfinished. *And I'm not hiding anymore.*

The transformation hadn't been magic. It had been a choice, made again and again, to show up as herself instead of who she thought others wanted her to be.

Her phone buzzed with a text from Victor: *Great class tonight. You're a natural teacher.*

Before she could reply, the door chimed. Victor stepped in, paint-stained and slightly breathless like he'd jogged from wherever he'd been.

"Forgot my sketchbook," he said, but he didn't move toward where he'd left it on the counter.

Instead, he stood there, wiping paint from his hands onto already ruined jeans, looking nervous in a way that made her pulse skip.

"So," he said, "I was thinking we could... eat. Together. Like, not in a room full of brushes. Somewhere with actual napkins."

Nora raised an eyebrow. "Are you asking me on a date, Mr. Sketchbook?"

"That was the intention, yes. Execution still pending." His smile was crooked, uncertain, absolutely perfect. "I know this might complicate things, but I think I'm falling in love with you. The way you see light. The way you teach people to be fearless. The way you're becoming exactly who you're supposed to be."

Nora's heart did something complicated in her chest.

Not the desperate, borrowed feeling she'd experienced with

Julian, but something steadier. More real. Less like finding a missing piece and more like discovering she'd been whole all along.

"I'd like that," she said. "Dinner. And... whatever comes after."

"Even if it's messy?" he asked.

"Especially if it's messy."

Because she'd learned something in that borrowed timeline, something the other Nora had tried to tell her through mirrors and memories:

Love wasn't about finding the perfect person or the perfect life.

It was about being brave enough to show up, imperfect and honest, and trust that someone would choose to see the beauty in your becoming.

Victor's smile could have powered the gallery for a week.

"Saturday?" he asked.

"Saturday," she agreed.

Outside, leaves spiraled past the windows like confetti, and Nora felt something settle in her chest.

Not completion.

But contentment with the ongoing work of becoming herself.

One brave brushstroke at a time.

# hope is quiet, too

· · ·

THE WINDOWS WERE OPEN.

Just a little. Enough to let in the sound of morning—bicycle tires humming down damp pavement, birds arguing over a bagel crust someone had dropped, the occasional whoosh of a too-hopeful jogger navigating puddles from last night's rain.

Nora stood in the center of the gallery with paint on her wrist and graphite on her cheek, watching steam rise from her coffee cup like incense in a temple she'd finally learned to tend.

She hadn't noticed the paint. Or the graphite. Or the fact that she'd been humming under her breath for the past twenty minutes —some nameless tune that seemed to emerge from the same place as her brushstrokes now, unbidden and unashamed.

She was smiling.

Not the careful, professional curve she'd perfected for customers and critics, but something real and unguarded that started in her chest and worked its way outward like light.

The gallery smelled like rosemary and rain and the lingering ghost of turpentine from last night's class. Her students had stayed late again, reluctant to leave the magic circle they'd created with easels and honesty and the permission to be beautifully imperfect.

"You're different when you teach," Joan had observed, adding another wild stroke of purple to her canvas. "Like you're more yourself."

"Maybe I am," Nora had replied, and meant it.

The self-portrait still hung on the far wall, but it had company now. Other pieces had joined it—bolder work, looser lines, more risk in the color choices. Her students' paintings dotted the space too, a gallery within a gallery showcasing the kind of fearless creativity that happened when people stopped apologizing for taking up space.

Nothing was perfect.

That was the point.

The bell above the door chimed—that familiar, delicate sound that used to make her brace for disappointment but now felt like possibility knocking.

A small child pressed her nose against the window, breath fogging the glass as she stared at the painting nearest to the street. Her mother tugged gently at her hand, but the girl was transfixed.

Nora opened the door.

"She's an artist," the child announced without preamble, pointing at the canvas that had captured her attention—one of Emma's pieces from Tuesday's class, all swirling blues and defiant yellows.

"She is," Nora agreed solemnly. "She painted her feelings."

"I paint my feelings too," the child said. "But Mommy says I shouldn't use the walls."

The mother looked mortified. "I'm so sorry, she—"

"She's absolutely right," Nora interrupted, crouching to the child's level. "Walls are for very special occasions. But paper works too. Would you like to see how we do it here?"

The child nodded vigorously.

Nora led them inside, past easels and brushes and the comfortable chaos of creation. She set up a small workspace with child-sized supplies—stubby brushes, washable paints, paper thick enough to handle enthusiasm.

"What feeling would you like to paint today?" she asked.

The child considered this with the seriousness of someone who'd never learned to doubt her own emotions. "Happy," she said finally. "But also a little bit scared. Like when you go down the big slide."

"Perfect," Nora said, squeezing yellow and orange onto a palette. "That sounds like adventure colors to me."

They painted together for twenty minutes—the child with fearless abandon, Nora adding gentle guidance when asked. The mother watched from a nearby chair, something in her expression softening as she witnessed her daughter's joy.

"You're very good with children," she said as they cleaned up.

"I'm learning," Nora replied. "They have a lot to teach about being brave."

When they left—the child clutching her dried painting like a treasure, already planning her next masterpiece—Nora felt that familiar warmth expand in her chest.

This was what she'd been missing. Not just creating art, but creating space for others to discover their own courage. To remember that they were allowed to take up room in the world.

Victor arrived as she was setting up for the afternoon's drop-in session—an experiment they'd started two weeks ago, offering an hour of unstructured painting time for anyone who needed it.

"Coffee delivery," he announced, balancing two cups and a paper bag that smelled like heaven. "And possibly the world's most perfect blueberry scone."

He looked different today. Not just the paint-stained clothes she'd grown used to, but something in his posture. A certainty that hadn't been there before.

"You seem pleased with yourself," she observed, accepting the coffee gratefully.

"I am." He set the bag on the counter and turned to face her fully. "I have news."

"Good news or 'we need to sit down' news?"

"Definitely good." His smile was radiant. "The community center approved our joint workshop proposal. 'Art as Emotional Expression' starts next month."

Nora nearly dropped her coffee. They'd submitted the proposal three weeks ago—a collaboration between Victor's established program and her growing classes, designed to bring art education to underserved communities.

"They said yes?"

"They said yes. They also said they want to make it a permanent offering if the pilot goes well." Victor stepped closer, his eyes bright with shared excitement. "We're going to teach together, Nora. Officially."

The weight of it hit her slowly. A real program. A chance to reach people who might never otherwise walk into a gallery. The opportunity to prove that art wasn't just for the privileged or the already confident, but for anyone brave enough to pick up a brush.

"That's..." she started, then found herself unexpectedly tearful. "That's incredible."

"Hey," Victor said softly, reaching out to catch a tear with his thumb. "What's wrong?"

"Nothing's wrong," she said, laughing through the emotion. "Everything's right. That's the problem—I'm not used to everything being right."

He pulled her into his arms then, a hug that felt like coming home and setting out on adventure all at once. She breathed in the scent of him—coffee and cedar and the lingering trace of charcoal that seemed permanently embedded under his fingernails.

"Get used to it," he murmured against her hair. "I plan on making things right for you as often as possible."

When they broke apart, his expression had shifted to something more serious, more weighted with intention.

"There's something else," he said.

"More good news?"

"Different news." He took her hands, studying their joined fingers like they held secrets. "I love you, Nora. Not the version of you that you think you should be, not some impossible standard you're trying to reach. Just you. Messy, brilliant, paint-covered you."

The words hung in the air between them, precious and fragile as spun glass.

"I love you too," she said, the admission feeling like the most natural thing in the world. "I didn't think I knew how anymore, but you reminded me."

"Good," he said, bringing their joined hands to his lips and pressing a kiss to her knuckles. "Because I was hoping you'd be willing to build something beautiful with me. Not just the work-shops—everything. A life. A future. All of it."

Before she could respond, the door chimed again.

Victor leaned in, his voice low and steady.

"You don't have to answer now. We've got time. I'm not going anywhere."

Mrs. Chen bustled in with her usual determination, followed by Franklin and three people Nora didn't recognize—two women and a man, all carrying the telltale signs of creative souls: paint-stained clothes, thoughtful eyes, the kind of restless energy that came from having too many ideas and not enough hours to execute them.

"Nora, dear," Mrs. Chen called out, "I brought reinforcements.

These lovely people heard about your classes and wanted to see the space."

What followed was controlled chaos—introductions and explanations, impromptu demonstrations of technique, the kind of organic community building that happened when people discovered they weren't alone in their desire to create.

Nora moved through it all with growing confidence, answering questions and offering encouragement, watching as strangers became potential friends over shared admiration for a particularly bold color choice.

This was her gallery now. Not a sterile showroom for other people's courage, but a living, breathing space where art happened in real time. Where mistakes were celebrated and breakthroughs were shared, and everyone was welcome to discover what they were capable of when fear stopped driving the brush.

Victor caught her eye across the room and winked, his expression full of pride and affection and the kind of steady certainty that made her believe anything was possible.

By evening, the gallery had emptied except for Victor, who was helping her clean brushes and stack canvases with the practiced ease of someone who'd made himself indispensable to her daily routine.

They worked in comfortable silence, the kind that came from understanding each other's rhythms. He washed while she dried. She organized supplies while he swept paint chips from the floor.

It wasn't romantic in any traditional sense—just two people taking care of their shared space, preparing for tomorrow's possibilities.

But it felt like the most romantic thing Nora had ever experienced.

"Question," Victor said as they finished up.

"Answer," she replied automatically, making him grin.

"When you were a kid, what did you want to be when you grew up?"

Nora considered this, wiping down the last of the palette knives. "An artist. Always an artist. But also..." She paused, remembering. "I wanted to be the kind of person who helped other people discover they were artists too."

"And now?"

She looked around the gallery—at the paintings that reflected a dozen different perspectives, at the easels ready for tomorrow's students, at the man who'd somehow become essential to her happiness without her noticing.

"Now I think I'm becoming exactly who I was always supposed to be."

Victor set down his towel and crossed to where she stood. "Can I tell you something?"

"Always."

"The first time I saw you—really saw you, not just in passing—you were standing in front of that self-portrait, the angry one with all the shadows. You looked like you were having an argument with it."

Nora smiled. "I probably was."

"And I thought—here's someone who knows that art is supposed to challenge you. Who's not afraid of the difficult conversations." He reached up, tucking a paint-streaked curl behind her ear. "I've been a little bit in love with you since that moment."

"A little bit?"

"Okay, a lot. Completely. Embarrassingly so."

She stood on her toes and kissed him—soft, certain, full of promise for all the beautiful, messy, imperfect moments to come.

When they broke apart, both breathing slightly harder, Victor rested his forehead against hers.

"So," he said. "Ready to build something amazing together?"

"I thought we already were," she replied.

He laughed then—head thrown back, completely unguarded, the sound echoing off the gallery walls like music.

Later, after Victor had gone home with promises to return tomorrow with fresh coffee and new ideas for the community workshop, Nora stood alone in her gallery and took inventory.

The space hummed with creative energy even in stillness. Easels stood ready for tomorrow's students. Brushes dried in neat rows, clean and purposeful. The self-portrait gazed out from its place of honor, no longer a monument to fear but a reminder of how far she'd traveled.

She thought about the other timeline—not with longing now, but with gratitude. That glimpse of what was possible had given her the courage to build her own version of extraordinary. Different from what she'd borrowed, but no less beautiful for being entirely hers.

Her phone buzzed with a text from Victor: *Sweet dreams, beautiful. Can't wait to create more magic with you tomorrow.*

She typed back: *Me too. Thank you for seeing me.*

*Always,* came his immediate reply. *Even when you can't see yourself.*

After she put her phone down, she pulled out her sketchbook—not with urgency, but affection. One line. Then another. Just the curve of a jaw mid-laugh. The tilt of a smile caught in pure joy. She didn't need to finish it tonight. She just wanted to remember how it felt to see him, really see him. And let herself be seen in return.

The light through the front windows had changed again—not the harsh fluorescent glare of before, not the golden magic of borrowed dreams. Just honest light. Cool and soft and entirely hers.

She didn't need a mirror to know who she was anymore. But somewhere—some version of her—might be smiling back.

Nora locked up the gallery and stepped out into the evening air. The street was quiet, painted in the soft pastels of dusk. A few blocks away, she could see the warm glow of the café where Victor sometimes met his other teaching friends. Closer, Mrs. Chen's flower shop displayed its evening bouquets in the window like small celebrations.

She belonged here. In this community, in this life she'd built with patient intention and stubborn hope.

As she walked home, Nora caught her reflection in a darkened storefront window. The woman looking back was paint-smudged and tired and glowing with the kind of satisfaction that came from work that mattered.

She looked like someone worth coming home to. And for the first time in forever, she believed it.

The End

# plans without passion

· · ·

SAGE TRAN HAD color-coded her life into submission.

Monday was navy blue—client meetings and damage control. Tuesday was forest green—project deliverables and passive-aggressive emails. Wednesday was burgundy—the day she pretended to care about quarterly projections while secretly wondering if her soul had died somewhere around her third promotion.

It was 7:43 on a Wednesday morning, and Sage was staring at her phone screen like it might spontaneously combust if she willed it hard enough.

**Calendar Alert:** 8:00 AM - Q3 Strategy Session with Mitchell & Associates

**Reminder:** Bring printouts of the Morrison deck (17 copies)

**Note to self:** Smile. Look engaged. Do not mention the existential void.

She took a sip of her third coffee—black, because adding cream required an extra thirty seconds she'd optimized out of her morning routine—and tried to remember when she'd started talking to herself in calendar notifications.

Probably around the same time she'd started sleeping four hours a night and calling it "efficiency."

Her apartment was a testament to the kind of organization that came from having absolutely no spontaneity left to organize around. Everything in its place, every surface gleaming, every corner optimized for maximum productivity. It looked like a magazine spread titled "How to Live Like a Very Successful Robot."

She'd been proud of it once. The sleek minimalism. The color-coordinated closet. The meal prep containers lined up like tiny soldiers in her spotless refrigerator.

Now it just felt like a very expensive cage.

The problem wasn't that Sage had forgotten how to be happy. The problem was that she'd systematically eliminated every opportunity for happiness to find her. Joy required spontaneity. Spontaneity was inefficient. Therefore, joy was inefficient.

It was a perfectly logical equation that had left her with a perfectly logical life devoid of anything resembling warmth.

Sage grabbed her laptop bag—black leather, professional, completely devoid of personality—and headed for the door. She had exactly twelve minutes to get to the office, grab the Morrison printouts from her desk, and transform herself into the kind of person who cared deeply about market penetration strategies.

She was halfway to the elevator when her phone buzzed with a text from Jenna, her assistant.

> Morrison meeting moved to 9 AM.
> Mitchell's flight was delayed. You have an
> unexpected hour of freedom! 🌿

Sage stared at the message, unsure how to process the concept of "unexpected freedom." Her calendar hadn't accounted for it. She didn't have a color for it.

What did people do with unexpected hours? When was the last time she'd had an unplanned moment that wasn't a crisis requiring immediate optimization?

She stood in the hallway of her building, briefcase in hand, and realized she genuinely didn't know.

The coffee shop wasn't part of her routine.

Sage's morning caffeine came from the machine in her kitchen—efficient, predictable, devoid of human interaction. But with fifty-seven minutes to kill and nowhere to kill them, she found herself pushing through the door of *The Daily Grind*, a place she'd walked past every day for three years without ever going inside.

It smelled like cinnamon and possibility, which immediately made her suspicious.

The interior was aggressively cozy—mismatched furniture, fairy lights strung with the kind of casual whimsy that suggested someone had actually enjoyed hanging them, local art covering every available wall space. A chalkboard menu offered drinks with names like "The Daydreamer" and "Inspiration Station."

Everything about the place whispered *softness*—the kind of gentle chaos that happened when people prioritized comfort over efficiency, connection over productivity.

Sage approached the counter like she was entering enemy territory.

"What can I get you?" asked the barista—a woman with silver-streaked hair and paint on her fingernails who radiated the kind of calm that came from never having attended a quarterly strategy session in her life.

"Large coffee," Sage said. "Black."

"Just black? Nothing fun? No flavor adventure?"

The question seemed to require more emotional bandwidth than Sage possessed. When was the last time anyone had asked her about adventure? About fun? About what she actually *wanted* instead of what she needed to be productive?

"Just black is fine."

The barista—her name tag read "Luna"—studied Sage with the intensity of someone who took coffee orders very seriously. "You know what? I'm going to make you something different. On the house. Call it a Wednesday rebellion."

Before Sage could protest, Luna was already moving, grinding beans and steaming milk with the fluid confidence of someone who'd never met a problem she couldn't solve with the right beverage.

Sage found herself at a small table by the window, watching Luna work and wondering when her life had become so beige that a stranger felt compelled to stage a caffeine intervention.

Her phone buzzed. Work email.

From: Robert Chen, Senior Partner

Subject: Morrison Account - Urgent Review Needed

Sage, need you to take another look at the Morrison projections before this morning's meeting. Something feels off about the Q4 numbers. Can you run a secondary analysis?

Sage's stomach clenched. Another task. Another fire to put out. Another reason to stay late and survive on vending machine dinners and the slowly dying hope that someday her work might matter to someone other than shareholders she'd never met.

She was reaching for her laptop when Luna appeared beside her table, setting down a mug that smelled like heaven had opened a coffee shop.

"Lavender honey latte," Luna announced. "With oat milk and a shot of rebellion."

"I didn't order—"

"You didn't order a lot of things," Luna said gently. "Doesn't mean you don't need them."

The coffee was perfect. Creamy and floral and completely unlike anything Sage would have chosen for herself. It tasted like *indulgence*—like someone had decided her preferences mattered more than her productivity schedule.

She took another sip, then another, feeling something in her chest loosen slightly.

"Thank you," she said.

Luna smiled. "Sometimes we need someone else to remind us of what we actually like."

After Luna moved away to help other customers, Sage sat with her unexpected coffee and her urgent email and a strange sense of displacement, like she'd wandered into someone else's life by accident.

She opened her laptop, pulled up the Morrison files, and tried to focus on quarterly projections while the coffee shop hummed with conversation and laughter around her—the sound of people who'd somehow figured out how to build joy into their ordinary Wednesday mornings.

But for some reason, her fingers kept drifting away from the spreadsheet and toward the notes app on her phone, where she found herself typing:

*What if there was a woman who'd forgotten how to want things?*

She stared at the sentence, wondering where it had come from. She hadn't written anything that wasn't work-related in years. Hadn't had a creative thought that didn't involve optimizing work-flows or maximizing efficiency.

*What if she met someone who reminded her she was allowed to be soft?*

The words appeared without her permission, flowing from some place she'd thought she'd successfully shut down years ago.

Sage blinked, deleted the sentences, and forced herself back to the Morrison account. She had work to do. Real work. Important work.

Work that paid for her efficiently organized life and her spotless apartment, and her color-coded calendar that left no room for lavender honey lattes or unexpected questions about softness.

But as she dove into spreadsheets and pivot tables, she couldn't quite shake the feeling that she'd left something important behind in those deleted sentences.

Something that tasted like rebellion and smelled like possibility.

The Morrison meeting was exactly as soul-crushing as expected.

Sage sat in Conference Room B—beige walls, fluorescent lighting, the kind of sterile corporate environment designed to kill creativity and inspiration—listening to Robert Chen discuss market penetration strategies with the enthusiasm of someone reading a grocery list.

"The Q4 projections look solid," Robert was saying, "but we need to be more aggressive with the digital marketing push. Sage, what are your thoughts on the social media engagement metrics?"

Sage looked down at her notes—perfectly organized, color-coded, completely uninspiring—and heard herself say, "I think we're optimizing for the wrong things."

The room went quiet.

Robert raised an eyebrow. "Come again?"

"The metrics," Sage continued, surprising herself with her own voice. "We're measuring clicks and impressions, but we're not measuring connection. We're tracking engagement, but not inspiration. We're building a brand that's efficient but not... meaningful."

The words felt foreign in her mouth—*connection, inspiration, meaningful*. When had she stopped using language that acknowledged humans had hearts as well as wallets?

Mitchell—a thin man in his sixties who'd built his fortune on the careful cultivation of meaninglessness—leaned forward. "Meaning doesn't drive revenue, Sage."

"Doesn't it?" The question emerged before she could stop it. "What if people bought things because they believed in them? What if we created campaigns that made people feel something instead of just convincing them to consume something?"

The silence that followed was deafening.

Robert cleared his throat. "That's... an interesting perspective. Very creative. But let's focus on the deliverables for now."

*Creative.* He'd said it like it was a diagnosis.

Sage nodded, made appropriate murmurs of agreement, and spent the rest of the meeting wondering when she'd started speaking in questions instead of conclusions. When she'd started caring about *feeling* instead of just *functioning*.

When the meeting finally ended, she escaped to the bathroom and stared at herself in the harsh fluorescent mirror. Same perfectly straightened hair. Same neutral makeup. Same blazer in a shade of burgundy that could only be described as "professional resignation."

But something in her eyes looked different. Restless. Like she'd accidentally remembered something important and now couldn't figure out how to forget it again.

Her phone buzzed. Text message from an unknown number.

> Sometimes the best strategy is knowing
> when to stop strategizing. - C

Sage stared at the message. She didn't know anyone with the initial C. She didn't give her number to strangers. She definitely didn't engage with cryptic texts from mysterious senders.

She typed back.

> Who is this?

The response came immediately.

> Someone who thinks you're ready for a
> different kind of meeting. Coffee shop on
> Fifth Street. One hour. Bring your questions.

Sage's finger hovered over the delete button. This was obviously spam. Or a scam. Or someone's idea of a very elaborate prank.

But something about the message made her pause. *Bring your questions.*

When was the last time anyone had asked her what her questions were? When was the last time she'd had questions that couldn't be answered with data analysis and strategic planning?

She looked at herself in the bathroom mirror again—at the woman who color-coded her life and optimized her mornings and had forgotten how to want things that couldn't be measured in spreadsheets.

*What if there was a woman who'd forgotten how to want things?*

The sentence floated back to her, unbidden and persistent.

*What if she met someone who reminded her she was allowed to be soft?*

Sage shook her head, slipped her phone back into her bag, and headed back to her desk.

But as she sat down to tackle the Morrison revisions, she found herself on Google searching "coffee shop Fifth Street" and wondering what kind of questions she might have, if she were brave enough to ask them.

She went.

Sage told herself she was being ridiculous. Told herself she had work to do and deadlines to meet and absolutely no business following cryptic instructions from strangers.

But at 3:47 PM, she found herself standing outside *The Daily Grind* again, clutching her laptop bag like a security blanket and wondering what exactly she was hoping to find.

The afternoon crowd was different from the morning rush— fewer suits, more artists, laptops and sketchbooks scattered across tables like evidence of lives lived on purpose. People who'd somehow figured out how to build careers around *joy* instead of just *survival*.

Sage scanned the room, looking for... what? Someone holding a sign that said, "Mysterious Texter?" A person radiating the kind of calm authority that sent cryptic messages to overworked consultants?

"Sage?"

She turned to find a woman approaching from the back corner of the shop—tall, elegant, wearing a flowing cream-colored cardigan that looked like it had never experienced a rushed morning or a crisis meeting. Her hair was silver-streaked, pulled back in a style that suggested she'd never wasted time worrying about whether she looked professional enough.

"I'm Celeste," the woman said, extending a hand. "Thank you for coming."

"How did you—" Sage began, then stopped. "Do I know you?"

Celeste smiled. "Not yet. But I know you. Shall we sit?"

Before Sage could formulate a proper response, Celeste had guided her to a quiet table in the corner, away from the afternoon chatter. Up close, there was something almost ethereal about her— the kind of presence that made you want to confess things you hadn't even realized you were hiding.

"I'm going to be direct," Celeste said, settling into her chair with fluid grace. "You're drowning."

Sage blinked. "Excuse me?"

"Not literally. Metaphorically. Spiritually, perhaps. You've built a life that looks successful from the outside, but it's slowly suffocating you from the inside."

"I don't know what you're talking about."

"Don't you?" Celeste tilted her head. "When was the last time you created something just because you wanted to? When was the last time you followed an impulse that couldn't be justified in a quarterly report? When was the last time you let yourself be soft?"

The questions hit like gentle arrows, each one finding its mark.

"I have a good job," Sage said defensively. "I make good money. I'm successful."

"By whose definition?"

The simple question hung in the air between them.

Celeste reached into her bag and pulled out a cream-colored envelope, thick cardstock with gold lettering that seemed to shimmer in the afternoon light.

"I'm here to make you an offer," she said. "A week in a different life. Yours, but... alternative. The version where you chose courage over safety. Where you followed your heart instead of your calendar. Where you remembered that efficiency isn't the same as fulfillment."

Sage stared at the envelope. "Is this some kind of therapy? Self-help seminar? Because I should tell you, I don't really—"

"It's an experience," Celeste interrupted gently. "A chance to see what happens when you stop optimizing your life and start living it. When you choose connection over productivity. When you let yourself want things that can't be measured."

"That's impossible."

"Is it?" Celeste smiled. "You wrote something today. In your notes app. Something about a woman who'd forgotten how to want things."

Sage's breath caught. She hadn't told anyone about those sentences. Had deleted them so Celeste couldn't have seen them in passing.

"How do you—"

"The woman in your story," Celeste continued. "What if she could meet the version of herself who never forgot? What if she could spend a week learning how to want things again? How to be soft again? How to choose joy over just... functioning?"

Sage looked around the coffee shop—at the artists bent over their work, at Luna behind the counter humming while she crafted drinks with care, at the walls covered in local art that someone had deemed worthy of display. At people who'd somehow figured out how to build lives around *meaning* instead of just *productivity*.

"What would I have to do?" she heard herself ask.

"Sleep," Celeste said simply. "Tonight, when you go to bed, hold this card. Tomorrow, you'll wake up in the life you might have lived if you'd made different choices. If you'd chosen risk over safety. If you'd chosen connection over efficiency. If you'd chosen to be soft."

She slid the envelope across the table. "No commitment beyond curiosity. One week to see what's possible. If you don't like it, you come back to exactly where you are now."

Sage picked up the envelope. It was heavier than it looked, substantial in a way that made it feel important.

"And if I do like it?"

Celeste's smile was mysterious. "Then you'll have some interesting decisions to make."

She stood to leave, then paused. "Sage? The woman in your story—the one who forgot how to want things? She's not broken. She's just been very, very careful. But careful isn't the same as alive."

After Celeste left, Sage sat alone with the envelope and her lukewarm coffee and the strange sense that she'd just been offered something she'd been unconsciously waiting for her entire adult life.

She opened the envelope carefully.

Inside, a single card with elegant script:

### Timeline Retreats
*For when your life just isn't it*

Below that, a simple message:

**One week. One choice. One chance to remember who you were before you learned to be safe.**

Sage stared at the card until the words seemed to shimmer and dance.

That night, she lay in her perfectly organized bed in her perfectly sterile apartment, holding the card between her fingers like a talisman.

*What if there was a woman who'd forgotten how to want things?*

She closed her eyes, clutched the card to her chest, and for the first time in years, let herself want something she couldn't plan for.

*What if she remembered how to be soft?*

Sleep claimed her gently, and her dreams tasted like lavender honey and rebellion.

# chaos & coffee

. . .

SAGE WOKE to the sound of something that definitely wasn't her alarm clock.

It was music—actual music, not the efficient buzzing of her phone—drifting through what sounded like an open window. Someone was playing guitar and singing off-key, and instead of being annoyed by the disruption to her morning routine, Sage found herself... smiling?

She blinked, trying to orient herself. The ceiling above her wasn't the pristine white of her apartment. This one had exposed beams painted a soft sage green, with fairy lights strung between them like captured stars. A dream catcher hung in the corner, feathers moving gently in a breeze that smelled like coffee and something sweet.

Pancakes?

Sage sat up slowly, heart hammering as she took in her surroundings. The bed was enormous and unmade, covered in a patchwork quilt that looked like it had been assembled from a dozen different vintage fabrics. Pillows were scattered everywhere

—some on the floor, some wedged against the headboard, all of them soft and inviting in a way that suggested someone who prioritized comfort over order.

The room was... chaotic. But beautifully so.

Books were stacked on every available surface—not organized by author or subject, but in teetering towers that suggested they'd been read and loved and abandoned mid-chapter when something more interesting came along. Mugs sat on the nightstand, some clean, some sporting rings from forgotten tea parties. A laptop lay open on a desk that was covered in papers, sticky notes, and what appeared to be the remnants of several different creative projects.

And everywhere—literally everywhere—there were plants.

Trailing ivy hung from macramé planters. Succulents crowded the windowsill. A massive fiddle leaf fig dominated one corner like a gentle green giant. The air itself felt alive, oxygenated, like being inside a greenhouse run by someone with excellent taste and terrible organizational skills.

Sage swung her legs over the side of the bed and froze.

Her feet found slippers—not the practical house shoes from her regular life, but ridiculous fuzzy things shaped like toast. Complete with butter patterns.

She was wearing pajamas she didn't recognize—soft cotton shorts covered in tiny typewriters and a tank top that read "Plot Twist Princess" in faded purple letters.

*Plot Twist Princess.*

What did that even mean?

Sage stood on unsteady legs and moved toward the desk, drawn by the scattered papers like a detective following clues. The laptop screen was dark, but the papers told a story she couldn't quite piece together:

- Handwritten notes in her own handwriting about "dual timeline structure"

- Printed emails with subject lines like "Deadline Extension Request" and "Manuscript Status Update"
- Sticky notes with cryptic reminders: "Fix the journal scenes," "More emotional stakes in timeline B," "Ask Theo about coffee shop research"

*Theo.*

The name sent a flutter through her chest, though she couldn't say why.

And then she saw it—a corkboard above the desk, covered in colorful pushpins and overlapping notes. Front and center, written in red marker with enough urgency to bleed through the paper:

*Thursday = final MS to Lila or she'll hunt you down with a red pen* 😊

Below that, a countdown in her own handwriting:

*Monday: 4 days left Tuesday: 3 days left Wednesday: 2 days left Thursday: Oh God!*

Sage stared at the board, panic rising in her chest like cold water. Four days. She had four days to finish a book she didn't remember writing, for an editor named Lila who apparently had strong feelings about deadlines and red pens.

She grabbed a printed manuscript page from the desk:

*Elena found the journal tucked behind a loose brick in the studio wall, its leather cover soft with age and secrets. When she opened it, she found not pages, but possibility—letters written in her own hand to someone she'd never met, love songs to a future that felt both foreign and familiar.*

*"I know you're reading this," the first entry began. "I know because*

*I've been writing to you my whole life, even when I didn't know your name."*

Sage stared at the page, something twisting in her chest. This was... hers? She'd written this?

The prose was nothing like the corporate communications she crafted for clients. It was soft, lyrical, full of longing and magic, and the kind of emotional honesty she'd trained herself to avoid.

It was beautiful.

It was also completely terrifying.

"Babe, you're gonna be late for your own deadline!" called a voice from somewhere deeper in the apartment—male, warm, tinged with laughter and just a hint of worry.

*Babe.*

Someone called her *babe* .

Sage wrapped her arms around herself, suddenly overwhelmed by the magnitude of what was happening. This wasn't just a different apartment or a different job. This was a different *her*—someone who wrote love stories and let plants take over her living space and owned pajamas that made jokes about plot twists.

Someone who lets herself be soft.

But what if she messed it up? What if she ruined this version of herself—this woman who'd somehow figured out how to build a life around creativity and love and beautiful chaos?

What if she destroyed something sacred?

"Coming!" she called back, her voice cracking slightly on the word.

The kitchen was where organization had gone to die a beautiful death.

Sage found herself in a space that looked like someone had taken her sterile apartment and fed it creativity supplements until it exploded into glorious, functional chaos. Copper pots hung from hooks, their bottoms charmingly blackened from actual use. The counter was covered in evidence of a life lived with enthusiasm—a coffee grinder surrounded by different types of beans, a stand mixer with bowl attachments scattered nearby, jars of spices with handwritten labels, and fresh herbs growing in mismatched pots on the windowsill.

And standing at the stove, spatula in hand and humming something that sounded like a cross between jazz and a lullaby, was the most beautiful man Sage had ever seen.

*Theo.*

He was tall but not intimidatingly so, with dark hair that looked like he'd run his fingers through it while thinking deep thoughts. His shoulders filled out a worn t-shirt that read "Books & Brew: Where Stories Steep," and his forearms—good god, his forearms—were dusted with flour and completely unfair.

He turned when he heard her footsteps, and his face lit up with the kind of smile that suggested she was the best part of his morning routine.

"There she is," he said, crossing to her with easy familiarity. "The woman who's going to revolutionize time-slip romance and break all our hearts in the process."

Before Sage could process that statement fully, he was kissing her forehead—casual, tender, like it was the most natural thing in the world.

She stood frozen, every nerve ending suddenly aware of his proximity. He smelled like coffee beans and something clean and warm, and when he pulled back to study her face, his eyes were the color of dark chocolate.

"You okay?" he asked, brow furrowing slightly. "You look like you've seen a ghost. Which, considering what you're writing, might be literal."

Sage blinked. "Literal ghost?"

"The journal spirits in your manuscript?" Theo grinned, moving back to the stove where pancakes were sizzling in a cast-iron pan. "Though you did say yesterday that the magic was more metaphorical. Something about 'emotional haunting' and 'love letters across time.'"

He flipped a pancake with the confidence of someone who'd never met a breakfast he couldn't conquer. "Coffee?"

"Please," Sage managed, still trying to wrap her mind around the fact that apparently she was writing a book about journals and spirits and emotional haunting.

Theo moved through the kitchen like a dancer who'd memorized every step, pulling down mugs and beans and what appeared to be at least three different methods of coffee preparation. "French press or pour-over? I got some new beans yesterday from this place downtown that roasts in tiny batches. The owner says each batch is like a love song, but honestly, I think she might be slightly unhinged."

"Pour-over is fine," Sage said, perching on a stool at the kitchen island and trying not to stare at the way his hands moved—precise but relaxed, like everything he touched was worth taking time with.

"So," Theo said, starting the coffee ritual with what appeared to be ceremonial attention to detail, "what's the plan for today? More wrestling with Chapter Twelve? Or are you finally going to admit that Elena needs to stop overthinking the journal entries and just trust what her heart is telling her?"

Sage stared at him. "Chapter Twelve?"

Theo paused mid-pour, coffee dripping forgotten from the filter. "Babe, you've been stuck on Chapter Twelve for three days. You kept saying Elena was being too careful, too scared to really connect with the letters. Ring any bells?"

*Elena. The character in the manuscript. Who was scared to connect.*

Sage felt something cold settle in her stomach. "How behind am I? On the book?"

"Behind?" Theo laughed, but there was a note of concern creeping into his voice. "Sage, you're supposed to turn in the manuscript on Friday. As in, four days from now. As in, the deadline you've been panicking about for two weeks."

That matched with what she saw earlier. Four days. She had

four days to finish a book she'd apparently been writing for months, about characters she didn't remember creating, in a genre she'd never attempted.

"I need to see the full manuscript," she said, her voice coming out higher than intended.

Theo set down the coffee pot and really looked at her then—not the casual glance of a boyfriend checking in, but the focused attention of someone who'd learned to read her moods like weather patterns.

"Sage," he said slowly. "Are you feeling okay? You're acting like you've never seen your own book before."

*Because I haven't.*

"I just... I'm having trouble remembering where I left things," she said, which was technically true.

Theo's expression softened. He came around the island and took her hands gently, his thumbs rubbing small circles on her knuckles. "Hey. You've been pushing yourself really hard. When's the last time you took a real break? Not just a coffee run or a quick walk, but actual time away from the story?"

The kindness in his voice nearly undid her. When was the last time someone had asked her about taking breaks? About taking care of herself?

"I don't remember," she admitted.

"That's what I thought." He squeezed her hands. "Okay, new plan. After breakfast, we'll take your laptop to the coffee shop. Change of scenery. I'll work on my open mic set, you can wrestle with Elena's commitment issues, and we'll both remember that creativity is supposed to be fun."

"Open mic set?"

Theo grinned. "Thursday night at Grind & Verse. I'm debuting a new piece about how coffee shops are just libraries for people who think better with caffeine. It's either brilliant or pretentious. Possibly both."

He released her hands and moved back to the pancakes, which

were somehow still perfect despite being temporarily abandoned. "Besides, I want to show you off. My girlfriend, the romance novelist who's about to make readers everywhere believe in love letters they'll never receive."

*Girlfriend. Romance novelist.*

The words felt foreign and familiar at once, like trying on clothes that belonged to someone with better taste.

Sage watched Theo plate the pancakes—perfectly golden, arranged with fresh berries and what appeared to be homemade whipped cream. He moved through the domestic routine with the same easy confidence he'd shown making coffee, like taking care of her was just another beautiful thing he did without thinking about it.

"Theo," she said carefully. "How long have we been together?"

He paused, syrup bottle halfway to the plate. "Four months next week. Why?"

"I just..." She struggled for words that wouldn't make her sound completely insane. "I feel like I'm still discovering things about you. About us."

His smile was soft, understanding. "That's the best part, isn't it? I'm still discovering things about you too. Like yesterday, when you told me about your theory that coffee shops are just speed dating for introverts and their future caffeine soulmates."

"I said that?"

"You did. Right after you figured out how to fix the pacing problem in Chapter Ten." He set the plate in front of her with a flourish. "You also said I was your caffeine soulmate, which was either the coffee talking or the most romantic thing anyone's ever said to me."

Sage stared down at the pancakes—fluffy, perfect, made with care by someone who'd learned her preferences and cared enough to remember them. She took a bite, and it was exactly what she would have ordered if she'd been brave enough to want something more indulgent than her usual protein bar.

"These are perfect," she said.

"You're perfect," Theo replied automatically, then caught himself. "Sorry, that was cheesy even for me. But you are. Especially when you're being all mysterious and thoughtful like this."

He settled on the stool next to her with his own plate, close enough that she could feel the warmth radiating from his skin. "Want to hear something weird?"

"Always."

"I had the strangest dream last night. You were in it, but... different. Sadder. Like someone had dimmed your light." He shook his head. "You were wearing this burgundy blazer and sitting in the most depressing office I've ever seen, and when I tried to talk to you, you looked right through me like I was invisible."

Sage's fork froze halfway to her mouth, pancake dripping syrup back onto the plate.

*Burgundy blazer. Depressing office.*

"That's... specific," she managed.

"I know, right? Dreams are weird. But when I woke up, I just wanted to hold you and remind you that you're seen. That you matter. That your stories matter." He bumped her shoulder gently. "Which is why we're going to get you unstuck today. Elena's going to figure out how to trust those journal entries, and you're going to remember why you love writing love stories."

She should have laughed it off. Called it "too much cheese for breakfast." Made some joke about his subconscious being overly dramatic.

But instead, she blinked hard and nodded, something cracking open behind her ribs.

Because somewhere inside her, the woman in the burgundy-blazer was still very, very afraid.

"Sage?" Theo's voice was gentle, concerned. "You okay? You look like I just described your worst nightmare."

"I'm fine," she said quickly, then caught herself. "Actually, no. I'm not fine. I'm terrified."

"Of what?"

"Of ruining this." The words tumbled out before she could stop them. "This life, this version of myself, this... *us*. What if I mess it up? What if I'm not as good at being her as she was?"

Theo set down his fork and turned to face her fully, his expression serious but not alarmed. "Babe, first of all, there's no 'her' and 'you.' There's just you. And second, you couldn't ruin this if you tried."

"You don't know that."

"I do, actually." He reached out, tucking a strand of hair behind her ear with infinite gentleness. "Because I've seen you at your most blocked, most frustrated, most convinced you're a fraud. And you know what? You're still the woman who writes love letters across time. You're still the person who turns coffee shop observations into metaphors for human connection. You're still *you*."

He paused, studying her face. "Whatever's got you spooked this morning—the deadline, or the general weirdness of being a creative human—it doesn't change the fact that you're exactly who you're supposed to be."

Sage nodded, throat suddenly tight with emotions she couldn't name.

Because the truth was, she didn't remember why she loved writing love stories.

She didn't remember writing them at all.

But sitting in this plant-filled kitchen with pancakes made by beautiful hands and coffee that tasted like someone had taken time to understand her preferences, she was starting to think she'd like to learn.

"Theo?" she said softly.

"Yeah?"

"Thank you. For taking care of me."

His smile was sunlight and certainty. "Always, babe. That's what love is—taking care of each other's dreams."

As Sage took another bite of perfect pancakes and tried to reconcile the woman who'd apparently built this life with the woman who'd woken up in it, one thought kept circling through her mind:

*This version of me knew how to let herself be soft.*

The question was: could she figure out how to be soft too, before her four-day deadline destroyed everything?

# the romance writer life

. . .

THE COFFEE SHOP was everything Sage's corporate brain told her was inefficient, and everything her suddenly awakening creative soul found irresistible.

*Grind & Verse* occupied the ground floor of a converted Victorian house, all exposed brick and mismatched furniture and the kind of organized chaos that suggested people came here to think rather than just consume caffeine. Bookshelves lined the walls, stuffed with everything from poetry collections to romance novels to manifestos on sustainable coffee farming. A small stage dominated one corner, surrounded by chairs that had clearly seen countless open mic nights.

"Our usual table?" Theo asked, nodding toward a corner spot by the window where someone had carved "Story happens here" into the wooden surface.

Sage followed him, laptop bag clutched against her chest like armor, trying not to notice how many people waved at them. At *her*. Like she was a regular. Like she belonged in this world of creative caffeination and artistic ambition.

"Sage!" called a voice from behind the counter. "The usual? Or are you feeling adventurous today?"

The barista was maybe twenty-five, with intricate braids and paint under her fingernails and the kind of smile that suggested she genuinely cared about matching people with their perfect beverage.

"Usual, please, Maya," Theo called back before Sage could panic about not knowing what her usual was.

"One lavender oat milk latte with an extra shot of creativity coming up," Maya announced. "And Theo, your normal liquid motivation?"

"You know it."

Sage settled into her chair—apparently *her* chair, judging by the way it seemed molded to her exact proportions—and tried to process the fact that she had a *usual* order at a coffee shop. That people knew her here. Expected her.

"You seem nervous," Theo observed, settling across from her with his own laptop. "More nervous than usual pre-writing session jitters."

"What if I can't do it?" The question escaped before she could stop it. "What if I sit down to write and... nothing comes?"

Theo reached across the table and covered her hand with his. "Then we'll sit here and people-watch and make up stories about the guy in the corner who's been nursing the same americano for two hours while staring intensely at his phone."

Sage followed his gaze to a man in his thirties, wire-rimmed glasses, stubble that suggested he'd been writing for hours and forgotten to shave.

"He's texting his ex," she said automatically, then blinked in surprise. "I mean—"

"See?" Theo grinned. "Your brain is already working. Keep going."

"He's texting his ex," Sage continued, surprised by how easily the story flowed, "but he keeps deleting the messages before sending them. He wants to tell her about the novel he's finally finishing—the one she always said he'd never have the courage to write."

"And?"

"And she was right. For a while. But now..." Sage studied the man's face, the way his thumb hovered over the send button. "Now he's remembering that courage isn't the absence of fear. It's writing the story anyway."

Theo's expression went soft, admiring. "That's why I love your brain. You see the emotional truth underneath everything."

Maya appeared with their drinks—Sage's lavender latte decorated with foam art that looked like a tiny book, and Theo's black coffee simple and strong.

"Any progress on the manuscript?" Maya asked. "I've been telling everyone who'll listen that I know a romance author who's about to be famous."

"Still wrestling with it," Sage said, which felt true even if she couldn't explain why.

"Writer problems," Maya said sympathetically. "My girlfriend's a poet. She once spent three weeks trying to find the perfect word to describe the color of regret. Turns out it was 'burgundy.'"

After Maya left, Sage opened her laptop with the reverence of someone handling a live grenade. The screen came to life, revealing a desktop background that was a photo of her and Theo—her head on his shoulder, both of them laughing at something outside the frame, fairy lights blurred behind them like captured stars.

She looked happy. Not just content or satisfied, but genuinely, radiantly happy.

When had she last looked like that?

"Just open the document," Theo said gently. "Don't think about it. Just... open it."

Sage clicked on a file labeled "Love Letters Across Time - Draft 3" and held her breath.

The document opened to reveal 187 pages of text. The word count at the bottom read: 67,891 words.

She'd written almost 68,000 words of a novel she didn't remember.

"I need to read from the beginning," she said.

"Babe, you don't have time to—" Theo started, then stopped when he saw her expression. "Okay. But maybe just skim? Get a feel for where you left off?"

Sage scrolled to page one and began to read:

*Elena Martinez had always been practical about love. She believed in compatibility over chemistry, in five-year plans over flights of fancy, in the kind of steady affection that wouldn't disrupt her carefully organized life.*

*Which was why finding the journal was so inconvenient.*

*It appeared on a Tuesday, tucked behind a loose brick in the wall of the art studio she'd inherited from her great-aunt. The leather cover was soft with age, the pages yellowed and slightly warped, as if they'd absorbed decades of secrets.*

*When she opened it, she found her own handwriting.*

*Letters addressed to someone called "M."*

*Love letters she'd never written.*

Sage's breath caught. The voice was hers—she could recognize her own rhythm, her own way of building tension—but it was looser than anything she'd ever written for work. More emotional. More... brave.

She scrolled down, scanning sections at random:

*Dear M,*

*I dreamed about you again last night. We were in a coffee shop that smelled like cinnamon and possibility, and you were reading over my shoulder while I wrote. Your hand was warm on my back, and when I turned to look at you, you said, "This is the story we're writing together."*

*I woke up missing someone I've never met.*

*How is that possible?*

*-E*

Sage's heart hammered against her ribs. The letter could have been about her and Theo, sitting here in this coffee shop while she read her own work.

"This is..." she began, then stopped. "Theo, this is about us."

"What?" He leaned over to read the screen, his shoulder brushing hers. "Oh, that section. Yeah, you said I inspired that part. Something about how being with me made you believe in love that transcends logic."

"I said that?"

"You did. Right before you kissed me and told me I was your muse." He grinned. "Which was either the most romantic thing ever or proof that writers are basically emotional vampires who steal material from their relationships."

Theo watched her with a softness that held questions he didn't ask. Like he'd seen her armor shift and didn't know what it meant —but knew better than to press.

Sage scrolled further, finding more letters, each one more intimate than the last:

*Dear M,*

*What if I told you I've been afraid my whole life? Not of failing, but of succeeding. Not of being seen, but of being truly known.*

*What if I told you that loving you feels like coming home to a place I've never been?*

*-E*

"I can't believe I wrote this," Sage whispered.

"Why not?"

"It's so... open. Vulnerable. I don't write like this."

Theo tilted his head, studying her face. "Sage, you've been writing like this for months. This is exactly how you write."

She scrolled to the end of the document, looking for where she'd left off. The last chapter was incomplete, ending mid-sentence:

*Elena held the journal against her chest, feeling the weight of all the letters she'd written to a love she couldn't remember but couldn't forget. Outside the studio window, rain began to fall, and she thought about courage. About the difference between being safe and being*

And that was it. The sentence hung unfinished, like a question waiting for an answer.

"I don't know how to finish it," Sage said, panic rising in her voice. "I don't even know how I started it."

"Hey." Theo's voice was calm, grounding. "Take a breath. This happens to every writer. You're not the first person to look at your own work and feel like a stranger wrote it."

"But what if I can't find the voice again? What if I've lost whatever made me able to write this?"

"You haven't lost anything." He closed the laptop gently. "You're just scared. And that's okay. Fear means it matters."

Sage's phone buzzed with a notification. An email.

**From: Lila Chen, Editor, Moonstone Press**
**Subject: Checking in on Love Letters**

Sage's stomach dropped. She opened the email with trembling fingers.

Sage,

Hope you're feeling better about Chapter 12! I know you've been struggling with Elena's arc, but remember—she's not broken, she's just learning to trust. Sometimes the most powerful love stories are about characters who have to overcome their own fear of being loved.

Looking forward to the completed manuscript on Friday. I have a good feeling about this one —early readers are calling it "The Time Traveler's Wife meets You've Got Mail with a touch of magical realism." Your dual-timeline structure is gorgeous, and the emotional stakes are chef's kiss*.*

Don't overthink the ending. Elena knows what she wants—she's just afraid to reach for it.

xoxo,

Lila

P.S. - Marketing is already brainstorming cover concepts. They're thinking something with vintage journals and fairy lights. Very on-brand for you!

Sage stared at the email, processing several devastating pieces of information simultaneously:

1. She had an editor named Lila who was expecting a completed manuscript in four days
2. People had already read early versions of her book and liked it
3. Marketing was designing covers, which meant this was *real*
4. She was apparently known for a particular brand of romance writing
5. She had absolutely no idea how to "not overthink the ending."

"Lila emailed," she said weakly.

"What'd she say?"

"She said Elena knows what she wants, she's just afraid to reach for it."

Theo smiled. "Sounds familiar."

"What do you mean?"

"Nothing," he said, but his expression suggested it was definitely *something*. "Come on, let's get you writing. Sometimes the only way through is forward."

Sage reopened her laptop, staring at the unfinished sentence. *About the difference between being safe and being...*

Being what?

Happy? Brave? Real?

She placed her fingers on the keyboard and tried to channel whatever part of her had written 67,891 words about love letters across time.

Nothing came.

The cursor blinked at her mockingly.

"I can't do this," she whispered.

"Yes, you can." Theo's voice was steady, confident. "Close your eyes."

"What?"

"Close your eyes. Now, what does Elena want more than anything?"

Sage closed her eyes, trying to picture the character she'd apparently created. A woman who was practical about love. Who found a journal full of letters she'd written to someone she'd never met.

"She wants to believe," Sage said slowly. "She wants to believe that love can be bigger than logic. That connection can transcend time. That she's worthy of the kind of love she writes about in those letters."

"And what's stopping her?"

"Fear. Fear that if she reaches for it, it'll disappear. Fear that she's not brave enough to deserve it."

"And?"

Sage opened her eyes, meeting Theo's gaze across the table. "And she's tired of being afraid."

"Then write that."

Sage looked down at the screen, at the sentence waiting to be completed:

*About the difference between being safe and being...*

Her fingers found the keys:

*...being alive.*

The words felt right. True. Like a door opening onto a path she'd forgotten how to walk.

She kept writing:

*Elena had spent so many years choosing safety over possibility that she'd forgotten the feeling of her own heartbeat when something mattered. But sitting here in the studio where her great-aunt had once painted love stories in watercolor and oil, surrounded by the scent of turpentine and old secrets, she felt something shift.*

*The journal was warm in her hands. The letters—her letters—seemed to pulse with their own energy, as if they were more than just words on a page. As if they were invitations.*

*What if love really could transcend time? What if the person she'd been writing to was writing back?*

*What if courage was just another word for saying yes?*

The words were coming faster now, as if she'd stepped onto a path her feet remembered even if her mind didn't. Each sentence felt like discovering something she'd lost, each paragraph like coming home to a language she'd forgotten how to speak.

And then her phone buzzed.

The notification broke her concentration like a stone through glass. Sage glanced down at the screen, expecting another email from Lila.

Instead, she found a message that made her blood run cold.

> Having trouble with your deadline?
> Borrowed inspiration only lasts so long.
> Some words have to come from you. -C

Sage stared at the message, heart hammering.

*Celeste.*

Somehow, Celeste knew she was struggling. Knew she was an impostor in this creative life. Knew that the words flowing so freely moments ago weren't entirely hers.

"Everything okay?" Theo asked, noticing her sudden stillness.

Sage deleted the message quickly. "Fine. Just... spam."

But as she turned back to the manuscript, the words that had been flowing so freely suddenly felt foreign again. Like she was wearing someone else's clothes and pretending they fit.

*What if courage was just another word for saying yes?*

The question stared back at her from the screen, and for the first time since waking up in this timeline, Sage wondered if she was brave enough to answer it.

Or if she even knew how.

# theo, the metaphor machine

. . .

"YOU'RE OVERTHINKING IT AGAIN," Theo said, closing her laptop with gentle finality. "Come on. Field trip."

"I have a deadline in three days," Sage protested, but she was already letting him pull her up from the chair.

"Which is exactly why we need to get you out of your head." He shouldered his messenger bag—worn leather covered in coffee stains and what looked like fragments of song lyrics written in Sharpie. "Trust me."

Twenty minutes later, they were sitting on a blanket in Meridian Park, surrounded by food trucks and fairy lights strung between trees like fallen constellations. Theo had somehow procured tacos, craft beer, and a small crowd gathered around a makeshift stage where a woman with purple hair was reading poetry about her ex-girlfriend's houseplants.

"This is your idea of solving writer's block?" Sage asked, taking a sip of beer that tasted like creativity and poor life choices.

"This is my idea of remembering why stories matter." Theo nodded toward the stage. "Look around. Everyone here is telling stories—through food, through music, through terrible poetry about succulents. We're all just trying to connect."

The poet finished to enthusiastic applause and bounded off stage, replaced by a man with a guitar who looked like he'd learned to play by studying heartbreak.

"Your turn," the guitarist called out, scanning the crowd. "Come on, someone brave enough to share something real?"

Before Sage could stop him, Theo was raising his hand.

"Theo, no," she hissed.

He grinned, already standing. "I'm debuting new material. You're my focus group."

He jogged up to the small stage, all easy confidence and infectious energy. The guitarist handed over the mic with a good-natured eye roll.

"Evening, beautiful humans," Theo said, his voice carrying over the crowd with surprising authority. "I'm Theo, and I have a theory about coffee shops."

Sage watched, mesmerized, as he transformed from her sweet, pancake-making boyfriend into something magnetic and sure.

"Coffee shops," he continued, "are just speed dating for souls. You walk in looking for caffeine, but what you're really seeking is that perfect moment of connection. The barista who remembers your order. The stranger who offers to share their table. The person reading the book you've been meaning to read for three years."

His eyes found hers in the crowd, and his smile deepened.

"Coffee shops are where we practice being seen. Where we test whether the world can handle the particular blend of chaos and creativity we bring to the table." He paused, letting the words settle. "And sometimes, if we're very lucky, we find someone who not only handles our chaos—they help us turn it into art."

The crowd was silent, hanging on every word.

"Love," Theo said softly, "is just two people agreeing to be caffeinated together. To share the good tables. To split the last blueberry scone. To sit in comfortable silence while they create separate beautiful things that somehow make one bigger, more beautiful thing."

He looked directly at Sage. "Love is finding someone who thinks your particular brand of weird is not just tolerable, but essential. Someone who sees your unfinished sentences and doesn't try to complete them—just sits with you until you find the words yourself."

Sage felt the crowd erupt around her, but all she could hear was the silence between heartbeats. Her throat burned with something dangerously close to recognition. He saw her. Really saw her. And instead of flinching—he offered a metaphor.

The applause was thunderous. When Theo returned to their blanket, slightly breathless and glowing with performance energy, she kissed him. Hard.

"What was that for?" he asked when they broke apart.

"For seeing me," she said. "For making me feel like my particular brand of weird is essential."

"It is." His voice was serious now, intimate. "Sage, your brain works in ways that constantly surprise me. You see connections that other people miss. You find emotional truth in the spaces between words."

"I'm stuck," she admitted. "On Elena's story. I don't know how she gets from fear to courage."

Theo was quiet for a moment, watching the guitarist return to the stage. "What if she doesn't get there all at once? What if courage is just... a series of small yeses?"

"What do you mean?"

"I mean, maybe Elena doesn't need one big moment of transformation. Maybe she just needs to start saying yes to the things that scare her. Yes to trusting the journal. Yes to believing in love that doesn't make sense. Yes to the possibility that she's worthy of the story she's writing."

Sage stared at him. "That's... actually brilliant."

"I have my moments." He grinned. "Plus, I've been listening to you work through this plot for weeks. I'm basically an honorary romance expert at this point."

"You should write your own book."

"Nah. I'm better at helping other people find their voices." He touched her cheek gently. "Speaking of which, what's one thing that scares you about finishing this book?"

The question caught her off guard. "What?"

"Right now. What's the scariest part about writing Elena's ending?"

Sage considered this, watching the fairy lights flicker above them. "That it won't be good enough. That I'll disappoint everyone who's already invested in the story."

"And?"

"And... that maybe I don't deserve to tell stories about love when I'm not sure I understand it myself."

But some small part of her—the one that still remembered spreadsheets and neutrality—whispered, *This isn't your life. You're borrowing someone else's happy ending.*

Theo's expression grew soft, serious. "Sage. Look at me."

She did.

"You understand love better than anyone I know. You understand that it's messy and complicated and requires daily choosing. You understand that it's not about finding someone perfect, but about finding someone whose imperfections complement yours."

He took her hands. "You write love letters across time because you believe love is bigger than logic. And you're right."

"How do you know?"

"Because you took a chance on me. A random coffee shop poet with questionable financial prospects and a tendency to speak in metaphors." His smile was gentle, self-deprecating. "You saw something worth investing in."

Sage felt something crack open in her chest. "Theo..."

"I know this deadline has you spinning. I know you feel like you're losing the thread of your own story." He squeezed her hands. "But Elena's journey isn't about becoming someone else. It's about becoming more herself. More honest. More willing to be known."

"What if being known is terrifying?"

"Then you write about the terror. You let Elena be terrified and brave at the same time." He paused, his voice growing softer. "You let her be a mosaic. Broken pieces and still something whole."

The guitarist finished his set to gentle applause, and the crowd began to disperse. Theo started packing up their picnic with efficient movements, but Sage remained sitting, processing the weight of what he'd said.

*You let her be human.*

When had she stopped letting herself be human? When had she started believing that vulnerability was a weakness rather than a superpower?

"Ready to go home and write?" Theo asked, offering his hand.

Sage looked up at him—this man who made poetry out of coffee shop observations, who saw her fear and met it with tenderness, who somehow knew exactly what her fictional heroine needed to hear.

"Yeah," she said, taking his hand. "I think I am."

As they walked back through the park, fairy lights twinkling above them like promises, Sage felt the story shifting in her mind. Elena didn't need to transform into someone fearless. She just needed to learn that being afraid and being brave could exist in the same breath.

That love wasn't about perfection.

It was about showing up, scared and hopeful and beautifully human, and trusting someone else to do the same.

"Theo?" she said as they reached the edge of the park.

"Yeah?"

"Thank you for being my particular brand of weird."

His laugh was warm and bright. "Always, babe. Always."

# words & withheld
# dreams

. . .

SAGE WOKE at 4 AM with Elena's voice in her head.

Not the panicked scramble of deadline anxiety, but something clearer—like tuning into a radio station that had been static for days. She slipped out of bed, careful not to wake Theo, and padded to the kitchen where her laptop waited.

The apartment was different in the pre-dawn darkness. Softer. The plants seemed to breathe in the shadows, and the fairy lights Theo had left on cast everything in gentle gold.

She opened the manuscript and began to write:

*Elena pressed her palm against the journal's leather cover and felt something shift—not in the book, but in herself. The letters weren't magic. They were memories. Not of things that had happened, but of things that could.*

*"What if," she whispered to the empty studio, "courage isn't about not being afraid?"*

The words flowed like water finding its level. For two hours, Sage wrote without stopping, watching Elena finally understand that the journal wasn't showing her a different life—it was showing her permission to want the life she already had.

For the first time since arriving in this life, Sage felt whole. It scared her, a little—how easily wholeness could become a kind of ache, when you didn't know if you got to keep it.

By the time Theo emerged, hair rumpled and squinting against the morning light, she'd written three thousand words.

"Morning, beautiful," he said, dropping a kiss on top of her head. "How long have you been up?"

"Since four. I think I figured it out."

"Elena's breakthrough?"

"Elena's everything." Sage gestured at the screen, where paragraphs of breakthrough sat waiting. "She doesn't need the letters to be real. She needs them to be *hers*."

Theo read over her shoulder, his presence warm and solid. "This is gorgeous, Sage. Look at this line—'Love isn't about finding the right person, it's about becoming the right version of yourself to love them well.'"

Sage paused, staring at the sentence she'd written without thinking. When had she become someone who understood love enough to write about it with certainty?

"Coffee?" Theo asked, already moving toward the kitchen.

"Please. And maybe—" She stopped, suddenly overwhelmed by a wave of something that felt suspiciously like panic.

"What?"

"What if it's not good enough? What if I'm just... borrowing insight I don't actually have?"

Theo set down the coffee pot and turned to face her fully. "Where is this coming from?"

Sage gestured helplessly at the screen. "This voice, this confidence about love and courage—what if it's not really mine? What if I'm just... mimicking something I've heard before?"

"Every writer is influenced by what they've read, what they've experienced," Theo said gently. "That doesn't make your voice less authentic."

"But what if—" Sage stopped, catching herself before she said something impossible to explain. *What if this whole life is borrowed? What if none of this belongs to me?*

Theo sat beside her, taking her hands. "Sage, you've been spiraling since yesterday. What's really going on?"

She looked into his concerned eyes and felt the weight of the secret she couldn't share. "I guess I'm just... afraid of not being enough. Of disappointing everyone who believes in this book."

"Including me?"

"Especially you."

His expression softened. "Babe, I fell in love with you before you ever wrote a word. I love the way you think, the way you see patterns others miss, the way you make ordinary moments feel meaningful." He squeezed her hands. "The writing is just... how you let other people see what I get to see every day."

Before Sage could respond, her phone buzzed with a notification. An email marked urgent.

**From: Lila Chen, Editor**

**Subject: Small panic but probably fine!!!**

Sage,

Okay, don't freak out, but I just got off a call with the publisher, and they want to move up the release date. Good news: they love the early chapters so much they want to fast-track publication. Less good news: we need the final manuscript by tomorrow (Thursday) instead of Friday.

I know, I know. But you're so close! And honestly, sometimes a tight deadline forces us to trust our instincts instead of overthinking everything to death.

You've got this. Elena's story is beautiful—don't let perfectionism kill it.

xoxo,

Lila

Sage stared at the email, blood draining from her face. "Tomorrow. She needs it tomorrow."

"What?" Theo read over her shoulder, his expression shifting to concern. "Okay, that's... intense. But you're almost done, right? You just wrote three thousand words this morning."

"I've written three thousand words. The book still needs an ending."

"So write an ending."

"I don't know how!" The words came out sharper than she intended. "I don't know how Elena and Marcus find each other across timelines. I don't know how to make the journal connection feel meaningful instead of gimmicky. I don't know how to—"

"Hey." Theo's voice was calm, grounding. "Breathe."

Sage breathed. Or tried to.

"What does your gut tell you about the ending?"

"My gut doesn't know anything about time-slip romance," she said miserably.

"But it knows about love."

Sage looked at him—at this man who somehow always knew exactly what to say, who believed in her even when she didn't believe in herself. "What if I mess it up?"

"Then you mess it up beautifully and we fix it in revisions." He smiled. "Sage, you've been telling me for weeks that this book is about taking emotional risks. Maybe it's time to take one."

She nodded, turning back to the laptop. The cursor blinked at her expectantly.

*What would Elena do?*

Elena would be terrified. But she'd also be tired of being afraid.

Sage placed her fingers on the keyboard and began to write:

*Elena walked to the easel where her latest painting waited—a landscape that had been fighting her for weeks. But looking at it now, she understood. She'd been painting Marcus without knowing his name. The way morning light caught in someone's hair. The shape of hands that knew how to be gentle.*

*"You're not letters in a journal,"* she said to the empty studio. *"You're every beautiful thing I've been afraid to hope for."*

The words felt right. True. Like finally saying something she'd been holding back for years.

She wrote for another three hours , barely aware of Theo moving around the apartment, bringing her coffee and silence and the occasional encouraging touch on her shoulder.

By noon, she had an ending.

Elena didn't find Marcus through magic. She found him because she finally stopped being afraid to look. The journal hadn't been showing her another timeline—it had been showing her permission to want love in this one. The journal hadn't been whispering secrets from another life. It had been echoing the parts of herself she'd silenced in this one.

"Done," Sage whispered, staring at the final paragraph.

"Really done?"

"Really done." She leaned back in her chair, suddenly exhausted. "Elena gets her happy ending. Marcus turns out to be the coffee shop owner she's been too shy to talk to. The journal was just... her own heart, learning to be brave."

Theo read the final pages, his expression growing soft. "Sage, this is beautiful. Really beautiful."

"Is it enough?"

"It's more than enough. It's honest."

Sage glanced over at Theo, warm and real in her periphery. She wanted to memorize this version of him—messy-haired and mug in hand—just in case she forgot. Just in case tomorrow brought changes she couldn't control.

As Sage prepared to email the manuscript to Lila, her phone buzzed with another text from the unknown number:

> Borrowed time runs out eventually. Hope
> you found what was yours to keep. -C

She stared at the message, something cold settling in her stomach. The week would be over soon.

"Everything okay?" Theo asked, noticing her sudden stillness.

"Fine," she said, deleting the message. "Just... tired."

But as she hit send on the email containing Elena's completed love story, Sage couldn't shake the feeling that she was about to lose something precious.

And she still didn't know if the words she'd written—the love she'd found—were truly hers to keep.

# the retreat proposal

. . .

SAGE SPENT Thursday in a haze of completion and dread.

Lila's response to the manuscript came within an hour: three paragraphs of gushing praise followed by a contract amendment for a two-book deal. Theo insisted on celebratory champagne at lunch. Maya at the coffee shop drew a heart in her foam and announced she was pre-ordering six copies for her book club.

Everything was perfect.

Which was exactly the problem.

"You're quiet," Theo observed as they walked through the farmer's market, his fingers laced with hers. "Post-deadline crash?"

"Something like that." Sage watched him select peaches with the careful attention of someone who believed fruit could be a love language. When had she learned to find such simple gestures devastatingly attractive?

They passed a vendor selling handmade soaps, and the woman behind the table brightened with recognition. "Sage! How's the book coming along?"

Sage froze, panic fluttering in her chest. This stranger knew her.

Expected updates on a creative project she'd supposedly been passionate about for months.

"It's... finished," she managed.

"Oh, wonderful! I can't wait to read it. Your last Instagram post about writing love letters to the future had me in tears."

*Instagram post? Love letters to the future?*

"Thank you," Sage said weakly, letting Theo guide her away before she could betray herself further.

A block later, they stopped at a cheese vendor, and Sage caught her reflection in the window of the shop behind them. For a split second, she didn't recognize the woman staring back—someone with looser hair and paint-stained fingernails and eyes that held secrets she'd earned rather than borrowed.

Who was that person? And how long could Sage pretend to be her?

"I have a surprise," Theo said, paying the vendor and tucking the cheese into his messenger bag alongside what appeared to be a collection of handwritten notes. "Well, more of a proposal."

Sage's heart stopped. "A what?"

The way he said it—gentle but weighted with significance—made her stomach clench. Was this it? Was he about to say something that would make leaving impossible?

She wasn't ready. She couldn't handle a love confession when everything would disappear tomorrow.

"Not that kind of proposal," Theo laughed, though something in his expression suggested the clarification might not be entirely accurate. "A weekend away. There's this writers' cabin about two hours north—my friend Jake owns it. No Wi-Fi, no distractions, just woods and a fireplace, and time to celebrate finishing your book properly."

Relief and disappointment warred in her chest. Not a declaration of love, then. Just a romantic getaway that would make her denature even more devastating.

The invitation hung between them like a bridge she wasn't sure she could cross.

"This weekend?" she asked carefully.

"Tonight through Sunday. I already checked—you don't have any editor calls scheduled, and I can move my Sunday workshop to next week." His thumb traced circles on her palm. "When's the last time you took a real break? Not just a coffee shop writing session, but actual time away from everything?"

*Never*, Sage realized. Even in her corporate life, she'd been addicted to productivity, to the illusion that constant motion equaled progress.

"I don't know," she said. "I should probably start thinking about the next book. Lila wants an outline for the sequel by—"

"Sage." Theo stopped walking, turning to face her fully. "The sequel can wait forty-eight hours. You just finished something amazing. Let yourself celebrate that."

The kindness in his voice nearly undid her. This man who wanted to take her away to a cabin in the woods, who'd planned a weekend celebration around her achievement, and looked at her like she was worth the effort of romance.

But Elena had been braver. Elena had chosen to stay in her own timeline, to trust that love could exist without magic. Elena had found the courage to want what was real instead of what was borrowed.

*I gave Elena permission to stay*, Sage thought. *Why can't I give myself the same?*

"What if I'm not good company?" she asked. "What if I'm all weird and in my head?"

"Then you'll be weird and in your head in a beautiful place with someone who thinks your particular brand of weird is fascinating." He grinned. "Plus, I brought new poems to test on you. Consider yourself a captive audience."

Sage looked at him—really looked. At the hope in his expression, the careful way he held her hand like she might disappear if he gripped too tightly. At the man who somehow made her feel seen and safe, and worthy of weekend getaways.

This would all be over soon. She's wake up in her sterile apartment with her color-coded calendar and her corporate job that paid well but didn't feed her soul.

Theo would be gone.

"Okay," she heard herself say. "Let's do it."

His smile could have powered the entire farmer's market. "Really?"

"Really. But I get veto power over any poems about coffee shop metaphysics."

"Deal," he said, already pulling out his phone. "I'll text Jake we're coming. You go pack something comfortable and maybe that blue sweater that makes your eyes look like they hold secrets."

"You've given thought to my sweater's effect on my eyes?"

"Babe, I've given thought to everything about you. It's kind of my thing."

The cabin was something out of a storybook—all rough-hewn logs and stone chimneys, tucked into a grove of pine trees that whispered secrets to the wind. A wraparound porch held two Adirondack chairs and a wooden swing that looked like it had supervised countless sunset conversations.

"Jake built this himself," Theo said, carrying their bags up the front steps. "Took him three years and approximately seventeen thousand YouTube tutorials."

Inside was a warm wood and soft lighting, with built-in bookshelves and a kitchen that somehow managed to be both rustic and efficient. But it was the living room that made Sage's breath catch— a massive stone fireplace surrounded by overstuffed chairs and a coffee table covered in art books and poetry collections.

On the mantle sat a vintage typewriter, its keys worn smooth by countless stories, and beside it, a framed photo of Theo and another man—Jake, presumably—grinning as they held up a badly constructed bird house.

Sage found herself drawn to the typewriter, running her fingers over its keys. In her corporate life, she'd never noticed things like this—the way objects could hold the weight of dreams, the beauty in tools that served creativity rather than productivity.

"Jake's grandfather's," Theo said, noticing her fascination. "Still works, if you're feeling analog."

"It's perfect," she said, meaning more than just the typewriter.

"Wait until you see the view from the bedroom." Theo set down their bags and immediately moved toward the kitchen. "I'm thinking pasta for dinner? Something that pairs well with celebrating your literary triumph?"

Sage wandered to the wall of windows that looked out over a small lake, its surface painted gold by the late afternoon sun. This was the kind of place where people wrote novels about second chances and love that transcended logic.

The kind of place where someone might fall so completely in love they'd forget it wasn't real.

But then she caught herself—caught the dangerous thought that maybe this *could* be real, maybe she could find a way to stay, maybe she deserved this happiness even if she'd borrowed it.

*No,* she told herself firmly. *This isn't yours. This is her life, her love, her happiness. You're just visiting.*

"Theo," she said carefully. "What are we doing here?"

"Making dinner?" He looked up from the cabinet where he'd been examining pasta options. "Or did you mean existentially?"

"I mean..." She struggled for words that wouldn't reveal too much. "What do you want from this weekend?"

His expression grew serious. He set down the pasta box and crossed to where she stood by the windows, and Sage could see something building in his eyes—something important he was working up the courage to say.

*This is the moment,* she realized with a spike of panic. *This is where I could say it—say I want this too. Say I'll stay. But I can't.*

"I want to watch you remember that you're allowed to rest," he said simply. "I want to see you without a deadline hanging over your head. I want to show you this place I love and maybe..." He paused, something vulnerable flickering across his face. "Maybe talk about what comes next."

"What comes next?"

"For us. For this." He gestured between them. "Sage, we've been dancing around something for months. This feeling that we're building toward something bigger than weekend coffee shop dates and deadline support."

Sage's heart hammered against her ribs. She felt herself reaching the edge of something—the place where she could say, *"I love you too,"* and mean it completely.

Instead, she choked it back. "Theo..."

"I know it's scary," he continued, misreading her panic. "I know you're worried about the career stuff, about balancing writing with... whatever this is between us. But I think we're good together. I think we make each other better."

He reached for her hands, and she let him take them even though every instinct screamed that this was dangerous territory.

"I'm not asking for answers tonight," he said. "I'm just asking for honesty. About what you want. About whether you can see a future where we're not just dating, but really building something together."

The question hung in the air between them like a confession she wasn't prepared to hear.

Because the truth was devastating: she could see that future. More than see it—she wanted it with an intensity that scared her. She wanted lazy Sunday mornings in his kitchen and joint creative projects, and the kind of partnership where they celebrated each other's victories like shared wins.

She wanted to wake up every day knowing that someone believed in her work, her dreams, her particular brand of weird.

But none of it was real. None of it was hers.

"I can't," she whispered.

Theo's expression shifted, hope fading into confusion. "Can't what?"

"I can't talk about the future. Not yet. Not..." *Not when I know it ends soon.*

"Okay," he said slowly. "Can you tell me why?"

Sage looked out at the lake, at the perfect golden light painting everything soft and romantic. At the cabin, where a man who loved her had brought her to celebrate an achievement that felt borrowed.

"What if I'm not who you think I am?" she asked.

"What do you mean?"

"What if the person you fell in love with was just... a version of me? What if the real me isn't brave enough for this?"

Theo was quiet for a long moment, studying her face like he was trying to solve a puzzle.

"Sage, everyone has versions of themselves. The confident writer, the scared human, the woman who makes terrible jokes when she's nervous." His smile was gentle, understanding. "I didn't fall in love with just one version. I fell in love with all of them."

"Even the scared one?"

"Especially the scared one. Because she's the one who's brave enough to write love stories even when she's not sure she believes in love."

The words hit like arrows finding their target.

"But what if—" Sage started, then stopped. Because how could she explain that her fear wasn't about being enough, but about deserving something that belonged to someone else?

"Hey," Theo said softly. "Whatever you're thinking, we don't have to figure it out tonight. Let's just... be here. Make dinner. Sit by the fire. Let the rest of it wait until you're ready."

He kissed her forehead, gentle and patient, and Sage felt something crack open in her chest.

This man. This beautiful, understanding man who wanted to build a future with her, who saw her fear and met it with tenderness instead of pressure.

She'd lose him.

Tonight, she could let herself pretend he was hers.

"Okay," she said. "Let's make dinner."

But as Theo moved back to the kitchen, humming contentedly while he filled a pot with water, Sage pressed her palm against the window and tried to memorize the feeling of being loved.

Just in case tomorrow brought nothing but spreadsheets and the echo of what could have been.

# plot twist: permission granted

. . .

SAGE WOKE before dawn to the sound of rain against the cabin windows and the weight of knowing this was her last morning. The weekend had flown by with more peace than she had the right to feel.

Theo slept beside her, one arm thrown across her waist, his breathing deep and even. She'd memorized the sound over the past two nights—the way he hummed sometimes in his sleep, the small smile that played at his lips when he dreamed something good.

She'd memorized everything. The joke he'd whispered in her ear while they brushed their teeth last night, something ridiculous about poets and dental hygiene that had made her laugh until she snorted. The way he'd kissed her shoulder blade yesterday morning while she'd typed notes for her next book, casual and reverent all at once. The poem he'd written on her wrist in purple Sharpie yesterday: *"She carries stories in her pulse"*—barely legible now but still warm against her skin.

She tried to memorize the exact weight of his arm across her waist, the precise temperature of his chest against her back. But already she could feel it slipping away, the way dreams faded when you tried too hard to hold them.

In six hours, it would all be gone.

Sage slipped carefully from bed and padded to the kitchen, where she made coffee with the ritualistic precision of someone trying to hold onto time. The rain drummed against the roof like a countdown, each drop marking another second closer to goodbye.

Through the window, the lake was gray and choppy, mirroring the storm in her chest. She'd spent the weekend pretending— pretending this life belonged to her, pretending she could keep it, pretending that love was enough to change the fundamental laws of borrowed time.

But pretending had its limits.

"Morning, beautiful." Theo's voice was rough with sleep, tender with familiarity. He wrapped his arms around her from behind, pressing a kiss to the top of her head. "You're up early."

"Couldn't sleep."

"Bad dreams?"

*No,* she thought. *Beautiful ones. That's the problem.*

"Something like that."

Theo turned her in his arms, studying her face with the careful attention of someone who'd learned to read her moods. "You've been somewhere else all weekend. Physically here, but emotional-ly... I don't know where."

Sage looked up at him—at this man who'd shown her what it felt like to be known, to be cherished, to be someone's first choice instead of their backup plan. Who'd made her believe, for just a few days, that she was worthy of love stories instead of just writing them.

"Theo," she began, then stopped. How could she possibly explain?

"Whatever it is, just tell me. Please." His hands framed her face, thumbs brushing her cheekbones. "I can handle it. Whatever's scaring you, whatever's making you pull away—we can figure it out together."

The kindness in his voice nearly broke her.

"What if I wanted to stay?" she whispered.

Theo's expression brightened with hope. "Then stay. God, Sage, of course, stay. We can figure out whatever's bothering you—"

"What if I told you I'm not who you think I am?" she interrupted.

"I'd say I already know that. I'd say everyone's more complex than they appear, and I'm looking forward to discovering all your layers."

"What if I told you I'm leaving?"

The hope died in his eyes. "Leaving when? For how long?"

"Today. And I don't know if I'm coming back."

The silence stretched between them like a chasm. Sage watched emotions flicker across his face—confusion, hurt, something that might have been panic.

"Is this about the book? About pressure? Because we can slow down, take things—"

"It's not about that."

"Then what?" His voice cracked slightly. "Sage, I love you. I know we haven't said it before, but I do. I love your messy hair in the morning and the way you see magic in ordinary things and how you make me want to write better poems just to be worthy of your attention."

*I love you too.* The words sat on her tongue like a confession she couldn't afford to make.

"I love that you're brave enough to write about love even when you're terrified of it," he continued. "I love that you see connections everywhere—between people, between stories, between moments that seem unrelated until you point out the thread that ties them together."

Each word was a knife, beautiful and devastating.

"Theo, stop."

"I love how you make coffee like it's a prayer and how you alphabetize your bookshelf but leave sticky notes in completely random places. I love that you're here, in this life, in my life, and I don't want to imagine it without you."

"You're going to have to."

The words hung in the air like a death sentence.

Theo dropped his hands from her face, stepping back as if she'd slapped him. "What does that mean?"

Sage wrapped her arms around herself, suddenly cold despite the warmth of the cabin. "It means this isn't real. None of it. I'm not supposed to be here."

"Sage, you're scaring me. You're not making sense."

She looked around the cabin—at the typewriter that had caught her imagination, at the books they'd read to each other by the fireplace, at the place where for three days she'd felt like she belonged somewhere.

On the coffee table sat her laptop, still open to the last chapter of Elena's story. The chapter where Elena chose to stay in her own timeline, to trust that love could exist without magic.

"I told Elena to be brave," Sage said softly, staring at the screen. "I told her she didn't need magic, just permission. But maybe I only knew how to write the truth—not live it."

"What are you talking about?"

"I have to go," she said simply.

"Where? Why?" Theo's voice rose, desperation creeping in. "Sage, talk to me. Whatever's wrong, we can fix it. I can fix it."

"You can't fix this. No one can."

She moved toward the bedroom to pack, but Theo caught her arm gently.

"Please," he said. "Just... explain. Help me understand what's happening."

Sage looked into his eyes—those beautiful, confused eyes that had seen her as worthy of love letters and weekend getaways and futures she'd never dared to imagine.

"What if I told you," she said carefully, "that sometimes people get chances to see how their life might have been different? To experience what happens when they make braver choices?"

"I'd say that sounds like the beginning of one of your stories."

"What if it wasn't a story?"

Theo was quiet for a long moment, searching her face. "Are you telling me you're from some kind of alternate timeline?"

"I'm telling you the woman you fell in love with built this life. Earned it. Deserves it. And I'm just... visiting."

"That's impossible."

"Is it?" Sage smiled sadly. "You're a poet. You believe in metaphors made real, in love that transcends logic. Is it really so hard to believe that sometimes the universe gives us glimpses of what we could have?"

Theo stared at her, and she could see him trying to process, trying to make sense of the impossible.

"The dreams," he said slowly. "The burgundyblazer woman in the office. That was... you? The real you?"

"Maybe. I don't know how the dreams work."

"And this version—this Sage who writes romance novels and makes terrible coffee and falls asleep reading in the bathtub—she's not real?"

"She's real. She's just not me."

Theo sank onto the couch, running his hands through his hair. "This is insane."

"I know."

"But it explains... things. The way you've seemed surprised by your own life. The questions about our relationship that you should have known the answers to."

"I'm sorry. I didn't mean to lie. I just... I fell in love with this life. With you. I wanted to pretend it could be mine."

"It is yours," Theo said fiercely, standing again. "Whatever timeline you came from, whatever brought you here—you're here now. That has to mean something."

"It means I got to spend a week learning what it feels like to be happy."

"And then what? You just leave? Go back to your burgundy-blazer and your corporate job and pretend none of this happened?"

Sage felt tears burning behind her eyes. "I don't have a choice."

"Everyone has a choice."

"Not about this."

Theo crossed to her again, taking her hands. "Stay. Choose this. Choose us."

"I can't."

"Why not?"

"Because it's not mine to choose. Because someone else built this life, someone else earned your love, someone else deserves the happy ending."

"What if I'm choosing you? What if I'm saying that this version of you, timeline-traveling or not, is the one I want?"

The offer hung between them like salvation she couldn't accept.

"What about her? The other Sage? What happens to her story if I take her place?"

Theo was quiet, clearly struggling with the implications. "I don't know."

"I do. She disappears. Her life, her choices, her love for you—gone. And I become someone wearing her face, pretending to remember things I've never experienced."

"Maybe that's not how it works."

"Maybe it is."

Rain lashed against the windows, and somewhere in the distance, thunder rumbled like the world was breaking apart.

"I have to go," Sage said again, more gently this time.

"When?"

"Soon. This afternoon."

Theo nodded slowly, accepting the inevitable even as it destroyed him. "Will you remember? When you go back?"

"I don't know. Maybe pieces. Maybe just the feeling of it."

"And will I remember you?"

Sage's heart shattered. "I hope not. It would be easier if you didn't."

"I don't want easier. I want you."

"You have me. You have the version of me who belongs here, who built this life with you, who knows all your stories and shares your dreams."

"It's not the same."

"It's better. She's better. She's brave and talented and deserves all of this."

"So are you."

Sage kissed him then—fierce and desperate and final. A goodbye that tasted like everything she'd never get to keep.

When they broke apart, both breathing hard, Theo rested his forehead against hers.

"I love you," he whispered. "Whichever version you are, wherever you came from. I love you."

"I love you too," she finally said, the words breaking free like birds she'd kept caged. "In any timeline, in any world, I love you too."

They held each other as the storm raged outside, and Sage tried to memorize the feeling of being loved completely, even as she prepared to walk away from it forever.

Because some gifts weren't meant to be kept.

They were meant to teach you what was possible.

She couldn't bring the cabin home. But she could bring the version of herself who'd been brave enough to love there.

And sometimes, that was everything.

# writing a wilder beginning

. . .

SAGE WOKE to the sound of her alarm—efficient, practical, devoid of happiness.

The ceiling above her was white plaster, not sage-painted beams. The air smelled like nothing, not coffee and possibilities. Her phone sat on the nightstand, displaying a calendar alert in corporate blue: `Monday Meeting - Morrison Account Review, 9 AM.`

She was back.

For a moment, she lay perfectly still, testing the weight of return. Her apartment felt smaller than she remembered, sterile in a way that had once seemed sophisticated but now felt suffocating. The silence pressed against her ears—no humming from the kitchen, no gentle breathing beside her, no whispered poetry about morning light.

But something was different.

Not in the apartment—that remained exactly as she'd left it, color-coded and optimized and emotionally vacant. The difference was in her chest, in the way she breathed, in the certainty that sat behind her ribs like a warm stone.

She remembered.

Not everything—the details were already softening at the edges like watercolors in rain. But she remembered the feeling of waking up excited to write. She remembered what it was like to be loved for her particular brand of weird. She remembered the taste of lavender honey lattes, the sound of her own laughter and the revolutionary concept that efficiency wasn't the same as fulfillment.

Most importantly, she remembered that she was allowed to want things.

Sage sat up, pulled her laptop from the nightstand, and opened a new document.

*What if there was a woman who forgot how to want things? And what if she remembered?*

The words felt familiar, like coming home to a language she'd always known but had temporarily forgotten how to speak.

She wrote for an hour before getting ready for work—not the frantic download of someone afraid of losing inspiration, but the steady output of someone who'd finally learned to trust her own voice.

When she finally closed the laptop and reached for her gray blazer, she paused.

In the back of her closet hung a dress she'd bought on impulse six months ago—soft blue with small printed birds, the kind of thing someone with personality might wear to work. She'd never had the courage to put it on.

Today, she did.

The meeting was so boring, Sage found herself taking notes about the people rather than the projections. Robert's nervous habit of clicking his pen. The way Mitchell's assistant kept checking her phone like she was waiting for news from a more interesting universe. The conference room's fluorescent lights that made everyone look slightly deceased.

These were characters. These were stories.

When Robert asked for her thoughts on the Q4 strategy, Sage heard herself say, "What if we focused on connection instead of conversion? What if we built campaigns that made people feel something instead of just buying something?"

The room went quiet.

"That's very... creative," Robert said, in the tone usually reserved for discussing communicable diseases.

"Thank you," Sage replied, and meant it.

After the meeting, she didn't retreat to her desk to optimize spreadsheets. Instead, she found herself in the break room, staring at the coffee machine and thinking about a barista named Maya who'd made foam art shaped like tiny books.

"Rough meeting?" asked a voice behind her.

Sage turned to find Kyle Lee—Robert's nephew, recently hired as a junior consultant, generally ignored by everyone including Sage. He was tall, with dark hair that looked like he'd run his fingers through it while thinking, and eyes the color of good coffee.

"Kyle, right?" she said.

"Yeah. And you're Sage. The woman who just told the partners that emotional connection matters more than market penetration."

"I did, didn't I?" Sage smiled, surprised by her own audacity.

"For what it's worth," Kyle said, moving to pour himself coffee from the sad office machine, "I thought you were right. Most marketing feels like corporate algorithms trying to manipulate human hearts. Gets exhausting."

Sage studied his profile as he doctored his coffee with the enthusiasm of someone making the best of limited resources. "You sound like you speak from experience."

"Poetry major, if you can believe it. Before I sold my soul to quarterly projections and KPI optimization."

"Poetry?" Sage's heart skipped. "Do you still write?"

"Sometimes. When the existential dread gets too loud." He grinned, self-deprecating. "There's an open mic night at this coffee shop downtown. *Grind & Verse*. I've been thinking about checking it out, but haven't worked up the courage to actually go."

*Grind & Verse.*

Sage felt something electric zip down her spine. "I know that place."

"Really? Have you been to the open mic?"

"Not yet," she said carefully. "But I'd like to."

Kyle's expression brightened. "Maybe we could... check it out together? Moral support for two reformed creatives?"

Sage looked at him—really looked. At the paint stain on his sleeve that suggested he still made art in his spare time. At the way he held his coffee cup like it contained possibilities instead of just caffeine. At the hope in his expression when he mentioned poetry.

He wasn't Theo. Would never be Theo. But maybe that wasn't the point.

Maybe the point was that she was finally brave enough to say yes to coffee shop poetry and reformed creatives and men who understood that emotional connection mattered more than market penetration.

"I'd like that," she said. "Thursday night?"

"It's a date," Kyle said, then blushed. "I mean—not a date date. Unless you want it to be a date. Which would be—"

"Kyle," Sage interrupted gently. "Thursday night sounds perfect."

That evening, Sage sat at her kitchen table with takeout Thai food and her laptop, working on the story that had been growing in her chest like a secret garden.

It wasn't Elena's story about journals and time-slip romance.

This was something new, something entirely hers—about a woman who'd forgotten how to want things until the universe reminded her that desire was just another word for hope.

She wrote until midnight, then called her sister.

She hadn't spoken to her sister in four months. Corporate life didn't leave much room for family relationships that couldn't be optimized or scheduled into quarterly reviews.

"Sage?" Claire's voice was cautious but warm. "Everything okay? It's late."

"I quit my job today," Sage said.

"You what?"

"I quit. Well, I gave my notice. Two weeks, very professional, but I'm done."

"What happened? Are you having a breakdown?"

Sage laughed, and it sounded like the first honest noise she'd made in years. "I'm having the opposite of a breakdown. I'm remembering who I used to be before I learned to be practical."

"Okay," Claire said slowly. "And who were you before practical?"

"A writer," Sage said, the word feeling strange and perfect in her mouth. "I wanted to be a writer."

"And now?"

"Now I'm going to try."

Claire was quiet for a moment. "That's terrifying."

"I know."

"And brave."

"I'm learning the difference."

They talked for an hour—about dreams and fear and the way corporate life could make you forget you had permission to want impractical things. About writing workshops and coffee shops and the revolutionary idea that maybe success wasn't just about salary and optimization.

"I'm proud of you," Claire said before they hung up. "For remembering."

Thursday night found Sage standing outside *Grind & Verse*, hands trembling slightly as she pushed through the door. The space was exactly as she'd imagined—exposed brick, mismatched furniture, the gentle chaos of people who prioritized creativity over efficiency.

Kyle was already there, sitting at a small table near the stage, two coffee cups waiting.

"You came," he said, standing as she approached.

"I came," she agreed, settling into the chair across from him.

The coffee was good—not life-changing, not poetry-inducing, but honest and warm and exactly what she needed.

"Nervous?" Kyle asked, noticing her fidgeting.

"Terrified," Sage admitted. "I signed up to read."

"Really? What are you reading?"

"Something I wrote. About second chances and borrowed time and learning to be brave enough for your own life."

Kyle's smile was warm, encouraging. "Sounds perfect for this crowd."

The open mic started with a woman reading poetry about her houseplants, followed by a man with a guitar who sang about coffee shops and soul connections. Then came a teenager with a piece about social media anxiety and an older woman who read what appeared to be a love letter to her late husband.

"Sage Tran," called the host—a woman with silver-streaked hair and paint under her fingernails.

Sage stood on unsteady legs, walked to the small stage, and looked out at the crowd of strangers who'd gathered to share their truths.

"This is about a woman who forgot how to want things," she began, her voice stronger than she'd expected. "And what happened when she remembered."

She read for five minutes—about corporate cages and timeline magic and the revolutionary discovery that you were allowed to choose joy over efficiency. About love that taught you to be brave and coffee shops that felt like home and the particular courage required to start over at twenty-eight.

When she finished, the applause was warm and real. Not thunderous, not life-changing, but the sound of people who understood the difficulty of being human in public.

Kyle was grinning when she returned to their table. "That was incredible."

"That was terrifying."

"Sometimes they're the same thing."

Sage looked around the coffee shop—at the people bent over notebooks and laptops, at the art covering the walls, at the stage where someone was now reading a piece about the emotional complexity of grocery shopping.

"Kyle," she said. "Would you like to get dinner? Somewhere that serves food you can't eat with one hand while typing?"

"I'd love that," he said. "But first—can I ask you something?"

"Sure."

"In your story, the woman who forgot how to want things—how did she remember?"

Sage considered this, thinking about timeline retreats and linen-wrapped women and the borrowed life that had taught her what was possible. Somewhere, maybe, a poet woke up with the taste of goodbye and lavender on his tongue.

"She met someone who reminded her that wanting was just another word for hoping," she said. "And hope was just another word for being alive."

Kyle nodded, understanding lighting his eyes. "And then?"

"And then she started again. Different than before, but still her. Still wanting things. Still hoping."

Outside, the first snow of the season began to fall, dusting the coffee shop windows with something that looked almost like magic.

This time, courage was the magic.

Kyle helped her into her coat, and together they stepped out into the soft snow and the infinite possibility of a Thursday evening with nowhere to be but present.

"Ready for dinner?" he asked.

"Ready for anything," Sage replied.

And for the first time in her adult life, she meant it.

The End

Did you enjoy Timeline Retreats?

Please consider reviewing it on Amazon, Goodreads, or Bookbub.

Reviews help me reach new readers.

Join my newsletter for writing updates, bonus content, FREE books, recommendations, and promotions at

www.daisylandishromance.com

# about the author

Daisy Landish is a clean romance and cozy mystery author whose clean and sweet novellas have tugged at readers' heartstrings around the world. When she's not writing stories, Daisy spends her time reading, hiking at dawn, and riding into the sunset on her horse, Rosebud.

www.daisylandishromance.com

facebook.com/daisylandishromance
x.com/daisy_landish
instagram.com/daisylandishbooks
amazon.com/author/daisylandish
bookbub.com/authors/daisy-landish
goodreads.com/Daisy_Landish

# also by daisy landish

**Clean Regency Romance**

Christmas with the Earl

The Lady Series - The Allington Collection

The Lady Series - The Gillingham Collection

The Lady Series - The Blackmore Collection

The Lady Series - The Norrington Collection

**Clean Contemporary Romance**

Timeline Retreats

Maplewood Grove Series

Love on Spruce Island

Second Chance

Cherry Tree Island

The Wedding Trio

Extra Credit

Counting on the Cowboy

Focusing on the Cowboy

Mistletoe Magic

Grounded at Christmas

**Cozy Mysteries**

Sophie Brooks Mysteries

Jane and Kennedy Daniels Mysteries

Pine Grove Mysteries

Annie Archer Paranormal Mysteries

Wilma Wade Holiday Mysteries

Mike and Maddie Mysteries

Mystic Moonhaven Mysteries

Sweater Weather: Cozy Mysteries for Fall

Summer Vibes: Cozy Mysteries for Summer

Let it Snow: Cozy Mysteries for Winter

Spring Break: Cozy Mysteries for Spring